Night Dance
Part I: Shadow Worlds

Kory Wynykom

© 2023 Kory Wynykom – all rights reserved.
c/o autorenglück.de
Franz-Mehring-Straße 15
D-01237 Dresden

Kory@nachttanz.net
www.nightdance.net

Editor: Nadja Bobik
Proofreading and editing of the (American) English version: Elise Ryan
Original version: *Nachttanz: Schattenwelten* (2022)
Cover design: Magicalcover.de
Layout: Autorenträume

NIGHT

Dance

Part I: Shadow Worlds

Kory Wynykom

ABOUT THE BOOK:

Night Dance is a healing voyage that takes us deep into the human abyss. Through the eyes of the British medium Zayla and the Lakota-American Logan, Night Dance connects the traumas and primal wounds of eight people on three continents. The trilogy is the story of the magic of life, the monumental power of love, and the embracing of our darkest shadows. Night Dance seeks to stir the hearts of its readership and inspire reflection and contemplation on the limiting and lopsided realities we too often blindly accept.

A **LIST OF CHARACTERS** can be found at the end of this book.

TRIGGER WARNING:

This book contains themes of deep despair, death, and suicide as well as a few scenes of violence and abuse (sexual, narcissistic and otherwise), which, in the context of trauma healing and (Jungian) shadow work, however, are vital for the plot.

To Majona

In memoriam Brock

With my deepest sympathy for your horrendous loss
and your broken heart.

You have my utmost respect for the love you have given
and will continue to give to this world.

Our deepest traumas held in love will heal humanity.
Grace Kane

Prologue

H er father routinely puts her into a trance. It's not the first trip into another dimension the professor has taken with his daughter. However, today's hypnosis session has a shadow looming over it right from the start. The relaxation suggestions take effect in record time. Within seconds, a leaden calm spreads over Zayla.

She deeply inhales the smell of moss and damp earth. Where does it come from? Where is she?

The part of her that remains awake and responsive even in hypnosis registers that her father bypasses regressing her to the scenes from her childhood. He also only briefly touches on the next stage, from before her birth while in her mother's womb, where Zayla recalls impressions and moods she and her mother experienced. When he asks her to dive once again into a past life that is of special significance to her, images she has long known rush past her as if in a rewound movie. She frowns.

"What do you see?" inquires the professor.

"The lives we've already looked at."

Zayla hears his surprised gasp.

In fast forward, she sees herself not only once again as a thief, a beggar, a victim of genocide and expulsion, but also as a murdering warrior queen and a devious priestess. Anchored most deeply in her, she has found, are those lives that demanded all her strength.

"Is it over?"

Zayla nods.

"Look down at yourself," her father asks her. "What clothes are you wearing this time?" When her answer fails to come, he asks her to look around. "Are you inside or outside? Are you alone or with others?"

"With others," she whispers, feeling a small child lying in her arms. Although Zayla gives herself permission to dive deep and unfiltered into her memory worlds, she flinches as the cruel rain of images comes crashing down on her.

Soldiers and civilians attacking a camp. She sees leather tents on fire. The slaughter of villagers, children pleading for their lives. Babies torn from their mothers' arms, their heads smashed on rocks. Panicked, she holds one of the children tightly. Zayla glimpses unborn babies, cut out of the bodies of pregnant women. Girls and women who are raped and whose breasts are cut off by their attackers. The bloodthirsty game of the beasts with their prey.

In the midst of the carnage, a lone soldier stands motionless beside the corpse of his horse. At the sight of the men in a bloody frenzy riding triumphantly past him with the genitals of "stinking redskins" cut out, he vomits.

Zayla is breathing heavily and her pulse is racing. The scene breaks off and changes to an icy snowy landscape on the Northern Plains many years later.

She hears the wind roaring and the wolves howling. In blood-red colors, the last rays of the setting sun sink into the horizon.

Her gaze falls on the warrior, marked by the long chase. He is sinewy and lean, and towers over most men. He stands tall in the snow, hands on his weapons, motionless, like a statue. His piercing eyes dart back and forth between his own men and the bluecoats who have surrounded him. Restlessly, the cavalrymen slide around in their saddles. Their horses snort and prance. The soldiers' tension is palpable.

Like animals, the headman and his people were hunted through their old homeland and captured just outside the Canadian border. The group he leads now consists of only a small band of warriors and a surplus of women and children. The survival of the defenseless is the sole reason the chief hesitates. Only if the women and children are spared, he shouts to the commanding officer, will I and my men not go to our deaths fighting.

Zayla looks into the leader's feverish eyes, then at the soldiers. She can feel the waves of hatred crashing over him, the lynch lust of the bluecoats. She senses the warrior's despair at the hopelessness of his situation. Countless times in his life he has already defied death and the devil. But the bitter defeat, so close to the frontier, is more than he can bear. He resembles a starving man who had food placed before him, but as if in mockery, just out of reach.

Zayla's eyes twitch searchingly. Where is the traitor? Her gaze lingers on one of the Indian scouts the army has hired for its hunt. Triumphantly, the traitor moves toward his former headman. The women and children will die if you don't let yourself be disarmed voluntarily, he barks.

The chief drops his rifle in the snow. The bow follows, then the quiver with the arrows, then the war club: a skull crusher. Threateningly, the scout points the revolver at one of the children. The headman spits and throws his knife to the ground. It is an unusually beautiful and intricately crafted weapon, its handle shaped like a black wolf's head. Greedily, the traitor reaches for it. For a moment, the chief turns his attention to the women. His eyes gleam moistly. Then he turns his head back to the scout and his expression becomes an impenetrable mask. He looks beyond his enemies and into the blood-red evening sky and intones his death song.

Suddenly, the chief lunges at the traitor with a mighty leap. The soldiers are in an uproar. Several shots crack. The warrior is hit, staggers, but straightens up again. With hatred, the scout thrusts his bayonet into his side. The leader collapses and falls to the snow, gasping. A shrill cry of victory sounds from the killer's throat followed by piercing screams from the ranks of the women.

Zayla also screams, but her throat is tight. No sound escapes her as her body twists and writhes on the couch. Tears roll down her cheeks. Her father places a hand on her arm. She hears his attempts to bring her out of her state of hypnosis, but they have no effect. Everything in her resists returning. Only when the professor gently but persistently pleads with her to retreat to the place she has designated as a safe haven for this journey do her tears dry up. Her pulse returns to normal, and she is once again on the snow-blown prairie.

Teary-eyed, she looks into the eyes of the commanding officer. With a barely perceptible movement of his head, the Colonel nods at her. He still loves her, she notes, but she wishes him dead. His men mutter witch as they recognize her. Along with the chief's two other wives, she kneels beside the dead leader. The widows inflict wounds on their arms and legs as a sign of mourning and cut their long hair. Incessantly they sway their bodies in the snow. From their throats resounds a lament so muffled and melancholy through the icy winter landscape that even the howling of the wolves and the raging of the wind fall silent. Nature listens to the grief of a defeated people and its lullaby of death.

Zayla hears her father's sharp intake of breath as she begins to hum and then sing in a language she never learned. He holds her hand.

"Are you ready to move to the moment when you leave this life again?"

Zayla answers in the affirmative. A cemetery appears before her eyes, a field littered with white wooden crosses. In its midst, she settles down, exhausted, and asks her body, over one hundred years old, to die. It is a quick and peaceful death.

"What happens now?" her father asks.

"I'm starting to come out of this avatar," she whispers. "Every weight has fallen off me ... and I'm floating upwards." She takes one last look at the body she left and feels relief and joy.

When Zayla turns around, she bumps into her mother, who embraces her wordlessly. Smiling, she takes her daughter by the hand and accompanies her part of the way. Near a clearing in the forest, Zayla says goodbye to her mother again.

Around a crackling campfire, Zayla sees the Colonel and the chief sitting together with the murderer. They are joined by the soldier who threw up during the massacre, the brother-friend of the murdered headman, and his friend's grandmother. Zayla approaches the small group. She sees the murderer shrug his shoulders.

I was not involved in the massacre, she hears him say. But I have contributed to driving the sandy-haired witch mad.

Zayla puts her head to the side and blinks at him. Something you won't succeed in doing a second time, she replies calmly.

The brother-friend of the murdered chief and the Colonel reach for her hand. The grandmother giggles and teases the three with such crude sayings that they bring a blush to their cheeks.

The killer looks at Zayla challengingly. Don't you want to try again? So far you haven't regained your old strength, he mocks.

The grandmother nods in agreement and gently pinches Zayla's cheek. All that you wanted to achieve, child, is still a long way off, she says.

The two bluecoats here, the traitor adds with a smirk, are just waiting to get another chance. While these two, he points to the murdered chief and his brother-friend, intend nothing less than to rewrite world history.

I'll think about it, Zayla murmurs. She strolls toward the lush green deciduous forest at the edge of the clearing. She wants to be alone with her thoughts. The wind comes up. With her eyes closed, she listens to the rustling of the treetops.

When she opens her eyelids again, she looks at a mighty cross of dark gray stone enthroned on a boulder where the forest path forks in front of her. A little girl emerges from the shadow of the cross and saunters toward Zayla. She is wearing a coat made of dark blue fleece with a pointed hood and colorful flowers, and she smiles tentatively. When Zayla returns her smile, the girl's face beams. A feeling of deep, all-encompassing love washes over the young Englishwoman, and for minutes she bathes in it as if in a fountain of youth. She kneels and pulls the girl to her. Deep sorrow pierces her heart. At the same time, she feels a tugging as if on an invisible string.

She snaps out of hypnosis as if she were flung from a rubber band that had been stretched and released. From one second to the next, she is pulled back into her body. She again feels the couch on which she rests, her arms and legs. Zayla recognizes herself in her father's house, in the English seaside resort of Brighton, and opens her eyes. "Papa," she whispers, throwing her arms around the surprised professor's neck. "Nell has been murdered."

Chapter 1

The Great Plains, South Dakota, USA

On top of a hill, Logan came to a stop. Panting, he sucked the midday heat into his lungs, which threatened to burst as he raced against time. Blood pulsed through his body with the force of a jackhammer. His legs were heavy as lead.

The majestic enchantment of the gently rolling hills and valleys of his old homeland commanded him to pause for a moment. The brilliant blue firmament and grassy ridges that seemed to wander into the boundary separating earth and sky touched the strings of his soul while the rugged beauty of the Great Plains opened his heart.

Logan Black Wolf Chief Diamandis loved this land. He turned his head and looked over his shoulder. Huge storm clouds towered behind him in shades of blue-gray and purple. With them, images long thought buried flooded back into his consciousness. Logan spat. The living conditions of his relatives out here were tearing him apart: an unemployment rate of eighty percent, an average life expectancy of fifty years, drinking water contaminated by uranium mines, over one hundred suicide attempts by teenage Lakȟóta in the past year alone. Apart from a bullet or the rope, often only drugs or alcohol succeeded in silencing the cries of the souls in their darkest nights.

Even as a young boy, death had been a constant acquaintance for Logan. He had had no illusions about who he was dealing with when, at the age of eight, he had accidentally walked under his cousin's body dangling from the rafters in a barn. The deeply unhappy girl had hanged herself.

For Logan, the desolation of the reservation, where the twenty-five-year-old had been born, stood in agonizing contrast to the proud history of the former lords of the Northern Plains. The cacophony of his kin's hearts lying in the dust held an inextricable contradiction to the magic of the songs and powerful voices the sons and daughters of the Seven Council Fires had once possessed.

The balmy wind that now rose from the south and floated across the prairie like a layer of velvet carried the breath of previous generations to his ear. The blood of the dead had soaked the ground on which he stood in their struggle for freedom and self-determination.

Come back to us, great-grandson of the Black Wolf Chief, they whispered. *You belong here.*

For a moment, Logan felt as if he could see in the distance the shadows of the dancers who had once honored the power of the buffalo grass. The men fastened it in dense tufts to their legs, hips, and torsos, swaying back and forth in the wind with outstretched arms that resembled the wings of birds. Logan felt the rhythm of the drums, the heartbeat of this land, in his veins. It was a rhythm that, more intense than the whisper of his ancestors or the caressing touch of the south wind, excited his every cell and revived his debilitated body.

He sharply inhaled at the sight of vultures on the horizon. They circled over a bush-covered area of a stream that had dried to a trickle in the summer heat. From the great distance, he could not tell what the scavengers were after. Was it possible his sister was down there?

He checked his phone and found he had no signal. The connection to the GPS tracker had also been lost. Logan's heart sank. His adopted brother, who had traveled after him from

Australia, would no longer be able to locate him on the prairie.

A horse would have meant a decisive time advantage for Logan. His mother's old pickup truck had stopped working at the same time she received the shocking news about her daughter's fate. Logan cursed his younger Lakȟóta half-brother who, along with a pack of teenagers, had grabbed the horses from their mother's paddock the day before.

Like most of the children on the reservation, his little brother had also grown up with horses. Some of the adolescent boys had formed gangs that captured the animals wherever they encountered them. These teenage gangs terrorized the communities on the reservation, often vanishing into areas where the tribal police could not follow them with their cars. *If Phoebe were to die now, her death would also be on the younger brother's conscience.*

Logan spat for the second time. He would make sure shame and guilt never let that little fucker fall asleep again.

The Lakȟóta started sprinting again toward the circling scavengers. The run lasted another half hour, and the closer he got to the bushes, the more his throat tightened. Upon finally arriving, he tore through the branches where he suspected the vultures' targeted prey would be.

Half-naked, with torn clothes and bleeding from wounds on her head and pubic area, the fourteen-year-old girl lay trembling on the ground. She was covered with bruises and her left eye was swollen shut.

"Phoebe!" Logan groaned in horror, touching his sister on the shoulder. "Phoebe, damn it!"

She let out a low moan. Then came a sharp cry and Phoebe's desperate attempt to defend herself. "Away! Away! Away!" The girl reared up, and her voice went into a hysterical scream.

Logan took a step back. "Phoebe," he whispered, choking

back tears. And then, following an impulse, he spoke in the language of his ancestors: "Miyé. Logan Šuŋgmánitu Tȟáŋka Sápe." *It is me, Logan Black Wolf Chief.*

At the sound of the grand old name, Phoebe raised her head and gave her brother a weak smile. Then, she slumped down and lost consciousness. Logan ran his fingers through his short sweaty hair, shaking with rage.

He dialed his mother's number. Twice, three times. Nothing went through. He changed his position several times, and then rushed up the nearest hill, but no matter what he did, he could not get reception.

Logan didn't dare leave Phoebe behind to go for help. He feared that when he returned, it would be too late for her. Her wounds were severe. *Those damned sons of bitches who did this to her ...*

He deliberated what to do next. Carry her back? How long would that take? Four hours? Maybe six?

Logan had already completed a tiring run of over two hours and was exhausted despite his excellent fitness. Carrying his unconscious sister home seemed like a hopeless undertaking. And yet, what alternative was there for him? He could leave Phoebe behind and get help. Alone, he could make much faster progress. It was possible he would get reception again on the way back. Perhaps he would not have to go far before he would be able to make a distress call. However, there was a storm coming up. What if Phoebe died in the meantime? What if she regained consciousness and found herself alone? What if the bastards who had raped her came looking for her, wanting to cover their tracks and dispose of their victim? What if the vultures pounced on her?

Logan suppressed a cry of rage at what seemed a hopeless situation. Then suddenly, he became aware of distant engine noises and looked up. A cloud of dust formed on the horizon. He saw a vehicle speeding toward him. Logan was torn between the hope of rescue and the fear of not being able to defend Phoebe and himself. He put his hand on his belt over the old combat knife with the black wolf head and watched as an SUV came to a stop just ahead of him. The driver's door pushed open.

"Nick!" groaned Logan in relief. "Damn, am I glad to see you."

A man in his mid-twenties with wise, sapphire eyes and shoulder-length brown hair, dressed in jeans, a T-shirt, and hiking boots, walked up to Logan and shouted in an unmistakably Australian accent, "Fucking hell, mate! What a bloody stroke of luck! Your sister ...?"

Logan returned the knife to the leather sheath on his belt and pointed grimly at the bushes behind him. With Nick's help, he parted the branches and carefully picked his sister up from the ground.

The Australian pulled a fleece jacket out of the travel bag in the trunk of the SUV and put it around the delicate girl's body. "Sorry," he mumbled. But Logan understood. It was the only gesture his adopted brother could think of to return some semblance of dignity to Phoebe. Logan thanked him with his eyes, and then Nick helped place the severely wounded girl in the back seat of the car.

"Where can we find the nearest doctor around here?" he inquired. Logan was glad his brother didn't ask any questions about what exactly had happened to Phoebe.

"No doctor," Logan replied. "We're taking my sister to my grandmother's."

Nick looked at him in surprise. "You rarely make decisions recklessly, my friend." He chewed on his lower lip. "I'm sure that's one of the reasons my father treated you with such great respect from the beginning." His gaze bored into Logan. "You're sure you want to avoid a doctor altogether?"

Logan nodded. "My grandmother is the best choice we have out here."

Nick sighed.

The drive became a stressful ordeal for both men. First, Nick got behind the wheel of the SUV while Logan held his sister in the back seat, but not long after, the brothers switched positions.

Nick, who did not know the way, kept following Logan's navigation instructions too late, and the Lakȟóta was unable to suppress angry outbursts. In response, Nick stopped the car and wordlessly joined Phoebe in the back seat. Logan bit his tongue and got out. For a moment, he thought about how he could calm his sister in case she woke up on the journey and found herself in the arms of a man she had never seen before. But he got behind the wheel anyway and started off at such a breakneck speed that Nick cursed, having trouble keeping himself and Phoebe in their seats. Logan cast a critical glance in the rear-view mirror. If Nick let his sister fall or bump her against the seat or car door, he would break his neck.

It took over an hour for the men to finally arrive with the wounded girl at Logan's grandmother's old log house, which stood secluded in western South Dakota. The back of the house bordered a strip of woodland, the only group of trees for several miles on the rolling grassy plain.

Uŋčí Black Wolf Chief, the mother of Logan's mother, appeared on the porch. She was an old but powerful and very slender woman with long gray hair hanging down to her waist in two braids. She wore washed-out jeans and a dark purple blouse. Dangling from a leather cord around her neck was one half of a pendant with two black wolves, the counterpart of which Logan wore. Even at her eighty years, Uŋčí faced her visitors upright and confident. With the hint of a smile, her pitch-black eyes caught the greeting glance of her favorite grandson, her gaze swallowing him up like quicksand.

Logan loved his grandmother dearly and held profound respect for her. His loyalty to her was boundless.

With great concern in her eyes but calm composure in her actions, Uŋčí asked him to put his sister on a sleeping place in the small room at the back of the log cabin. The chamber was dark and smelled pleasantly of herbs and concoctions stacked on shelves up to the ceiling. Eagle feathers, hand drums, animal figurines, animal teeth and claws, along with healing stones lay scattered everywhere in assorted colors and shapes. Massive bear and bison skins covered the floor.

The heads had not been severed from an especially thick, white-yellow buffalo hide and the shaggy, brown-black fur of a grizzly bear. Their skulls rested on the ground, staring out from bony, dark eye sockets like sentinels from a bygone era.

At the small fireplace in the kitchen of the log cabin, Uŋčí was busy burning aromatic spicy herbs and plants. Within seconds, their smell permeated every corner of the cottage like rising mist. The scent of sage stood out particularly strongly and impregnated the air. Then the healer heated a bucket of water. When finished, she approached Logan and asked him to leave the cabin with Nicholas for a while. For what she was about to do, she needed to be alone with Phoebe. Logan rose and led Nick out to the prairie.

"What a woman," Nick was full of admiration for Logan's grandmother. "She didn't even want to know what kind of stranger you dragged in here with you."

A smile played around Logan's lips, which did not reach his eyes. "Uŋčí knows very well who you are, Nick."

"Oongtshi?" he tried to repeat the word. "What does that

name mean?"

With both hands, Logan rifled through his jet-black hair. "Uŋčí means grandmother. She is an ancient soul who guards the secrets of my people," he added. "She is a bridge between this world and the next. A holy woman and a spiritual guide. She has mastered the high art of healing like no other."

His grandmother's abilities had fascinated Logan since he was a child. She was clairsentient, clairaudient and clairvoyant and walked back and forth between the physical and non-physical worlds. His Uŋčí was an extraordinary woman who, although fully accepted and honored by her and Logan's people, had sought a place of her own to live outside of their community.

For his grandmother alone, Logan as a fourteen-year-old would have refrained from escaping the desolation of the reservation. For Uŋčí alone, he would have abandoned the opulent life he now led as a twenty-five-year-old with his influential family of choice in Australia.

Logan leaned against the hood of the SUV and hung his head. He inhaled deeply and heavily. The exhalation that followed was accompanied by a dark whistling sound, a wailing sound that could no longer be suppressed, breaking through a body that refused to obey its exhausted owner. "Phoebe is … practically … still a child. How could those cursed sons of bitches do this to her?"

Nick was silent.

Logan bit his lips, and then literally spat out each word one by one. "She … is … practically … still … a … child." His voice broke.

"What can we do?" whispered Nick.

Logan raised his head. "I'm going to find these guys," he replied icily. "I'm going to cut off their hands and their dicks and shove them down their throats. They will writhe in pools of their own blood and die in agony. I will look into their eyes during their pathetic death throes and enjoy it. And then the damned justice system in this country can inject a poison into my veins and send me to hell with these scumbags so that there, I can avenge in a thousand more ways the suffering they caused my sister."

Bitterness drove Logan to the edge of a precipice from which his return was threatened to be cut off.

"I don't think Phoebe will ever get over this," he continued again. "She'll spend her life recoiling from any man who tries to get close to her. Those pigs have destroyed her, something this miserable life on this damned reservation has yet to accomplish." He paused. "Raped Lakȟóta women often used to commit suicide."

"That's utter insanity," Nick snapped. "She's not a disgrace to you because she is the victim of such monsters."

Logan shook his head. "Of *course* she's not. But the sense of degradation and the unbelievable brutality ... many of our women didn't want to go on living like that."

He saw that Nick was frowning. "Didn't your men rape in war, too?"

Logan rubbed the fatigue from his eyes. "In the old days, rape may have been part of warfare for some tribes. But a people like mine — who had their heads set straight by a woman, not a man, when they forgot to treat the buffalo and the land properly, a people who revered a woman as the bearer of their most sacred ceremonies — do not disgrace their daughters, Nick. A nation that knows it can only be as strong as the hearts of its women does not tolerate rape. Such a nation honors the female and the male way. And it respects the way of its *wíŋkte* and Two-Spirit People who do not fit into binary gender roles."

After a pause, Logan continued his reflections. "The struggle of the European settlers for our land, however, had increasingly changed the position of our women. So did capitalism, the Christian missionaries, the alcohol, and the fur trade. Our women became dependent upon the economic and power interests of their fathers, their brothers, their husbands. These changes were not to their advantage. In the old days, our men were raised to honor the women in their families: their mothers and grandmothers, their sisters, cousins, and aunts. If a woman was raped, it was tantamount to a death sentence. The council would put a knife in the perpetrator's hand with instructions to go onto the prairie and take his own life. A man who rapes is attacking his family. He goes against the Creator and against society. Thus, he no longer belongs to humanity.

"Nowadays, however, even among my own people, rape is no longer an exception. Neither is domestic violence or even child abuse." Logan clenched his fists. "And we are struggling with the epidemic level at which our women and girls are disappearing and being raped and killed, especially by non-Lakȟóta. The police, the courts, to a large extent the media — none of them give a damn. It is the legacy of racist colonialism in this country. It is like a cancer."

A long pause arose between the two men. Logan knew his adopted brother had also experienced terror and loss long before he matured into a man. Nick knew of the existence of traumas that cut like swords through the soul, and both brothers were familiar with the coping mechanisms people developed to protect themselves from the darkest episodes of their lives.

Logan observed that Nick seemed to drift off into his own mind. His adopted brother broke out in a sweat and shivered. Had the images of his captivity flooded him? Scenes he had once described as dozens of billiard balls in his head, played simultaneously against the table cushions? Balls that shot back and forth with full force, wounding him again and again to the core?

Under Logan's searching gaze, Nick turned his face away from him. He made a gruff hand gesture, signifying that his attention was unwanted. Logan respected that. His brother knew how to focus on the part of his personality that was able to look at itself with sober, analytical eyes in such moments. In this observer role, akin to that of a scientist during a field experiment, Nick had learned to dismiss the scenes that threatened to consume him, which was accompanied by the mantra that he was watching the horror of his captivity but did not need to relive it.

Relieved, Logan noticed Nick's breaths become deeper and steadier. He had once again successfully refused to surrender his fears to his tormentors. Logan put a hand on his shoulder. "Those monsters couldn't destroy you, Nick. You've gotten so much stronger than they were."

"If you hadn't insisted on playing the hero back then," Nick snorted sarcastically, "those guys would have put me six feet under."

Logan's fingers dug supportively into Nick's shoulder. Then he clenched his hands into fists, playfully punched his brother's arm, and took a step back.

Logan knew the immense gratitude that Nick and his father still felt toward him. Nick's mother, however, had from the beginning only seen "the Indian" in him, the foreigner, the vagrant, the gang member, and a killer. All roles that had been scary to her. Logan, for his part, had recognized in Nick's mother nothing more than a conceited white woman who used her privilege to demand her own way at the expense of others. He had taken immense pleasure in playing on her fears toward him. When his adoptive father finally split up with this woman after a bitter divorce, he had quietly celebrated the day.

"I'm sure you thought the *killer* would come through in me again," Logan taunted, also alluding to his plans for revenge for the crime against Phoebe.

Nick countered, "You should never have heard what my mother said about you back then. You're *not* a killer. You weren't one when you pulled me out of that hellhole, and you're not going to be a killer now." He looked at him firmly. "We'll deal with these assholes differently, Logan. There are plenty of ways to destroy these pigs' lives once we find out who they are. If we get our father on board, with the help of his tracking dogs, we'll find a way to make these guys pay."

Logan liked the matter-of-factness with which Nick now spoke of *their* father. He appreciated his sympathy and forced himself to smile. "We'll see," he replied thoughtfully. "We'll see."

Chapter 2

Canary Wharf, London, United Kingdom

Marrock Lovell was furious with his superiors. The investment banker hated them for the lies they had spread about him. He despised them for their lack of backbone and loss of leadership. He looked down on the gang of gentlemen in their dark tailored suits who had stabbed him in the back and declared him the scapegoat. With the corners of his mouth turned up and his arms folded, he had followed their lecture on culture change in investment banking. He had endured the rebuke that the bank needed to move with the times and get rid of its risk-takers. But the content of that sermon had rolled off him like water off a duck's back.

A colleague, leaning his hip against the door frame with his arms crossed in front of his chest while Marrock was clearing his desk in his office, smirkingly commented that Marrock would have had to pay more attention to having integrity. The fired banker was annoyed by the gloating expression on this man's face and was already hatching a plan to get back at him. Nobody made fun of Marrock Lovell!

He hated the smugness with which his boss had rubbed salt in his wounds when the man pointed out that he had been passed up for a promotion again.

"We appreciate your dedication, Marrock," and then his boss had added, "but amidst these vexatious allegations of the me-too vultures after your stunt with the corporate sociologist, there's no way we're going to keep you around any longer. What the hell possessed you to go after that cute little thing so aggressively when she had made it abundantly clear to you she wanted to be left alone?"

Marrock snorted, and almost bared his teeth. He knew exactly what to think of such a "rebuke."

A few years earlier, the banking giant had introduced a surveillance system that put many ideas from George Orwell's *1984* to shame. Big Brother had long been a reality at this investment bank. Comprehensive video surveillance of offices, corridors and the cafeteria, the recording of telephone calls, the reading of e-mails, and the creation of movement and purchase profiles with the help of chips in the in-house ID cards were part of everyday life. Under the pretext of not only regulating but predicting misconduct on the part of its employees, however, the existing surveillance systems had been raised to a whole new level in the current year: Data and profiles were evaluated automatically, and a computer calculated the likelihood that an employee would or would not harm the financial giant.

Marrock's *advances*, as he would call them, had been digitally documented and were, in the current social and political climate, sufficiently offensive in nature to prevent him from taking any future legal action against the dismissal. Instead, he had to settle for the severance pay he had been awarded. The corporate sociologist had been hired as an independent observer only to give the investment bank's façade a better coat of paint. Marrock knew that much. Was it possible his boss had used her to set a trap for him?

Frustrated and undecided about what to do next after his expulsion, the 41-year-old had randomly stuffed a few articles of clothing into a travel bag and left for the Caribbean on the next available flight. There he would take a two-week break.

At the breakfast buffet of his hotel on the very first day, he met a young Swedish woman who introduced herself as a

London psychology student. The blonde, who didn't fit the profile of Marrock's usual prey, turned out to be a stimulating flirt. She carried a very analytical perspective. Coupled with her gift for witty conversation and her talent for stroking the banker's ego to the point where he almost started purring, she was a more-than-pleasant pastime for him. Her inexperience in bed was compensated by her never-ending enthusiasm. She was eager to please and learn from a *sex god*, as she called him.

The sacked banker did not, however, measure the real value of his flirtation by the sex he enjoyed in abundance with her during his vacation, but by the information he received during the breaks in between. At first, Marrock had dismissed the student's astonishing case histories on the healing potential of hypnosis from the practice of her mentor, Professor Dr. Matthew Kirkpatrick, as nothing more than sheer entertainment. He found it hard to believe that hypnosis and transmigration, or *the journey of souls,* could be the specialties of a highly intelligent and enlightened university professor. Marrock whistled between his teeth when Silja told him what fees the professor, who had a two-year waiting list, was able to collect for such hocus pocus. Then, however, the banker had started to become fascinated by the case of a multiple sclerosis client of the professor, which Silja told him about after they had met a young woman in a wheelchair at the evening buffet.

"Professor Kirkpatrick put this client under hypnosis," Silja chatted blithely, pouring him more wine. "She told of her lives in the avatar of several warriors. Among other things, she had also lived as a Viking, in the style of the legendary Ragnar Lothbrok, for example. It was this life that she was particularly fond of. Under hypnosis, she raved about the power and elegance of this avatar. Of his cat-like movements, his conquering moves, the freedom he had to take what and who he wanted. Professor Kirkpatrick asked her during the hypnosis session if that meant the Viking had raped. Her response was that indeed he had on occasion, but the Viking warrior had never felt guilt in doing so. It had been a rough and wild natural life. She said forced copulation and sexual coercion were common enough in the animal kingdom, too. Orangutans and chimpanzees do it, as do dolphins, which are so dear to humans. The Viking did not behave much differently in his natural state, she told Professor Kirkpatrick."

Marrock raised his eyebrows.

Silja looked at him and grinned. "Exciting, isn't it? Professor Kirkpatrick then asked this woman why her soul chose to live in the avatar of an MS patient today."

"What did she say?"

"Her response was hesitant," Silja recounted. "Still under hypnosis, she finally explained that she had to learn to stay with herself and look inward, instead of fulfilling her needs solely on the outside. She needed to learn to live with love — in particular for herself."

Marrock had followed the student's words with great attention. In her stories, he immediately recognized the entire manipulative and financial potential of hypnotherapy if a person like him managed to maintain the façade of philanthropy and altruism.

Back in London, he googled the name of Silja's mentor. Surprised, he found that Professor Dr. Matthew Kirkpatrick was not only highly regarded at a London university, but worldwide as a lecturer, psychologist, and hypnotherapist. *This man holds more academic honors than a decorated war hero medals,* Marrock thought enviously. Then he clicked on the YouTube video embedded on the website of the professor's practice.

When he first glanced at the man's daughter, her beauty hit

him like a bolt from out of the blue. His eyes were glued to the highly attractive creature on his computer screen. Thick and heavy dark hair, like Shehrezâd from the Persian tales of *The Thousand and One Nights,* hung down to her hips and framed an even face with high cheekbones, green-brown shimmering eyes, and sensual lips. She took Marrock's breath away. In the opulent leather chair where he had taken a seat, his pelvis jerked forward, unable to control this small but lustful movement.

What a beauty this girl was! Even dressed in loose-fitting jeans and a baggy sweater, Zayla Victoria Kirkpatrick could not hide that she possessed the body and grace of a goddess. Lust and desire flooded the banker like water to a wadi after a downpour. In his mind's eye, he made her the object of his darkest fantasies. With a trophy like Zayla at his side, he would surely be the envy of the men with whom he saw himself in incessant competition for the fleshpots of this world. Close cooperation with Zayla's father might also open opportunities for him to reclaim his social status outside of investment banking and reprise his favorite role as master manipulator. He admired his fellow Englishman Sir Alfred Hitchcock and was a great lover of the entire twentieth-century black-and-white film era. The maneuvers of Ingrid Bergmann's sinister husband in the crime film *Gaslight,* aimed at having his spouse committed to a mental hospital, would have been no more than child's play for Marrock. A liaison with the professor's daughter could bring him into the fold of the scientific teaching and research community if he were smart enough about it.

Marrock's attention turned back to the YouTube video. Overheated by his manifold fantasies, he was about to start relieving himself when the presenter's words hit him like a bolt of lightning. *Seventeen fucking years old?* Had he actually heard correctly? Zayla had just turned seventeen? Bloody hell, the girl looked like she was in her mid-twenties. Professor Kirkpatrick would flay him alive.

Marrock himself was the father of two young daughters and always eager to defend his own flesh and blood, at least to the outside world. The very idea that a man his age could begin an affair with one of his own girls had the potential to turn him into a ferocious beast. However, it was not the awareness of doing wrong that gave Marrock pause. After all, in many ancient and in most non-Western cultures, girls fourteen and younger were considered sexually mature and were married off. No, what stopped the ex-banker was the knowledge of social ostracism. The fear of the light that could fall on the sensory-deprived darkness within him — the life-threatening confrontation with an old powerlessness.

Marrock sighed and pushed himself away from the desk in his leather chair. Then he went into the bathroom, yanked open the shower door and turned on the water. He undressed, reduced the temperature, and forced himself to withstand the ice water assault on his libido and loss of control. Only when he began to shiver with cold did he allow himself to turn the water off again and dry his body. Then he slipped on his boxers and a T-shirt. On the way back to his study, he reached for a red wine glass and the last bottle of a sinfully expensive Château-Mouton-Rothschild. He placed both on his mahogany desk which, much like its owner, attracted the gaze of every visitor and took up more space than seemed appropriate. Cursing, Marrock dropped back into his leather chair and ruffled his raven hair. Then he reset the YouTube video to the place where Zayla was introduced in a short segment and clicked start.

"Zayla Victoria Kirkpatrick is the only child of internationally renowned psychologist, human scientist and hypnotherapist Professor Dr. Matthew Kirkpatrick," the presenter began.

"Professor Kirkpatrick graduated with honors from the University of St. Andrews and subsequently completed his PhD there. He has researched and taught at Stanford in the U.S. as well as at the University of Arizona. Since returning to the United Kingdom, he has been active in the country's top universities while maintaining a private practice.

"As you can clearly see from the pictures now played, Professor Kirkpatrick's daughter, who has just turned seventeen, is an exceptionally attractive girl, but also — as our sources have confirmed — a young woman with outstanding intellect: father and daughter are members of a network for the highly intelligent whose entry qualification requires an IQ of at least 150. By comparison, 68% of the population is in a normally intelligent range with an IQ between 85 and 110. The most intelligent have an IQ in excess of 150. Along with Zayla and Matthew Kirkpatrick, about two percent of all people are at this level.

"Geniuses such as Albert Einstein and the British physicist Stephen Hawking are said to have had an intelligence quotient of 160. Psychologists attribute an IQ of 210 to the German poet and natural scientist Johann Wolfgang von Goethe, 205 to the Swedish scientist, mystic and theosophist Emmanuel Swedenborg, 190 to the Russian chess world champion Garri Kasparov and 154 to the American actress Sharon Stone.

"Another unique attribute, aside from Zayla Kirkpatrick's exceptional intelligence, is that she is said to be mediumistic, telepathically inclined, and an empath, or a person who can sense feelings around her — including other people's fears or their states of health. Zayla is said to be clairsentient and clairvoyant and generally able to sense energies and moods that are hidden from other people. Zayla Kirkpatrick, we were told, has a personal interest in this case because Nell, the eleven-year-old girl who recently disappeared here in the London borough of South Kensington, lived in her immediate neighborhood and maintained close contact with Zayla. Zayla claims she can help the police in the search because the soul ..." here the presenter paused meaningfully, "... yes, indeed, because the *soul* of the missing child had allegedly contacted her. After three days of fruitless searching by the police, Nell's desperate parents have now agreed to enlist Zayla's help. And we, BBC Two's Carl Norris, and Amelie Jones, get to accompany Zayla on her search for the missing girl.

"Professor Kirkpatrick is so convinced of his daughter's abilities that he hopes the presence and documentation by — let's put it cautiously — *skeptical* journalists will be a breakthrough for the acceptance of paranormal abilities in science and in the international mainstream. We are excited about what is in store here, especially because someone of Professor Kirkpatrick's internationally acclaimed status has contacted and invited us to film. Still, we wonder if a father should be allowed to subject his underage daughter to such a potentially sensitive situation, one that could make the girl a target of public ridicule."

Following sudden inspiration, Marrock stopped the video and opened another browser window. He typed "Dr. Matthew Kirkpatrick" into the search bar and immediately received results linking to the professor's practice and the Internet addresses to his university activities and private website. After a brief time, Marrock found what he was looking for. Fascinated, he studied the posting of a year-long training opportunity as a hypnosis and regression coach for fifteen selected people in a pilot project under Professor Kirkpatrick's direction.

Grinning broadly, the banker toasted himself with his glass of 1er Grand Cru Classé Pauillac Magnum Bordeaux. Then, with the deviousness and calculated emotion that rivaled the insidiousness of Shakespearean villain Richard the Third, he began writing an application to Professor Kirkpatrick.

Chapter 3
The Great Plains, South Dakota, USA

*T*here is dead silence on the prairie. Moon and stars are hidden behind a blanket of clouds. Darkness has settled over the grassy plain like a cloak, enveloping the camp with its three dozen bison-skin tents set up in a circle and tapering upward in ghostly silence. Although not a breath of air stirs, the tinkling and jingling of wind chimes made of animal bones underscore the surrealistic scene. It is the calm before the storm. The deceptive idyll in which nature holds its breath and sucks the world around it into a vacuum where even the singing of birds and the buzzing of insects die.

Powerful squalls are coming. Minute by minute, they whip more violently across the land. Lightning bright as day flickers on the horizon, giving an awe-inspiring foretaste of Wakíŋyaŋ, the thunder beings, the mighty electric forces of nature that will soon be unleashed over this part of the northern prairies.

The heavy leather walls of the teepees beat in the wind, but the melodic swinging of animal hooves hitting each other resounds in the same rhythm as before. And just as the bending water of the river erodes the rigid rock and the seemingly powerless triumphs over the strong, the sound of the wind chimes gains the upper hand over the roaring of the storm ...

A warrior in the full bloom of his years enters one of the larger tents inside the camp circle. He is the husband of the sandy-haired woman who, along with the grandmother, kneels beside the wounded man on the teepee floor lined with bison and bear hides. Although not wearing any badge of his rank, his demeanor alone identifies him as one of the foremost of his people. He grasps both the critical state of his injured brother-friend and the unstable emotional condition of his wife with just a glance. The friend's body is littered with wounds that the diligent hands of the two women still cannot close. Blood flows in rivulets, like water from a leaky container, and has stained the floor and parts of the women's leather clothing a dark red. A twitching and trembling run through the body of the warrior lying on the ground. His muscles spasm in rapid succession, giving him an almost grotesque appearance. His breath comes shallow and brittle. The sweat of the man fighting hard for his own life mixes with his blood. His skin glistens in the glow of the fire.

The wounded man tosses his head and whispers unintelligible words. The master of the house, who is still standing at the entrance of the tent, watches as his wife dips a clean piece of leather into a bowl of water and strokes the wounded man's face. Then she brings her ear close to his mouth and backs away, startled. The husband sees her glance at the grandmother, who is covering the warrior's wounds with an herbal paste. Full of concern, the husband sees that his wife's movements become agitated. Her eyes gleam moistly. All too well he knows the emotions raging within her. The grandmother hands her a bowl of herbal tea to give to the injured drop by drop.

A scratching at the tent entrance announces a visitor. It is a dignified old man, tall like all males of the people, and of lean build. He is a Holy Man of high reputation through whom the powers of the universe work and who knows how to heal the sick like no other.

Troubled about what he has seen, the husband signals his wife to follow him outside and frowns when she hesitates. The couple shares a deep concern for the wounded man's condition. But the look his wife casts at the warrior lying on the ground before she bows to her husband's request and rises has the effect of a punch to his stomach. The couple exits the tent, leaving the Holy Man alone with the grandmother to care for the injured warrior. The sandy-haired woman expresses her wish to go to the river to clean her hands from the blood of the wounded. With a nod, her husband indicates his agreement, but he stops her from going to the women's bathing area of the camp without his company. Instead, he urges her further upstream, beyond the bathing area, to a secluded spot that his wife immediately recognizes. A smile settles on her face, which is lined with worry. She spins in circles with outstretched arms, stroking the air, and then faces him.

"Iyótaŋkilakštó," she whispers to him. *I love you.*

A shiver covers the husband's body as his emotions overwhelm him. In this place, he once made the sandy-haired girl his wife.

She moves light-footedly toward the bank of the river and kneels at the water's edge. She lowers her arms into the cool water and follows the blood with her eyes as it slips off her hands, darkens the water, and drifts downstream. Her husband watches every emotion cross her face as intently as an eagle on the hunt. She raises her head and looks at him, straight on, not lowering her eyes out of respect and politeness, as is customary among their people. She stands and approaches her husband. Her left hand gently rests on his bare torso, marked with the deep scars of Wiwáŋyaŋg Wačhípi, the Sundance, and lingers where his heart beats. Her delicate touch triggers a tingling sensation inside him. Then she begins to speak.

Did her husband have to lead her to this place just to get confirmation that she still loves him? Did she hide her feelings so badly at the sight of his wounded brother-friend that she made her husband and herself the subject of gossip in the village? Does he not know that she would never try to take advantage of the fact that the people expect a man of his rank to bear even the loss of his own wife with composure, refraining from any retaliation? Does he really fear she might leave him? Does he not know that she loves him? And will always love him?

Rain begins to fall. The man's reaction to his wife's words is outwardly cool, but he knows that she can feel how much they have touched him. The Holy Man asks for the flesh of those who are closest to my brother-friend and want to see him alive, he says. He also asked *for yours, he adds silently.*

The warrior pulls his hunting knife from his belt and cuts out tiny pieces of his wife's flesh from her forearms, dropping them into small tobacco pouches. Then he hands her the knife, and she performs the same action on him.

Bright as day, a jagged flash of lightning shoots over the heads of the couple. A deafening crash sends the tip of the knife the sandy-haired woman holds deeper into her husband's arm than she intended.

While the couple sacrifices their flesh and puts it in the small leather pouch filled with tobacco ready for the ceremony of the Holy Man, the blood of the husband mixes with that of his wife. Defenseless against the powerful elements of nature, the couple prays in loud, clear voices for the life of their gravely injured friend, thanking Wakȟáŋ Tȟáŋka, the universal spiritual force, for the return of the outcast to his people. The husband's chanting becomes one with that of his wife, and the prayers of both unite with the sound of the rain pouring down and the crashing of thunder. In the background, the soft sound of wind chimes made of animal hooves is heard and settles more and more gently over the thunderstorm, until the quiet finally defeats the loud and silence reigns again on the prairie.

In the darkness of the early morning hours, Logan awoke for the second time that night in his grandmother's log cabin. With his fingertips, he felt the fine beads of sweat that coated his body like the late summer gossamer of young crab spiders. His breathing was shallow and irregular. The images of his dream had seemed more tangible and pressing than anything he had dreamed before. Excitement flooded through him, making his neural pathways crackle like high-voltage wires. The people in his dream seemed as familiar to him as the people closest to him in *this* world, and yet he knew none of them by name.

The sandy-haired woman was the epitome of everything he

could have wished for in a wife. *The woman of my dreams*, Logan thought, and couldn't quite take himself seriously at the thought. He laughed silently and shook his head.

A family of his own ... Logan hung on this thought for a while. For the first time, he admitted to himself that, at twenty-five, he was at an age when a man in the traditional Lakȟóta world would have long demonstrated his skills as a hunter and his prowess as a warrior. He also would have done so for the privilege of being able to woo a woman with his head held high instead of subjecting himself to the ridicule of his own people in this attempt, outed as a young buck. Had he proved himself? Was he capable of providing for a family and protecting them? Did he want to?

From the opposite side of the main room in Uŋčí's log cabin where he lay, he heard Nick's steady breathing and, farther away, the quiet breaths of his grandmother and his still unconscious sister. *Phoebe.* She had been the victim of brutal violence, and he had just had dreams with erotic undertones? Feelings of shame flooded him. He closed his eyes and exhaled slowly. What had he become? Who had he become? Should he perhaps never have left the reservation and the United States? If he had not turned his back on his family more than a decade ago, he would have been able to stand by their side over the years and protect Phoebe.

He was the eldest son of a Lakȟóta who had died as a U.S. soldier in Iraq in the war against Saddam Hussein. He had almost no memory of his father. And yet, shouldn't he have taken over his role long ago instead of allowing himself to be so absorbed by the luxurious life of his Australian family? Had it been wrong to enjoy the last eleven years as the adopted son of Deimos Aleksander Diamandis, who was so tremendously influential and devoted to him?

Logan took a long, deep breath and exhaled just as slowly and deliberately. Then he rose, slipped on his jeans and sweatshirt, and glanced at his smartphone.

It was three o'clock in the morning. Sleep was out of the question for him, so he strode out onto the shadowy prairie toward the creek that meandered closely behind Uŋčí's log cabin. Logan squatted down on the bank, letting out another deep sigh. Lost in his thoughts and at odds with himself and his decisions, he let his hands and forearms glide through the cool water.

When he looks up, following a soft sound in the water, he sees the sandy-haired woman striding unclothed into a river. Without shame and with a smile on her lips, she approaches him, the warrior already standing waist-deep in the water, having invited her by a hand signal to follow him. As she stands less than an arm's length away from him, he playfully slaps his hand on the water, splashing the cooling droplets onto her body. The sandy-haired woman lets out an amused squeal, but when she tries to get back at him for his teasing, he puts up with it for only a few moments. With a quick grip, he pulls the young woman toward him. While his right arm is wrapped around her waist, the fingers of his left hand slide along the sensitive skin on her neck. With gentle movements, he washes her body with the river water. She nestles against him and listens to the song he has begun to sing, telling her of his love and desire to honor her and make her his wife in the right way.

But then his song is carried by a second voice, and Logan sees his brother-friend standing on the other shore. He gestures to this man to leave the place where he wants to make the sandy-haired girl his wife. But the warrior on the bank has already taken the first step toward the young couple. When his foot meets the river, the water ripples turbulently around Logan.

The outlines of other Lakȟóta men and women now appear on the shore, and to his confusion, Logan hears the approaching muffled murmur of a monotonous "Wógluze!" They marry their own! Wógluze! A forbidden relationship that leads to incest. Some women interrupt the repetitive shouts and start singing an indignant tremolo. Logan's gaze falls back on his brother-friend. With every step he takes closer toward him and the woman, the waves become higher and higher until they finally spill over the banks. By the time the brother-friend reaches the couple, the calm stream has turned into gurgling white water. Logan watches the water climb up his own body and the bodies of his wife and friend. The skin of the three liquefies where they are touched by the water. In this way, the brother-friends and the sandy-haired woman merge first with the water and then with each other.

The last image etched in Logan's memory before his body obeyed him again and he could tear his arms out of the river and retreat from the shore was the sight of three heads with a single body cast in water, accompanied by the echoing laughter of three voices. Then, the water suspended in midair, dissolved, and became one again with the rippling of the small river that bordered Uŋčí's log house.

Once again, sweat had broken out all over Logan's body and his pulse was racing. Had he been dreaming with his eyes open?

The hairs on the back of his neck suddenly bristled, sensing someone behind him. Wheeling around with all his might, he nearly brought down the petite old woman who had silently approached him. Logan cursed.

His grandmother soothingly put her hand on his upper arm. "The blood of Šuŋgmánitu Tȟáŋka Sápe flows in your veins, my grandson. The voices that call you are the voices of the Black Wolf Chief and his brother-friend, Heȟáka Nážiŋ, the Standing Elk."

The power and clarity of these words struck Logan to the core. He shuddered, every hair on his body standing on end. Uŋčí's insights into the long-ignored challenges her favorite grandson would be faced with once again upon his return to his old homeland provided the impetus for the course correction that would dramatically change Logan's life yet again that night.

"Šuŋgmánitu Tȟáŋka Sápe, the Black Wolf Chief, was one of our most controversial leaders, but also one of our greatest. The young warriors followed him in droves. Our people need their young men back, Logan. We need men like you, *tȟakóža*, my grandson, especially here on the reservation."

Logan remained silent. Uŋčí's words struck him where he was most vulnerable. His thoughts wandered back to the three people in his two dreams, and he now understood who he had encountered. The wounded man in mortal danger and the man on the shore had been the Black Wolf Chief. The warrior, however, who had made the sandy-haired girl his wife, was the Black Wolf Chief's brother-friend, the Standing Elk. Logan rubbed his forehead with his index and middle fingers. But why had he experienced both dreams from Standing Elk's point of view and not from that of his ancestor, the Black Wolf Chief?

"Šuŋgmánitu Tȟáŋka Sápe had been cast out by our people," Logan murmured as he pondered his thoughts.

Uŋčí nodded and then calmly told the story of the Black Wolf Chief — as if she wanted to remind her grandson in her very own way whose descendant he was.

"The father of the Black Wolf Chief killed a warrior of his own tribal group in a dispute. For this act, the tribal council expelled him from the Lakȟóta people. Šuŋgmánitu Tȟáŋka Sápe was only fifteen years old, but he followed his father, whom he loved and revered and whom he believed to be unjustly condemned, into exile. Unprotected and homeless, father and son roamed the prairies from then on. Every day they ran the risk of being attacked and killed. In search of the protection of a community, they let themselves be recruited the following summers and winters as scouts for the white soldiers and lived for some years among our enemies on the Northern Plains as well. There the Black Wolf Chief passed the tests that made him a man and a warrior, and that also gave him his name. When his father lost his life in a raid of hostile tribes, Šuŋgmánitu Tȟáŋka Sápe returned to the Oglála-Lakȟóta. As an exile, he had expected to be killed by our warriors. But his fame and skill as a scout among the white soldiers and his daring and courage as a fighter among our enemies had preceded him. Our young men and especially Heȟáka Nážiŋ, the Standing Elk, the old brother-friend of the Black Wolf Chief, fought for his return to our people against the will of the elders.

"Many older Lakȟóta men distrusted Šuŋgmánitu Tȟáŋka Sápe and saw him as a threat to the cohesion of the tribe. They did not like his influence on the young warriors and were eager to ostracize the Black Wolf Chief as a traitor and renegade. For the young men of the Lakȟóta, however, Šuŋgmánitu Tȟáŋka Sápe embodied the ideal of the warrior across camps. He was an exceptional fighter and a brilliant strategist. He combined many of the old warrior virtues that were considered exemplary among our people: inner strength, perseverance, and endurance as well as a sense of honor, a willingness to sacrifice, and a love of truth and bravery. The young men admired and revered him. And since the Lakȟóta would have also offered a brave enemy a place within their own ranks, Šuŋgmánitu Tȟáŋka Sápe was welcomed back as a true son of his people. The Standing Elk and the other young men forced the Black Wolf Chief's opponents to pay him the respect he deserved as a glorious warrior and self-elected leader of those Lakȟóta groups who wished to follow him. Thus, the tribal council finally recognized him as one of our headmen and a leader of warriors."

Logan was familiar with the main points of the tales surrounding his great-great-grandfather. He knew that the warrior virtues of his people included not only those mentioned by Uŋčí, but also humility, respect, generosity, and wisdom. These four virtues had not been ingrained in the Black Wolf Chief in the same way as those for which he was still admired and revered today.

Logan's thoughts wandered back to the young woman in his two dreams, who both Šuŋgmánitu Tȟáŋka Sápe and Heȟáka Nážiŋ had loved. "Who was the sandy-haired girl, Uŋčí?"

The old woman's eyes flashed. She looked at her grandson for a moment as penetratingly as if she were able to see to the bottom of his soul. Then she lowered her eyes and chuckled. "Ah. So, you did see her ..."

Uŋčí's tone told Logan that she had decided at that moment to tell her grandson more about this woman, who was only mentioned in passing in the Lakȟóta oral traditions about their legendary leader.

"Her name was Tȟuŋkáŋ Hetȟúŋ-wiŋ. Rock-With-Horns-Woman," she continued with a smirk. "She was the twelfth and youngest child of French and Irish settlers, and she had grown up among our people from birth. In her heart, the Rock-With-Horns-Woman had always been a Lakȟóta."

Logan wondered what reason his grandmother might have had for emphasizing that last sentence so clearly.

"Both the Black Wolf Chief and the Standing Elk loved the Rock-With-Horns-Woman," Uŋčí continued. "She had been brought to the Standing Elk's family after her biological father did not want her because he blamed the little one for the death of his beloved wife. The sandy-haired girl's father was a French fur hunter and trapper. He had become the friend of one of our warriors after finding him wounded in the Black Hills years before and nursing him back to health. The Lakȟóta then allowed him to build a log cabin near their winter camps and live there with his wife and children. Our mothers quickly shook their heads at the fact that the trapper's wife became pregnant again year after year, giving birth to one child after another. Lakȟóta women rarely bore more than three or four children in their lifetime. Our men were far less lustful than the white man. *Iglúonihaŋ*, treating oneself with respect through self-control and self-discipline, was a skill the trapper lacked. He would have done better to curb his physical needs through fasting, hard running, swimming, and the sweat lodge. Moderation in eating was considered by our warriors to be as necessary to meet the high ideal of manly strength and beauty as were restraints in the sexual act.

"Instead of blaming himself, the trapper faulted his youngest daughter for the death of his wife, who died after giving birth to the sandy-haired girl, their twelfth child. The grandmother of the Standing Elk, a healer who had been brought to assist in the painfully long and difficult birth, took care of her. She, like every Lakȟóta child, was given a second family among our people and was later named Tȟuŋkáŋ Hetȟúŋ-wiŋ, Rock-With-Horns-Woman. The grandmother of the Standing Elk was a holy woman, a Waphíya Wíŋyaŋ. She fostered the sandy-haired girl's understanding of *Wówakȟaŋ,* the spiritual force that was unusually strong in her even as a child, and which enabled her to maintain a particularly close connection with the spirit world throughout her life.

"According to Lakȟóta customs, the Rock-With-Horns-

Woman was considered an equal daughter and sister among our people. Still a child himself at the time, the Standing Elk was fascinated by the sandy-haired girl from the beginning and avoided any sibling-like contact with her. He must have seen in her, even as a boy, the girl he wanted as his wife when he became a man. Heȟáka Nážiŋ moved from his parents' tent to that of his second parents. He met the gossip he later caused in the village because he wanted to marry a member of his own family — even though they were not related by blood — courageously and defiantly."

Wógluze! They marry their own! This exclamation of the Black Wolf Chief, when he had approached the Standing Elk and the sandy-haired woman in the river in Logan's dream, took on a whole new meaning for Logan.

Thoughtfully, Uŋčí continued her narrative, "The presence of the Rock-With-Horns-Woman among our people brought death to the Standing Elk and the entire village when years later, white soldiers used the girl and one of her biological brothers as a pretext to raid the camp to free alleged white prisoners. The Black Wolf Chief had by then returned from exile and become one of our most feared leader of warriors against the white invaders. But when the bluecoats raided the camp, he was out hunting with a band of his followers. Upon his return, he found the village completely burned down and vowed revenge. The Standing Elk, who had stayed behind sick, was also dead. The whites had dragged the Rock-With-Horns-Woman away with them. The daughter who the Standing Elk had with her had also been killed. The son of the two was still an infant and the soldiers let him live. Surely they would have killed him, too, had it not been for a white woman holding him in her arms.

"The Black Wolf Chief found the Rock-With-Horns-Woman

and her young son again a year later during peace negotiations as an interpreter and took care of both. He made her his wife because he had never forgotten his childhood love, but also because it was expected of a man to care for his deceased brother's widow and children. Šuŋgmánitu Tȟáŋka Sápe loved Tȟuŋkáŋ Hetȟúŋ-wiŋ, and the two were each other's salve for the many wounds they shared. But the Rock-With-Horns-Woman also turned out to be a barbed thorn in the flesh of the Black Wolf Chief, for after the massacre of our people, Šuŋgmánitu Tȟáŋka Sápe hated the whites with a passion that bordered on obsession. At the same time, in Tȟuŋkáŋ Hetȟúŋ-wiŋ he had a woman at his side who not only embodied what he loved and should protect, but constantly reminded him of what he had learned to hate.

"Šuŋgmánitu Tȟáŋka Sápe was one of our best warriors and an excellent hunter. When the buffalo herds were numerous, meat was never in short supply in the tent of a good hunter. Guests came and went, especially in a chief's teepee. For a single woman, there was more work in such a home than she could manage on her own. Men who were good providers could afford to have more than one wife. Šuŋgmánitu Tȟáŋka Sápe stole a second wife from our enemies, the tribal group he had lived with during his exile, and then courted a third from among the Húŋkpapȟa-Lakȟóta. Your great-great-grand-mother, Logan. A prudent husband, however, would have discussed such a move with his first wife. He would not have put a woman of an enemy tribe in front of her. Perhaps such a man would have married two sisters from the beginning who he could assume were fond of each other, would get along, and would share their work and chores. This way, however, it became a difficult marriage between Šuŋgmánitu Tȟáŋka Sápe and his three starkly different wives.

"The sandy-haired Rock-With-Horns-Woman eventually left the Black Wolf Chief and her grown children and lived in seclusion among the whites for a while. But even here she was not happy. When she returned to the Lakȟóta, and Šuŋgmánitu Tȟáŋka Sápe was later betrayed and murdered high up on Northern Plains, the Rock-With-Horns-Woman managed to preserve her husband's body from the hatred of the whites and thus from mutilation. She managed to protect his memory and legacy. No one knows how she did it or who helped her, because after the death of the Black Wolf Chief and the death of her children, the Rock-With-Horns-Woman's spirit gradually slipped into madness. No one learned where the chief's body had been buried. The Rock-With-Horns-Woman and her helpers took this knowledge with them to *Wanáǧi Wičhóthi* – the place where the spirits of the dead dwell."

Uŋčí again fell into a long silence. Her grandson struggled to grasp the full scope of what he had just heard, and his grandmother allowed him the space and time he needed to do so. Uŋčí's tales had stirred in Logan a yearning that powerfully overwhelmed him and for which he could not pinpoint the real cause. On that early morning on the prairie, a whole series of questions that burned in his soul came to mind. If only he could have found words for what had struck him right in the heart. But as it was, he kept silent, because he had no language for all that was churning inside him. He only asked the one question that burdened him more than any other.

"What will become of Phoebe, Uŋčí?"

The old woman sighed. "Whether her body and soul will heal depends on her ability to accept what has happened. If she can hold this horror in love to herself, she will be able to free herself from its stranglehold."

Logan did not understand his grandmother's words. They

seemed unfathomable to him. Superhuman. But the respect for age he had been raised to have, commanded him to remain silent.

"Your family needs you back here, *t̃akóža,*" she said, looking at him thoughtfully with her dark quicksand eyes. Throughout his life, Uŋčí had accepted all of her favorite grandchild's decisions. She had never pushed Logan, had never asked him for anything. But that morning on the prairie, she had made the same request to him twice.

Logan nodded. He was the oldest son in a fatherless family, and it was his job to protect his younger siblings. "I know," he replied quietly.

Chapter 4

The Lucid Dream I: Mount Rushmore, South Dakota, USA

*I*t was like looking through iced glass as a gray haze clouded the view of the Great Plains. The endless expanse of the prairie rushed past the window of the train in yellowed black-and-white scenes until a crashing bolt of lightning bathed Mount Rushmore in a rich, golden-orange light.

Zayla is the only one of the passengers to be ejected from the train and lands gently, buttocks first, on the head of Thomas Jefferson. On Abraham Lincoln's head already sits the grandmother and old healer she has known since her soul was born. The healer's granddaughter has taken a seat on Theodore Roosevelt's head.

Sisters! Zayla exclaims delightedly when she recognizes the two women. How nice that I have met you here.

The healer smiles. It was time, my child, it was time. Lost in thought, the old woman pats Abraham Lincoln's face beneath her.

Do you remember, she asks, how this President, who spoke of his white forefathers having begotten a new nation on this continent in freedom and dedicated it to the principle that all men are created equal — all men, except of course those who first dwelt here, she adds — how this man then, who advocated for the end of slavery, also consented to the hanging of thirty-eight of our warriors?

The granddaughter and Zayla nod. It was cruel news that, after the violent uprising of starving Dakȟóta, had also spread like wildfire among their relatives, the Lakȟóta.

Hundreds of our warriors, the healer murmurs, were sentenced to death because their living space had become so scarce that they could no longer feed their families. Men accused of rape and murder were sentenced to death with nearly no evidence presented against them.

Which is why President Lincoln had many of those sentences

commuted to imprisonment, Zayla recalls. But that did little to change the blatant injustice.

This old white man here, the healer's granddaughter explains, tapping President Roosevelt's head with the flat of her hand, was talking about how, while he wouldn't go so far as to say that the only good Indian is a dead Indian, he did believe that such a statement was true nine times out of ten.

The three women shake their heads. What foolish ignorance!

Zayla points to President Washington next to her and President Jefferson below her. And these two gentlemen here were slave owners, she says, giving Thomas Jefferson's face, on which she has taken a seat, a soft nudge with her heel.

The granddaughter looks at her thoughtfully. My brother is looking for the sandy-haired Rock-With-Horns-Woman. She then explains to Zayla, adding cryptically: But he doesn't know yet that he is looking for her.

The name awakens a memory in Zayla that she can't quite place.

My brother dreamed of this woman, for whose life he once went to his death, the granddaughter tells. He is longing for the old times. What is your name in this life, sister?

When Zayla gives her full name, she realizes in her sleep that she is dreaming.

I am the daughter of a Persian family of priests and the great-granddaughter of the High Priestess of the Isle of Glass, England's most sacred earth, she adds.

The healer and her granddaughter giggle.

Sure, this is what you are in this life, child, the old woman laughs, but what does that mean? You have been everything and will be everything. Just like everyone else. The universal force of life is at work in us. We are every gender, every skin color, every culture, every religion. We are all the same, all made of the same stuff. But again and again we choose oblivion when we begin a new life as human beings.

That is true, Zayla reflects. Her ancestry is meaningless, and yet nothing happens without reason. Does your brother know how to find the sandy-haired Rock-With-Horns-Woman? she asks.

The granddaughter shakes her head. He dreamed about her, but he doesn't know who she is. My brother feels guilty for leaving his family and forgetting us on the reservation. He feels guilty for the crime I just became a victim of. But this crime is also what will finally bring him back to us! Her voice sounds almost triumphant at these words. Then Zayla sees that the energy field of her old friend changes. The radiant royal blue turns to a gray-brown, then slimy black color. Blood runs down her legs in streams.

Zayla slaps her hand over her mouth. Oh God! Not again! Not again!

She sees the girl in the clutches of the men. She feels the cruel pain that tears her body apart. She feels her soul burst open and the past suffering of women spill out of her like the fetuses cut from the bodies of pregnant women. Women whose bodies were desecrated by the conquerors with the same cold-heartedness as they desecrated the earth and all its human and other-than-human inhabitants. Zayla feels the festering wounds in her old friend's soul and then in her own.

Suddenly she hears a light murmur. Her mother takes a seat next to her on President Washington's head.

Mother! Zayla's tears tighten her throat.

Even the female animals, their mother greets the three women with a nod, know this cruel pain that those men, standing in the darkest shadows of their masculinity, have cast on women. In war. On their campaigns of conquest. In peace. In their marriages. With their children.

An orangutan appears next to Zayla's mother.

The Indonesians call these wonderful animals forest people, she reports, ruffling the neck of the female ape. It projects its short life into the minds of the women, chained belly-down to a bed frame and abused by workers on the palm oil plantations.

Nausea rises in Zayla. Disgusted, she jumps off Mount Rushmore and burrows deep into the soil of Mother Earth. She wishes to die in her protection and never return to this world. She hates the people and the planet, which she feels is increasingly like a prison.

Her mother's hand pulls her out of the ground, back onto Mount Rushmore and Thomas Jefferson's head. You cannot close your eyes to the suffering of this world, she admonishes her daughter. You must learn to hold the world's pain if you are to regain your full power. You must also meet your own pain with love and thus transform it.

Zayla shakes her head. I can't do this, Mother. I don't want to feel pain anymore!

Her mother looks at her for a long time. Has the murderer's evil spell already reached your father? she asks gently.

The evil spell of the murderer? Zayla blinks. She glances at the healer and her granddaughter. Does her mother mean the man who killed the two women's relative, the Black Wolf Chief?

Her mother smiles.

Zayla feels a chill run down her spine and her pulse races. She blocks out everything around her, closes her eyes and listens to the rhythm of the ancient language in which her mother speaks. The healer joins in.

Your daughters, Zayla, the two women speak to her in thought, will far surpass what you can accomplish in this world. You are likely to become a beacon, child, but your daughters will be the spiritually exalted women of a new time. A time when the women of this world and their allies will stand up and speak out. Be careful not only to raise the child of an ancient love and let go of them both, but also to find a way back to the child the murderer will give you. Meanwhile, the great-grandchildren of the Black Wolf Chief will succeed in paving ways that can change the future of the First Nations. It will be the wounds of all humanity through which the light will shine that will advance the healing of the women and the men of this world, the intermediate beings, the human and the other-than-human relatives. Wise and visionary beings will take care of an earth where humanity can live and breathe in freedom again.

First dozens, then hundreds, and finally thousands of beings begin to gather around the granddaughter of the old healer to stop the blood dripping incessantly from her body. The beings come from everywhere. They descend from the sky and emerge from the presidential stone heads, reducing them to rubble. They bed the girl's body on soft grass and draw an ever-tightening circle around the wounded young woman. Countless hands lay themselves on, around and under her in brown, black, white, and yellow colors. The ethereal figures begin to sing:

We love you, sister. We feel your pain. You are Mother Earth's daughter. You are the heart of all of us.

Zayla opened her eyes.

Chapter 5

Narrabeen, North of Sydney, Australia

Tahnee Freeman stopped the video of her cousin Zayla and Uncle Matthew on her iPhone and rolled her eyes. She brought both hands together behind her head and tied her light brown hair into a lush ponytail. Then she glanced at her brother, Carl, who was lounging wide-legged next to her on the couch, ruffling his dark curls.

The professional surfer had returned from training half an hour ago and was still in his sponsor company's T-shirt and board shorts. He cursed like a sailor and hit his forehead with the palm of his hand.

"Bloody fucking hell! Isn't it enough that Dad and I have been subjected to hate speech and death threats for our socio-political views? Do we also have to make a mockery of our family with such a bizarre video?"

Tahnee sighed. Uncle Matthew was a highly renowned psychology professor and hypnotherapist, and the video, immediately after it had been posted online, caused fierce hostility and heated debate. "You're afraid of a shitstorm if your critics link you to Zayla and Uncle Matthew?"

Carl snorted. "Are you surprised, after all we've been through? I'm going to ignore this video for as long as possible, and I'm also not going to show it to Travis for now. If we're lucky, the storm of embarrassment will pass us by without doing any major damage."

Tahnee nodded. "If push really comes to shove, you can only answer for yourself anyway, and not for the shortcomings in judgment of your family. Or what people might consider shortcomings in judgment."

Her brother looked up, a wry grin on his face. "Wise words, Sis!"

Tahnee and Carl's mother was Professor Kirkpatrick's only sister and, after her marriage, had made a good name for herself in Sydney as an artist and gallery owner. Their father was Yarran Freeman, a well-known and well-connected Australian journalist, a Wiradjuri Aboriginal whose ancestors had made their home in what was now known as central New South Wales.

Yarran was an Indigenous and international affairs analyst at the Australian Broadcasting Corporation, and a few weeks earlier he had given a sensational speech about the dark side of the Australian dream. He had shared a heartfelt personal account of what it meant to him as a Wiradjuri to have grown up in a society that had, in his view, been consistently built on the backs of indigenous people, against their will. He had told of his children. Of Tahnee, his daughter, who had inherited her mother's fair skin and light brown hair, while his son Carl took after his father in appearance. Yarran had emphasized that Carl, who had been born into the same family and advantageous socio-economic circumstances as his sister, had nevertheless had to walk a rockier road than Tahnee, who was superficially accepted as a white Australian. Yarran had also briefly addressed his divorce, now final and widely reported in some media, and touched on the challenges of his marriage to a non-indigenous woman.

Full of enthusiasm, he had highlighted Australia's uniqueness at the end of his speech. "This country is an outstanding and unprecedentedly beautiful country!" he had shouted. "A country that has become the object of envy by many other nations around the world."

The journalist, who had already worked as a war correspondent for CNN in Afghanistan and Iraq and lived as a correspondent in Abu Dhabi, loved his homeland and was proud to be Australian.

"I feel even more pride about being the father of one of the most successful Australian surfers ever. My son is a two-time World Surf League Champion. Carl represents both Australia as a whole and us, the indigenous people of this country in particular, with this title in the world ranking."

Tahnee knew her father looked with great favor on the fact that her brother's increasing popularity had not gone to his head. Carl had recognized his responsibility and embraced his status as a role model wholeheartedly. She was also proud of him and loved her brother very much.

"My son," Yarran had shouted to his audience, "has become a beacon for those Indigenous young people in this country who want to share in the Australian dream. Carl is fully committed to the social advancement of our young people, whose chances of ending up in jail are still higher than earning a high school diploma!"

In an environment that tends to be homophobic, Carl had also courageously made an opening for the acceptance of gay surfers of all skin colors with his unexpected public acknowledgement of having a same-sex partner.

"Also, and especially in a country where homosexuality is against the rules of some of our indigenous cultures, where same-sex relations are considered 'wrong' in some cases, Carl's coming out is a damned brave decision that demands all my respect!"

Her father had divided his audience and the commentators of Australian newspapers and news programs with the honest words he had chosen for his speech. For some, he was a charismatic and eloquent man who had put his finger in several Australian wounds with force and backbone. For others, he was seen as someone fouling his own nest, an attention seeker and self-promoter.

Tahnee, who adored her father, knew that Carl was her parents' favorite child. She had always only ever felt her younger brother's preferential treatment subconsciously, yet at no time would she have entertained the illusion that she was the sibling of whom her father and mother were particularly proud — whether it was the school successes for which Carl was celebrated but Tahnee received only a smile, or the day her brother won a surfing competition for the first time and Tahnee had wondered what she would have to achieve to elicit the same uncontainable joy and pride on her parents' faces. Carl's first heartbreak had even taken its toll on her mother almost more than it had on him.

Although Tahnee's fair complexion might have contributed to her living a more advantaged life "in the outside world" than her brother, within the family, Carl had sat on the throne and been afforded privileges, as her father had emphasized in his speech much to Tahnee's chagrin.

Her parents loved her, too. She had no doubt about that. But they were more critical of and reserved with their daughter than with their son. Carl heard praise and encouragement more quickly and with more enthusiasm than his sister.

The hate comments and snide remarks under the YouTube video of her cousin Zayla and her uncle Matthew, which the siblings had finished watching together, considerably dampened Tahnee's anticipation of Nick's return from the U.S. that day. Had Uncle Matthew really hoped for such a powerful "breakthrough for the acceptance of paranormal abilities in science and the international mainstream," as the BBC reporter had described in her introduction? Could he really dare to risk his and his daughter's good reputations for such a questionable film report?

"Mum?" Tahnee called out to the patio.

No response.

"Mum?" she called out again, a little louder.

Her mother poked her head through the door. "What is it, Carly?"

Tahnee rolled her eyes. "Carly? I thought you and Dad had finally given up on that nickname for me and left it to Nick!"

Her mother pursed her lips. "Old habits die hard, sweetie." She smiled. "Why did you call me?"

Tahnee pointed to her iPhone. "Have you seen this new video of Uncle Matthew and Zayla?"

Florence shook her head.

"It was just uploaded yesterday. It's a recap of what happened when Zayla found the body of Nell, that little girl she was such close friends with. Remember? Whose parents live near Zayla and Uncle Matthew and who suddenly disappeared?"

"Oh my God!" exclaimed Florence. "Have they found the little one?"

"A totally fucked up story," Carl interjected. "I can't believe Uncle Matthew and Zayla actually went public with this *psychic detective* nonsense!"

Florence raised her eyebrows. "May I remind you, son, that your partner also has very special talents?"

Carl waved it off. "Don't say that too loud, Mum. Travis is pretty reserved about his abilities, thank God. He would never make himself a public target for ridicule like Zayla and Uncle Matthew did in that video."

Florence sat down on the sofa with her children, and Tahnee played the YouTube video again. Thirty-five minutes later, her mother was also shocked.

"Unbelievable, isn't it?" Tahnee encouraged her to comment.

Florence tugged on her earlobe. "Even as a small child, Zayla spoke about your great-grandmother, who had passed away long before Zayla was born."

She paused for a moment. "Zayla kept saying that your great-grandmother had been at her bedside at night," Florence continued. "Uncle Matthew and Aunt Nazneen were often at a loss for words because Zayla would talk about things that happened long before she was born."

Tahnee frowned. "What kind of things was she talking about, Mum?"

Florence stroked her chin with the back of her hand. "Like that time your grandmother had a stillborn and aborted later two children. How would Zayla have known that as a three-year-old? She would walk up to Grandma, hug her, and tell her she didn't have to worry about the children she'd lost anymore. Zayla knew they were fine, and the little ones said they loved their mother. Your grandmother started crying uncontrollably when she heard that. I stood by and was just stunned."

"That sounds like one of Travis's whacky childhood memories," Carl grumbled.

Florence tapped her chin gently with two fingers. "There was this strange story about an old family ring that had been passed down to Zayla's mother, which she had lost during her move from Cornwall to London. Zayla hadn't been born yet when her mother lost that ring. Yet she knew about it."

"Couldn't Zayla have put this together somehow?" asked Tahnee.

Florence shrugged her shoulders. "Possibly. But Zayla's mother was so devastated at the loss of that ring that she didn't say a word about it to anyone for a long time. Not even to Uncle Matthew. The strange thing was that a few days after Zayla first mentioned it, the ring suddenly reappeared. It was in the kitchen on the windowsill. Just like that. No one knew how it had gotten there. Zayla was three or four years old at the time.

She was adamant that your late great-grandmother had returned the ring. It was all so absurd to me at the time that I decided not to bother with Zayla's stories any longer. She always scared me a little, much like Aunt Nazneen with her Second Face. I was so glad I never had to deal with Zayla's abilities, which far exceeded those of her mother."

Tahnee made a sound of understanding. The family had admired her uncle's Persian-born wife for her graceful beauty, kindness, and goodness. That her aunt had possessed the second sight, which her mother feared, Tahnee heard for the first time today. "What I find even stranger, Mum, than all you just told us, is that Zayla actually managed to track down little Nell. No one knew where to look for the girl. Nobody knew if Nell was even alive. And then Zayla comes along and insists on knowing that the little one was murdered. Uncle Matthew puts her under hypnosis, and the spirit or soul of Nell — or whatever the hell that was supposed to be ..."

"I do not like that swearing, Tahnee!"

Tahnee rolled her eyes. Her mother tolerated her brother's strong language as long as Carl didn't overdo it. For Tahnee, however, different rules applied. She started a second time.

"So, something seemed to have taken possession of Zayla, and she's telling details about the murder of Nell in this unnaturally childlike voice. On camera! I find that part of the video incredibly hard to digest. It still makes me shiver."

Florence brushed a strand of hair from her face and sighed.

"Obviously, though, the cops believed Zayla," Carl indicated. "Otherwise, they *never* would have gone with some nut job to find the place our cousin described to them in such detail."

"The police did find it then," Florence added. "If it hadn't been for Zayla, they never would have thought of looking in Whitechapel. I really have no idea what to make of this video," she admitted.

After a short pause, she continued, "However, to Zayla's credit, she is an honest girl who wouldn't hurt a fly. In no way could she have anything to do with Nell's murder. And I firmly rule out the possibility that she or Uncle Matthew would intentionally mislead anyone."

Tahnee threw her arms up in the air. "I just wonder why, if all this information was available to her, she couldn't also say who Nell's murderer was. After all, the fact that she couldn't describe him was made abundantly clear in that documentary. That's something I don't understand. With the abilities she allegedly has, shouldn't such information have been brought to her? None of this makes sense to me. Scientists like Stephan Hawking have always maintained that there can be no life after death. And Dad would certainly not approve of this video!"

Her mother smiled. "Yes, I'm sure your father would have something to say about this. Especially since so many Australian First Nation cultures forbid showing pictures of the deceased or mentioning their names. I have never been involved with the afterlife research that Uncle Matthew does and can't really form an opinion about it. But didn't Shakespeare let Hamlet say there were 'more things in heaven and earth, Horatio, than are dreamt of in your philosophy'?"

"Whatever meaningful value such a quote might have," Tahnee muttered. "You know what the worst thing is about this video, Mum?"

Florence shook her head.

"These hate comments. What many people have posted in the comments section is awful. We are used to a lot in this family, but I wish Zayla would have been spared this savage abuse and that Uncle Matthew would have disabled the comments section. Listen ..." Tahnee reached for her phone, called up the video again and scrolled down the screen. She avoided reading out to her mother and brother the most vulgar comments where Zayla had been viciously sexualized and degraded, instead limiting herself to a selection of derogatory but moderately hurtful comments relative to the others:

"Ladies and gentlemen, I present to you with this video: 'The Manipulation of Mourners. – The Documentary.'"

"All scammers and rip-off artists who prey on desperate and stupid people who have lost a loved one."

"A medium that helps the police is truly not a new concept. It's been tested all over the world and then abandoned because these guys do nothing but waste the police's time."

"It is a shame that so many people are naïve enough to want to BELIEVE paranormal claims instead of doing reasonable research. Because anyone who seriously studies it for even a few minutes can immediately see what manipulation techniques people like this girl use."

"This is ridiculous! The two Kirkpatricks are either charlatans or delusional psychotics. In either case, they should be institutionalized."

"I love this kind of television. But only as entertainment because I can't believe a word of it. There have also been cases in the U.S., Australia, New Zealand, and Spain where the police asked a medium for help, and then nothing worked panned out. I wish it were true, but all these TV shows are just scams, just like Matthew and Zayla Kirkpatrick are nothing but frauds."

"Check out James Randi on YouTube. He exposes them all."

"Who is James Randi?" Florence sounded dismayed.

"A now-deceased magician," Tahnee replied. "He is the founder of an organization that investigated paranormal claims, wanting to test them under controlled conditions. He even offered prize money for a while for successful demonstration of supernatural abilities under scientific testing conditions. However, no one ever received the money. Without exception, he denounces the followers of the paranormal as frauds who want to harm others and enrich themselves at the expense of other people."

"One thing I can say about Travis," Carl grumbled, "is that he wouldn't want to hurt anyone or get rich off anyone. They're not all charlatans."

Tahnee agreed. Like her cousin Zayla, her brother's partner was a person of honesty and integrity. She glanced at her phone's clock and emitted a shriek. "Damn! Mum, can I have your car keys now, please? If I don't leave right now, I'm going to miss the boys at the airport!"

Florence smirked. "Well then, hon. Give my love to Nick. And Logan, too, of course. Tell them to feel free to drop in on us sometime. Are you staying with the Diamandises tonight?"

Tahnee nodded. "Can I bring your car back tomorrow night? Or, better yet, Carl, can you come with me and drive Mum's car back later? You have time now, don't you?"

Carl shrugged his shoulders. "Can do. Maybe I'll run into Travis at the Diamandises', too. He's been waiting eagerly for days to see Logan again and find out how he and Nick did in South Dakota. I'll drop him a line and see what he's up to."

Tahnee pressed a big kiss on Carl's cheek. Grinning from ear to ear, he waved her off.

"It's okay. It's okay. But you owe me, Sis."

"Don't stress the two men so much," Florence admonished her daughter. "Nick and Logan have had a long flight. They'll be tired."

Why her mother felt the need to say that at that very moment was beyond Tahnee's comprehension. She said nothing in reply but felt criticized one more time for something she couldn't put her finger on.

Tahnee longed to fall into Nick's arms. She longed for his

undivided attention. Even more than before, she now felt an urgency to get to the airport on time. Hastily, she took the car keys from her mother's hand, kissed her goodbye, and pulled Carl up from the sofa. With her brother in tow, she ran out the door.

Chapter 6

Brighton, County of East Sussex, United Kingdom

Zayla was sitting in a plain folding deck chair on the pebble beach of the English seaside resort of Brighton, an hour's train ride south of her hometown of London, gazing out at the restless sea. Over the English Channel, the sun had moved in a wide arc to the west. Its last rays, lost in purple hues on the horizon, could no longer warm the gusts that blew her dark curls into the girl's face.

Zayla was exhausted from the long seminar weekend that lay behind her, and she was hungry. The raw sea air made her shiver. She reached for her fleece jacket and leaned back in one of the wooden deck chairs available for public use on the beach. Disregarding the world's tallest tower with a movable observation platform advertised in tourist brochures, she took a long look at the cast-iron skeleton of the West Pier to her right: a two-hundred-year-old pier that had been left to deteriorate from salt water and corrosion after two fires, its gloomy romanticism highly prized as a photo motif by visitors to the seaside resort.

Zayla closed her eyes. What a weekend.

Zayla's father had received several hundred applications for the offer, previously published only on his private webpage, to enable fifteen hand-picked people to undergo further training as hypnosis and regression coaches. The professor's program consisted of twelve weekend sessions over twelve months under his personal guidance in the calm ambience of his second home in Brighton.

Matthew Kirkpatrick wanted to attract disciples for his work outside of his teaching position at the university. The professor's goal was to gather people around him who felt called to help others with his methods. He liked to see a degree in social or psychological education, but it was not a prerequisite because the program he was offering was off the conventional path anyway. The pilot project was to be free of charge for the selected applicants except for travel, bed, and board expenses. But Zayla's father was already thinking about what he could require for his subsequent training programs after the unexpectedly large demand. From the pool of applicants, he had selected ten participants according to his own preferences, leaving the other five to the evaluation of his daughter.

Despite her young years, Zayla had long since grown into the demanding role of the professor's personal assistant. She loved working with him at this task. At her own request, her father had taken her out of both the British school system when she was nine years old and later the American school system during his six years of teaching and researching in the U.S. Instead, he had paid for private tutors for his only child as much as possible. He thought highly of Zayla's sharp mind and metaphysical abilities. With her gifts, however, judged by many to be unsettling, she had been relegated to the role of outsider from an early age, shunned by those who were afraid of anything they did not understand.

Zayla's differences, being bullied during her school years, and the death of her mother had brought father and daughter closer together in a relationship based on great respect and deep love. They understood each other intrinsically and shared a fascination for the possibilities of hypnosis to answer the ancient questions of humanity: Who are we? Where do we come from? Why are we here? Where are we going? Her father pursued clues that could lead to some of the answers with more consistency and impartiality than almost anyone else.

Rarely did a day go by when he and Zayla did not have a lengthy conversation on these topics and his work.

Among the 348 applicants for the twelve seminar weekends offered by Professor Kirkpatrick was a former London investment banker. Zayla's first impulse had been to ask her father to reject the banker's application she had spotted in the pile marked "shortlisted." In her opinion, he didn't fit the application profile, and reading his documents made her uncomfortable.

At dinner, she had approached her father about the banker and expressed her concerns. The professor, however, even after a face-to-face interview, had been so consistently impressed by Marrock Lovell's depth, candor, and eloquence that he questioned Zayla's intuition for a rare time. Unsettled by her father's enthusiasm and confused by her own unusually ambivalent feelings, which warned against Marrock while at the same time wanting to give him a chance, his application ended up in the pile of the fifteen accepted.

When Zayla first came face to face with the banker, the immense force of his presence, the dark eroticism oozing from every pore, and the oppressive feeling that she had met him before had shaken her to the core. Contrary to her initial fears, however, Marrock had been consistently polite to her, her father, and the seminar participants and had kept a respectful distance. And yet, at moments, she felt the heat of his gaze burn into her body like volcanic embers. Even when she focused all her attention on this man, it was impossible for her to read him in the same way she managed with most other people. It was as if tremendous powers had stretched an invisible protective shield around the banker against which her highly developed abilities bounced like children's wooden arrows against a war shield.

Zayla sighed.

One thing at least was certain, namely that Marrock was attracted to her like a moth to the moonlight. Whether she should take his fascination as a compliment or dismiss it as a nuisance, she had not yet decided.

She found his interest in her rather disruptive to his training as a hypnosis and regression coach, although the banker had so far made no attempt to get closer to her.

"I'm gay, by the way."

Zayla's eyelids fluttered open. *Excuse me? Had this sentence been directed at her?*

She looked up and saw a young man standing in front of her, slim and of medium height. He wore faded jeans and a light-colored tank top that pleasantly accentuated the dark brown tone of his skin and athletic arms. Despite the heat he was used to in his native Australia, with which Brighton could not compete even in the height of summer, he was visibly less sensitive to the cold than she was that evening. With a disarming smile exposing flawless teeth, he handed Zayla one of the two bags of fish and chips he held in his hands.

Zayla beamed at him. "Oh, thank you so much, Travis. You're a lifesaver."

"My pleasure," he grinned.

She began to eat with delight. "Is *I'm gay* your way of telling me you don't want to hit on me?"

Travis's dark eyes sparkled, and he was all smiles. He dropped into one of the deck chairs next to Zayla and ran his hand through his black-brown curls. Then he cocked his head to the side and his gaze locked with hers.

"I think that sums it up pretty well," he admitted. "With your looks, you must be used to guys hitting on you all the time."

Zayla shrugged and lowered her eyes.

"So, it makes things easier," Travis said, "when you know I can't be interested in getting you into bed."

She snorted softly. "As soon as men realize what abilities I have, they lose all interest anyway."

She devoured another bite of cod.

"I scare a lot of people," she added with a composure she didn't feel. "And what do you mean by *it makes things easier*?" she wanted to know before bringing the third morsel to her mouth.

Travis eyed her. "Making friends with you."

Since the round of introductions of the fifteen participants two days ago, Zayla also felt a bond with the young Australian that she could not explain.

"This first seminar weekend was fabulous," he changed the subject. "Your father is a gifted teacher and truly impressive psychologist and hypnotherapist. I will have to chew on what he gave us in the seminar breaks for weeks to come. Just his explanations about Atlantis and the Japanese underwater pyramids of Yonaguni yesterday during lunch – my goodness. Completely new perspectives on this world emerge when you quietly listen to him for a while."

"He has his moments," Zayla agreed.

Travis regarded her closely, and her cheeks grew hot. "I could stare at you like this for hours," he confessed. "Like the hyper-realistic paintings of New Yorker artist Alyssa Monks. Do you know that painter?"

Zayla shook her head.

Travis pulled his phone out of his pocket and showed her the American's website. "When I first stood in front of the paintings in her 'Water Series,' I was just a boy and in the home of a powerful man whose passion for this woman rubbed off on me and whose adopted son became like a brother to me. I love Alyssa Monk's painting technique and her ability to cloud and

69

obscure human forms while at the same time giving each of her paintings the sharpness and precision of a photograph." He stroked the screen with the flat of his hand, as if he could touch the artist's paintings. "I'm moved by the subtle eroticism, the intimacy in many of her paintings. Even my partner, who is barely interested in art and is leading a new generation of confident Aboriginal and Torres Strait Islander surfers in my homeland, can relate to her."

Zayla enjoyed the matter-of-factness with which Travis talked about his feelings, and she liked the admiration that was in his voice when he mentioned his partner.

"So, men who are interested in you run away as soon as they realize you have abilities that are beyond their comprehension?" he asked.

Zayla gave a guttural groan.

Travis nodded. Bitterness resonated in his voice as he said, "Welcome to my world, my dear. Most people freak out about my abilities on a regular basis. Men even more blatantly than women. Sometimes being endowed with gifts like ours is more of a curse than a blessing. But at least we're spared the stake these days." He shook his head. "How did the police react to your help in finding Nell, anyway?"

Zayla raised her eyebrows. "You've already seen the YouTube video? It is the assignment for our second seminar next month."

Travis pretended to be embarrassed. "I was curious. However, the comments under the video broke my heart. People can be so cruel and ignorant. What they don't understand, they immediately demonize."

"Yes," nodded Zayla, "it was an attempt to make people think about how incredibly limited the realities they accept are. Unfortunately, we didn't succeed in the way we had envisioned. But we'll leave the video online for now anyway. There have also been some nice and encouraging responses from people who have written to my father personally. Maybe we just have to get through this shitstorm. It's always the critics who come out of the woodwork first. Possibly people who think like us will follow suit later. As for your question about Nell, a Detective Chief Inspector later called me and asked if I would be willing to work for the police more often. He would never admit it publicly, but he and his colleagues found my cooperation surprisingly helpful."

"He said that to your face?"

"Yes, but he wasn't unkind about it. He was just honest."

"How did you answer?"

"I refused. Criminal investigations are associated with such a dark energy field that I am hardly able to escape it. The work of a psychic detective does not suit me. It has far too many pitfalls. It's a job that other mediumistic people can do, if they feel called to do it. Nell's murder was an exception for me because I loved this wonderful little girl so much, but also because she wanted me to bring closure to the unanswered questions that have worn down her parents. Nell's parents are in complete despair. Their entire lives have been turned upside down. Their daughter was a powerful source of love for everyone who came in contact with her. She was like a Godsend to this world."

"Can you still perceive her sometimes?"

Zayla sensed Travis giving her a sympathetic look. "Rarely," she replied softly. "When we were searching for her body, it was different. I had an intense and much more consistent connection with her. When my father put me under hypnosis, it was as if I put my personality aside for a while and her soul used me as a mouthpiece. That was a new and not always pleasant experience for me."

Travis snorted. "That part of your video really pushed me to the limits of what I consider believable myself," he admitted. "How do you view what happened, Zayla? Why was Nell murdered?"

She was silent for a long time, and Travis followed suit. Zayla enjoyed the sensitivity with which he had already attuned himself to her. Throughout the seminar weekend, she had noticed that his empathic abilities were similarly well developed. Was *he* able to read the banker's feelings?

"I suspect ..." she finally replied, looking at him cautiously from the side, "that this is about something much bigger. You need a certain view of the world, though, to be able to appreciate this 'bigger' thing."

Again, she lapsed into a long silence, and again Travis waited patiently for her to continue.

"My father will go into these topics in greater depth in the next sessions. Then you can decide for yourselves whether you think his view is sound or not. It takes an open mind and an open heart to do so. Most people automatically resist when confronted with the idea that on a higher level, even murder can have meaning. Maybe not necessarily that it has to, but *can* have. Looking back on my father's countless regression sessions, I find it hard to ignore the fact that the souls he works with incarnated on this planet because it is an excellent place for them to work on their various developmental issues under the challenging conditions here. Now, is what his clients report to him the entire or maybe even the only picture of a reality beyond our 3-D world? Certainly not. Has my father found incontrovertible answers to all questions that move mankind? No, of course not. But what he does do points to important mosaic stones in a larger whole — just as your and my glimpses behind the veil and our mediumistic experiences with other realities do as well, but in a unique way and from a different perspective than my father's work."

Travis nodded thoughtfully. "My glimpses into these otherworlds have shown me that the meaning of our lives can only be to love and to learn. Not so easy when you have to face your own shadows and the insane pain this world has experienced again and again."

Zayla was moved by the depth of his insight. "When I think of Nell's parents," she said, "I think their challenge might be to work on love and forgiveness, too. Superhuman when your own child has been killed, and yet at the same time an opportunity ..."

"... as in any crisis," Travis interjected. "Isn't that word in the Chinese script made up of the characters for *danger* and *opportunity*?"

Zayla nodded. "Funny, isn't it, how it's always so difficult for us to discover our opportunities for growth amid our crises and grief," she observed.

"Nell's death may be an opportunity for her parents," she continued her thoughts, "to achieve perfection in living in love, and forgiving themselves — perhaps even their daughter's killer at some point. When Nell's parents have fully lived through their grief, they may be able to put something in place that could help other victims of violent crime."

There was another long pause.

"How do you respond to someone who asks you what you know with absolute certainty, not just believe, about the things beyond our 3-D reality here?" asked Travis.

Zayla shrugged. "That consciousness is immortal, and that consciousness is the building material of everything that is cast into form in the universe. That's something I know with certainty. Even the physicist Max Planck knew that matter as such does not exist, but that something like an intelligent mind is the foundation of all that we perceive as matter. Planck knew that everything we humans consider as *existing* presupposes consciousness. He called this mysterious creative power — as all civilized peoples of past millennia also did — *God* and explained that he, as a physicist who had to deal with matter, therefore departed from the realm of matter and entered the realm of spirit. With it he saw the task of physics finished at this point and handed over the additional research into the hands of philosophy. Perhaps with a twinkle in his eye. Beyond Planck's basic insight that consciousness must be considered fundamental, there is certainly much that is very probable. There is a lot that my own experiences, with my mediumistic abilities, or the work of my father or of those scientists who dare to do research outside the mainstream all point to. But those who claim to have answers set in stone are, in my view, manipulators, fanatics, or neurotics."

"I wonder if there can even be such a thing as one single truth," Travis pondered. "After all, our lives always take place from unique perspectives. So don't we have to accept that right and wrong remain human designations and have no validity in the grand scheme of things?"

Zayla smiled. "Do you know Dischalâl ad-Dîn Muhammad Rûmî?"

"Rûmî? Yes, I've heard that name before, but I don't know anything about him."

"He was one of the most important Persian-language scholars of the Middle Ages, and he is my parents' favorite poet. Rûmî once said something I find beautiful: 'Out beyond ideas of wrongdoing and rightdoing, there is a field. I'll meet you there. When the soul lies down in that grass, the world is too full to talk about. Ideas, language, even the phrase *each other* doesn't make any sense.' "

Zayla felt the Sufi mystic's words touch Travis's soul, and in her heart, she embraced her new friend like her greatest treasure.

"There is a video of two men on the topics of the meaning of life and forgiveness, which shows ideal human behavior, in its highest form. The two make clear everything that becomes possible through forgiveness. For humans, clinging to hate and anger is the same as first eating rat poison, and then sitting down and waiting for the rat to die."

Travis raised his head. "Isn't this a TED Talk you're referring to? It's about a young American who, as part of a gang ritual, shot a college student who was working as a pizza delivery boy that night, right?"

Zayla nodded.

"I remember," Travis continued, "that the victim's father sought contact with the killer's family. He established a foundation in the name of his murdered son and made it his mission to teach the principles of peace and nonviolence to school children, first with the killer's grandfather, but then with the remorseful murderer himself. Their stated goal is to help victims of violence heal their traumas."

"Exactly. That story is the perfect example of what I meant when I said Nell's murder might be about something much bigger."

"You mean the only way forward is through forgiveness and acceptance? Hmm, certainly a promising path, if one can take it. But how many victims of murder, genocide, torture, or rape can accept that? You said yourself, it requires something almost superhuman."

Zayla thought back to the many sorrowful scenes of her past-life regressions as well as her lucid dream at Mount Rushmore. Travis was certainly right, and yet, it was the only way forward. "Rûmî taught that harmony with oneself and the universe could only be achieved if we learn to love source, the universal force, all that is, and thus to love all that has been created — even that which we condemn or judge as repugnant and repulsive. It is a rocky road, but I am convinced that it is the only direction of travel that can really take humanity forward. However, no one should be forced to take such a route. Each of us has the right to make our own decisions."

Travis reached for Zayla's hand and looked at her for a long time. Under the force of her gaze, he lowered his lids. But then he seemed to take heart and raised his head again.

"Zayla Victoria Kirkpatrick," he whispered, "you are an incredibly fascinating person. And pretty as a picture, to boot. What a damn shame you're not a man. I'd have to propose to you right here and now!"

Zayla felt the blood rush to her cheeks. "I wouldn't be much good as a man," she replied with a smile. "But thank you for that flattering compliment, Travis. The soul connected to my body has a high affinity for the women of the world and their collective history. The scenes from other lives that came up in childhood memories, in dreams, and in hypnosis sessions with my father were rarely memories of men, but mainly of women, and from a wide variety of eras and cultures of this world. And from completely different walks of life and ethnicities. I would feel quite uncomfortable in a man's body, I think."

Travis rubbed his forehead. "How can you be sure that what you describe during a hypnosis session is actually something you've personally experienced?"

"A good question," Zayla admitted. "I know because I suffered and cried along with the experiences. Everything I saw felt real and genuine. The tremendous intensity of my feelings is my proof. I saw myself as an African woman on a slave ship, chained together with other diseased women, men and children and thrown overboard. I have seen myself in Rwanda as a mother who was drowned when the Hutu went after the Tutsi.

She had her dead young children tied to her arms and legs so she would go under. I experienced myself as a Mongolian warrior queen who had every good-looking man she slept with killed so as not to jeopardize her leadership position.

"I found myself as a Spanish healer in the clutches of the Inquisition, a Scottish thief on the English prison ships to Australia, a powerful priestess in ancient Egypt, and one of the three wives of a man who fought with all his might on the American Great Plains against the subjugation of his people. These and other memories that were part of all these lives felt profoundly personal and real. The lives of these women turned my insides upside down and some of the information, some of the names and places I mentioned under hypnosis, were so detailed that we were able to research them and prove that some of these people indeed lived."

It had become dark. The wind was gusting across the sea. The dancing lights of the beach promenade and the numerous couples enjoying romantic summer night walks conveyed a feeling of safety and security. More and more of the deck chairs on the beach were occupied. Only in the immediate vicinity of Zayla and Travis did it remain strangely vacant, as if the two of them were sitting in a hidden nook that no one could enter.

"However, if you look at it objectively," Zayla continued, "there is no absolute certainty that it was about *my* memories and *my* past lives. In addition, time is an illusion, presumably created so that we can understand and comprehend the world in which we find ourselves as humans. The past is made up of our memories, the future is made up of our expectations. All that I perceive in a regression as part of my *past* lives runs simultaneously after all. Perhaps you can think of it as having a bucket in front of me filled with all my human experiences. When I scoop out water, I only get to grasp one part at a time.

The rest continues to play out in that one bucket and at the same time.

"But even if the images I saw and the feelings I suffered through were not memories of my own past lives, and what emerged during hypnosis sessions were entirely different events — perhaps completely unknown to us — their healing potential remains enormous. I can report first-hand about the fascinating spontaneous healing of countless people. They came to my father because they suffered from a fear of heights or had a fear of drowning. Some had severe physical pain that they had not been able to get rid of for years. But when they returned under hypnosis to an unresolved traumatic situation that could not have taken place in their current lives, they were freed from their fears and their pain."

Zayla again fell into a long silence. Gently, she scanned Travis's energy field, feeling his great strength and the current of melancholy and love pulsing within him. Never before had she felt connected to another human being in such a profound way as with this young Australian on that magical summer night in the English seaside resort of Brighton.

The connection opened her heart unexpectedly wide. She turned to him and no longer had any doubt that he, too, understood who they were to each other. Travis reached for her hand again. The gentle contact of their fingers struck Zayla like a lightning bolt. The quiet, deep connection, the unhurried exchange of energies and feelings between them turned into a sparkling high-voltage line and information superhighway. Images from other lifetimes burst upon them. The two shared four scenes before the spell broke.

Brother and sister in the first scene. The woman in her early twenties, the man a little older. Both are children of the powerful ancient Celtic priestesses ordained near Glastonbury, on one of England's most sacred grounds.

Next to the siblings squats a middle-aged man dressed from head to toe in black. He has the habitus of a warrior and the dark charisma of a magician. The black and white arts that he and the daughter of the high priestess, who now nestles close to him, know how to wield, terrify the people. Accused of heresy, the former Templar wants to flee with his beloved. Under torture, however, her brother reveals the hiding place of his sister and brother-in-law and is then forced to watch them both be burned alive.

Then, a second scene on the Great Plains of the North American continent. A burned Indian village. Corpses, blood, and destruction dominate the scene. A white man and a warrior of the Plains' tribes face each other. The warrior curses his guilt-ridden friend from their childhood days. Blind with rage, the warrior goes after the trapper and would have slain him if the white had fought back. His refusal to stand up to his old childhood friend, however, saves his life. The warrior lets go of him again.

The scene changes to the killing of the warrior many years later on the snowy plains near the Canadian border. The white hunter's sandy-haired younger sister, with whom he has had a special relationship since childhood, sways back and forth in the snow. Blood oozes from wounds on her arms and legs. The hunter approaches his sister and kneels down beside her. When he realizes that her mind has slipped into madness, his heart breaks.

The fourth scene switches to the Australian outback. An Aboriginal couple on the run from the imminent kidnapping of their children. The Stolen Generations: Sons and daughters snatched from their mothers' arms and put into homes and missions or given up for adoption to European families to make them useful and socially acceptable to the conquerors. The father kneels before his children and swears in a tear-strained voice that he would rather kill himself and them than allow

*them to be stolen from him. The mother crouches beside him,
suppressing a sob. As her gaze falls on her young daughter's wide eyes,
Travis recognizes her.*

"Oh my God!"

"Yes," whispered Zayla, "you and I. We were mother and daughter in one life and brother and sister in two others. I don't know the father of the Aboriginal girl or the former Templar. But you know who they are?"

Travis threw his hands in the air and groaned without answering. Together they shed tears of sorrow for the painful memories of a divided past. And they shed tears of joy that they had found each other again.

"How old were you when you understood that your abilities weren't those of other people?" asked Travis, when the storm of emotion had subsided and the tears of both had dried again.

"That took a little while. I never thought anything of it as a child. The downloads, visions, and information I have gotten from a young age come to me in all different ways and have never been threatening. Not even once. What I sometimes perceive of beings from other dimensions comes through channels that I can also turn off again. I can set limits to these beings. If I don't want to see, hear or feel them, it is enough that I carry the intention in me not to be available for any communication. Or I simply go to another frequency, like changing a radio station. It works both ways. However, it is difficult for me to escape the energy fields of people. This flooding with foreign energies drives me to be alone a lot. Fortunately, my parents never made me feel weird. That only came with my other relatives and the whispering about me that followed, and I didn't really understand that either at first. I thought that what I could sense, all other people could sense or see as well. The first real shock came when I started school, and the bullying began. It was merciless. My father therefore later had me taught by private tutors. The experiences from my school days put my abilities on hold for a while."

"A defense mechanism," Travis muttered.

Zayla was moved by his understanding and deep sympathy for her pain. "Yes, a protective measure," she confirmed.

"What was the trigger for your abilities to start working again?"

"My mother's death."

Zayla thought back with much love to the woman who had given birth to her and who could trace her ancestry back to a family of priests in ancient Persia. They had lived at a time when Persian women had more rights and freedoms than most other women in the world at that time. Until hordes of Arab Muslim horsemen had brought the empire to its knees, burned its libraries, enslaved its inhabitants, and given its women a male guardian for every step they took.

"Contact with your mother made you open up again?"

Zayla nodded.

"How old were you?"

"Twelve."

"How old are you now?"

"Seventeen."

Travis whistled between his teeth. "Seriously? I had you pegged in your mid-twenties."

Zayla smiled. "That's what a lot of people think. Were you born with your psychic abilities like me, Travis?"

"I come from a pretty shitty family background ..." he began evasively. "Not such an educated home, not such a posh existence as your family's. I didn't mean that in a derogatory way," he added apologetically. "I have a First Nation father I've never met. My mother thinks he was a drunk and a good-for-nothing. She's a white Australian with British roots, and she had to juggle three jobs at once to keep us afloat. I was the product of a brief affair between her and my father."

Travis looked out to sea, humming the tune of an old nursery rhyme.

"I was born with my mediumistic abilities, yes. They were always part of me. But my mother didn't have the time or interest in taking anything I said as a child seriously. Mostly she just attributed everything to my 'creative imagination.' However, she never actively hindered my abilities either."

"And at school?"

Travis thoughtfully shook his head. "It would never have occurred to me to talk about all that I can see and feel at school. I was bullied because of my background or because I was too 'soft' and not interested in girls. Unlike you, though, my mediumistic abilities helped me stand up to all the guys who made my life difficult."

"How so?"

"For example, by being able to read them accurately and adapt to them, or to avoid them when the situation demanded it. Sometimes something was placed into my head that I could use against those fuckers to make them keep their hands off me: a picture, information about a person close to them, sometimes a warning. In any case, something that was concrete and stunned them enough to get them off my back. I've never been one to back down easily."

Zayla put her hand in Travis's. "How do you manage to commute back and forth between Australia and England every month for a year for my father's seminars?"

"With various jobs and a gracious sponsor," Travis said with irony. "That's a pretty long story. The short version for the rest of this evening would be that I hung out on the streets a lot as a kid. When I was ten years old, Logan ran into me for the first time. He's like an older brother to me today. He's not Australian, he's Native American. A Lakȟóta. Totally crazy story how this guy came to Australia."

"Another story for another night?" asked Zayla, chuckling.

"In fact, if you don't want to sit here with me until the early hours of the morning, I'd better share it with you some other time. I will let you in on this much though: My life and my story were in many ways also Logan's life and Logan's story. Deimos Aleksander Diamandis, a well-known tycoon and media mogul in my country — have you ever heard of him?"

Zayla was familiar with this name. She nodded.

"Deimos picked Logan up on the street and later adopted him. Probably because he had freed his biological son Nick from the hands of kidnappers who had fucked him up pretty badly. Logan was in the right place at the right time. Another one of those whacky stories. Anyway, Logan became Deimos's adopted son. He had never forgotten me, though, and in his new role as the adopted son of this immensely powerful man, he had offered me some fantastic opportunities to live a better life. Damn lucky I ran into him, really. On the other hand," he continued after a brief pause, "nothing in this world just happens. There were dynamics at work other than luck or coincidence. But to answer your question about the flights between Australia and England over the next eleven months, let's say I have a sponsor: Logan. At least, if the money I make from my jobs isn't enough."

Finally, Zayla blurted, "I know Deimos and Nick Diamandis by name, Travis! Nick is the boyfriend of Tahnee, my father's niece. Oh my God, it's truly a small world!"

"Tahnee is your father's niece? Then she and my partner Carl, World Surf League champion *Carl Freeman*, are *your cousins*? Oh, come on, Zayla, you've got to be kidding me!"

Zayla grimaced. "No, of course not. After all, Carl just won this title for the second time, and we're all incredibly proud of him. He's such a great athlete! Aunt Florence must have known that my father was going to offer his pilot project in Brighton. Or was it Carl who brought it to your attention?"

"No, it was your aunt. She took me aside and showed me your father's website after she must have heard through Carl that I had mediumistic abilities. She didn't mention that your father was her brother, though."

"That was wise of her. Personal connections of any kind were undesirable for my father. He wanted participants with fresh and impartial perspectives. If you had referred to Aunt Florence in your application, I'm not sure you'd be sitting here with me tonight."

"But that's how your father chose me!" Travis grinned.

Zayla appeared amused. "Actually, it was me who picked you out of 348 applications."

"That many? Well then, I'd say you having chosen me makes this weekend the beginning of a very special friendship. What do you think?" Travis squeezed Zayla's hand, his face beaming.

"I have a good feeling about you," she confirmed with a smile and placed a kiss on his cheek.

"You know," Travis said, "one of the many things I've always appreciated about Logan, as well as Deimos, is that they both have a much more open-minded view of the world than most people I've met. The fact that I have a connection to the supernatural has never scared or frightened either of them. It never ceases to amaze me how naturally they accept my abilities. The totally unnatural distinction between *normal* and *paranormal* is not shared by either of them. Logan once told me that it has always been meaningless in the traditional Lakȟóta world anyway. The same is true, I suspect, of my ancestors. But

I'm afraid I no longer have access to their knowledge, nor do I have any contact with my father or his family.

"Spirituality is profoundly ingrained in Logan and Deimos," he mused further. "Both are deep thinkers. Logan is also always looking into the philosophies of martial arts. He and Nick are avid kickboxers and skilled jiu-jitsu athletes. Together, with a Japanese man named Stom — he's a friend of the three of us — they work with disadvantaged youth in Sydney. They offer martial arts therapy to those kids to help channel their misdirected energies and pent-up frustration. Logan and Nick went through this school themselves as teenagers. I, too, was shown this path through Stom and Logan, and I must confess, it has changed my life. Logan has a fascinating grandmother, by the way. Your abilities remind me a little of her, Zayla. Uŋčí is one of the very great last treasures in this world. I was able to meet her once. She supported me tremendously in going my way and not giving up on myself. I just wish I could still locate my father somehow. It's a shitty feeling when you don't know where you come from. I can't even tell you what people my father is from."

Zayla stroked Travis's hand and he turned his face to her.

"I'd still like to warn you about something, Zayla." His mood had become even more serious.

Zayla frowned. "Warn? About what?"

Travis stared over at the decaying metal skeleton of the West Pier. "The banker. Did you fish him out of 348 applications, too?"

Zayla shook her head. "Not really."

"Your father, then. What was your first reaction when you met Marrock the day before yesterday?"

"Darkness ..." she answered slowly. "Only for a first, brief moment. But it was there. Sensory-numbing darkness."

"And then?"

85

"I couldn't read him. But he's been consistently polite and respectful so far."

"Go with that first impression, Zayla. He's up to something. I've felt it every moment this weekend. Whatever he's up to, it's not good. And it clearly has to do with you."

Chapter 7

South Dakota, USA

Logan's heart contracted as he watched tears glimmer in his great-cousin's eyes. The teenager was standing in front of a stripped-down mobile home on the reservation, the home of Logan's aunt. The boy's mother, Logan's cousin, stepped toward her son, but he kept his back turned. His face reflected the disgust, but also the pain, of a child shoved aside. His mother had returned from a drinking binge, and Logan couldn't help but hear her boy's bitter reproaches. He felt reminded of his fourteen-year-old self.

"You promised me, Mom," he heard Vincent say with a tremor in his voice. "And yet you've been drinking again!"

His mother responded to him insistently. They were words of justification, amends, self-loathing, and finally despair as she seemed to realize that in addition to his respect, she had lost her boy's trust. The idea of something snapping in the teenager's heart made the hairs on the back of Logan's neck stand up, and he closed his eyes. His grandmother's words reverberated in his head like an endless echo: *Our people need their young men back, Logan. We need men like you, my grandson, especially here on the reservation.*

Uŋčí was right. But the people also needed their daughters back. They needed to regain sovereignty over their land. They needed new and old ways to heal the wounds that had been created in the more than five hundred years since 'the Indian' had been killed in order to 'save the man' in him.

We are not American!

Logan thought of the impassioned words of Hawaiian patriot Dr. Haunani-Kay Trask in her speech commemorating the one hundredth anniversary of the island nation's forced incorporation into the United States.

We are not American, she had shouted, raising a warning finger. *We will die as Hawaiians! America is the most powerful imperialist country in the world. It claims to be democratic. Lies! It has never been democratic with native people. America gives death to native people. And the only way to fight the United States of America is to be political!*

Unlike Dr. Haunani-Kay Trask, however, a part of Logan felt very much American. His biological father — half Lakȟóta, half white — had died as a highly decorated U.S. soldier in Iraq. Both of his grandfathers had served in Vietnam. His maternal great-grandfather had been used as a code talker against the Japanese in World War II. Even the best cryptographers in Nippon, Uŋčí had proudly reported, had been unable to decipher the intercepted messages of Diné and a few Lakȟóta code talkers. When a journalist mentioned to a Japanese general after the end of the war that American indigenous languages had been used for coding, the general laughed and thanked him for the information. The impossibility of deciphering the messages, the Japanese explained, had been a mystery his country thought would never be solved.

Logan exhaled and closed his eyes. He and his Lakȟóta family were the descendants of a revered but controversial headman and warrior leader. *Šuŋgmánitu Tȟáŋka Sápe*, the Black Wolf Chief, was elevated to legend and had fiercely resisted the European conquerors until his death. Logan was also the adopted son of Australian power player Deimos Aleksander Diamandis, a tremendously respected and immensely influential media mogul with Greek-Iranian ancestry and primary residence in Sydney.

Logan was a citizen of the Lakȟóta Nation and held

Australian as well as American citizenship. He knew that some Lakȟóta traditionalists disparagingly referred to him as an *apple*: a person whose exterior appeared "red" but whose feelings and thinking had become "white." He, however, saw himself merely as a man with broad horizons. He had heard of the suspicion with which people on the reservation looked at the opulent life he had led for more than a decade now. He also knew of the hope that rested on him to finally bring his influence to bear on his own people as the adopted son of one of the most powerful men in the world. But he had not yet used his privileged position to improve their lives.

The descendants of those Lakȟóta families who had followed the Black Wolf Chief at the height of the "Indian Wars" still showed exuberant patriotic respect for the leader and his descendants. Other families, however, who had already crossed paths with the contentious war chief in the 19th century, also regarded his great-grandchildren with suspicion. Only Uŋčí was held in the highest esteem by both parties.

A third group among the Lakȟóta chose neither side and waited to see if Logan, who had left the reservation as a teenager, would find a way back to them as an adult. His stay in South Dakota had confronted him with a momentous choice: He could shoulder the burden of the historical trauma that was rampant and metastasizing like a cancer in the souls of indigenous peoples, or he could turn his back on the enormity of the challenges once again and return to his adoptive family in Australia.

Logan rose to his full height. Then he entered his aunt's mobile home and looked straight into the hostile eyes of his mother, who sat next to her sister in the kitchen. She had her elbows propped on the table and was clutching a coffee mug with both hands. She must have seen the flash of surprise in his gaze because a mocking smile curled around her lips. She raised her hands and made the sign for seven.

Seven months she had been dry now?

"You didn't think I was capable of it, did you?" she asked bitingly.

Logan was relieved and also a little proud. He stacked the boxes of groceries he had bought before his visit next to the kitchen table. He placed all the cash he was carrying on top of them. His aunt thanked him with her eyes and invited him to stay. Logan sat down with his mother and sipped from the mug of coffee she had slid to him.

"Did your white family give you enough pocket money?" she asked, pointing her chin at the dollar bills on the food boxes. The tone of her voice dripped with sarcasm, earning a displeased look from her sister.

Logan eyed his mother impassively, but inside he was seething. He did not know how Deimos had managed to persuade Mary to agree to the adoption of her eldest son. To this day, his mother and adoptive father avoided any explanation of this. And still Mary seemed to have forgiven neither Logan nor herself for him becoming the Australian's adopted son.

"Shouldn't your first concern be for your daughter?" he replied coolly.

His mother lowered her eyes.

Outside, the voices of Logan's cousin and her son had fallen silent. Had Vincent perhaps run away?

"No one can take better care of my daughter than Uŋčí," Mary stated. With a sense of satisfaction, Logan noticed the guilt in this mother's voice.

"What's going to happen to Phoebe?" his aunt asked.

Logan exhaled slowly and heavily. He thought of his grandmother's words when he had asked her the same question. *If she can hold this horror in love to herself, she will be able to free herself from its stranglehold.*

Logan shook his head and remained silent. What he didn't say hung in the air like black smoke.

He heard the patter of horses' hooves. Shortly after, the door opened and a tall, lean boy entered the room. He and Logan cursed at the same time as they recognized each other. Immediately the boy turned on his heel and bolted to escape. Logan jumped up, nearly knocking over the kitchen table, and rushed after him. Even before Háŋska was back on his horse, Logan had pulled him to the ground. The teenager was nimble and knew how to fight back but had no chance against his martial arts-skilled older half-brother.

"You fucking rat!" hissed Logan, holding him in a chokehold. "I could have found Phoebe a lot faster if your dumb ass hadn't stolen the horses with your toddler gang!" Angrily, he gave him a hard shove with his knee.

"Fuck you!" cursed his brother.

"Logan! Let go of Háŋska!" he heard his mother call.

"You can't protect this little skunk," he replied, pushing his brother's face into the dust.

"Logan!" his aunt admonished him. "Let Háŋska go!"

Logan loosened his grip.

His brother got up, spitting out dust, and looked at Logan with contempt. "You think because you suddenly show up here again, you have the right to play head of the family?" he sneered. "Have you looked around? Have you helped us even once? What have you done, you coward, except run away?" Háŋska bared his teeth, his words hitting Logan harder than any war club could.

"Take me to my daughter!" demanded Mary sharply. Addressing her younger son, she hissed, "And you, Háŋska, are as much of a good-for-nothing as he is."

The apple does not fall far from the tree.

Logan winced. He glanced at his mother, but she didn't seem to have heard anything. Then he studied his brother's features. Had Háŋska said those words out loud, or had the two brothers just thought them together?

Háŋska grimaced bitterly. He swung himself on his horse and rode away without a word.

The drive to Uŋčí's log cabin was uneventful. Logan kept the *Lakȟóta Nation's Voice* playing, the reservation's radio station, to fill the oppressive silence between him and his mother. When he parked the rented SUV in front of his grandmother's log cabin an hour later, mother and son had not exchanged a single word.

Uŋčí greeted her daughter Mary with a nod of her head. What it was exactly that made the two women freeze when they met, Logan didn't know. But a careful glance was enough to find his old suspicion confirmed that his mother felt inferior to his grandmother. Perhaps it had been her drunkenness and neglect of her three children that had contributed to their fractured relationship.

To Logan's surprise, it was Phoebe who warmed the icy mood between the women. She leaned her head against her mother and pulled her grandmother near her, so the two had to stand close together and couldn't avoid each other. Then she looked at her brother.

"You brought an interesting friend with you," she explained, pointing to Nick, who was standing in the background. "He speaks with a funny accent and told me about all the strange animals that exist in his homeland."

The smile she gave Logan left him speechless. It was incomprehensible to him where she found the strength to do it.

The fact that she was back on her feet at all was as much a miracle as the fact that she treated Nick, who was not only a man but also a stranger to her, like a friend.

"My favorite part was the video with the man fighting with the kangaroo to rescue his dog from it," she shared.

Nick stepped up to the siblings and grinned. Logan introduced him to his mother.

"I still like the look of the dog best after the kangaroo picked him up and pinned him with his paws!" His adopted brother turned to Phoebe when Mary made no effort to acknowledge him with more than a grunt.

The two laughed and Logan shook his head. Then he became distracted by a visitor of Uŋčí's unknown to him, who stepped out of the log cabin. She was an attractive woman in her mid-twenties with brown skin and long black cornrows that reached her hips. Besides the African braided hairdo, Logan took note of her intelligent dark eyes and her full, feminine body shape of which many African American women were so proud. An ironic smile twitched around the corners of her mouth when she noticed his gaze appraising her. Logan feigned being caught and shrugged.

Uŋčí introduced her visitor as Tiya-Alea Redbird, member of the Ojibwe-Anishinabe, *the beings created out of nothing,* who were native to the areas around the Canadian and U.S. American Great Lakes.

Logan's mother was delighted by the unexpected visit and hugged the young woman. "Tiya's mother is a friend of mine," Mary explained, and Logan wondered why she even bothered to tell him. "Her father is from Antigua. Her mother lives on the Black River in Manitoba, up in Canada. Tiya lives here in South Dakota, in Rapid City. She's a journalist, radio host, and successful podcaster!" Logan registered the enthusiasm for the

Ojibwe-Anishinaabe woman in his mother's voice.

Tiya gave him a long look. "In the language of my mother's people, I am *makade Anishinaabe ikwe.* A black indigenous woman."

This confirmed what Logan had suspected. Uŋčí invited her visitors to take a seat in her kitchen and have lunch together. Together with Phoebe, she set the table and served a hunter's stew of bear meat with wild mushrooms and onions, chopped juniper, fresh oregano, and sumac. As a side dish, she passed corn cakes. Logan's mouth watered. He had not eaten such a dish in years and enjoyed it to the fullest. He learned that Tiya had a strong relationship with Uŋčí and had already recruited her as a teacher for a project to revive indigenous languages.

Tiya had heard about the horror Phoebe had endured and found herself as a guest in Uŋčí's home because she wanted to support the old woman's granddaughter. At the same time, it was her intention to enlist Uŋčí's support for a second project that could provide a space for healing for the relatives of the many disappeared, raped, and often murdered indigenous girls and women.

Inspired by the ancient Lakȟóta and Ojibwe-Anishinaabe societies in which young and old men and women came together based on their abilities and interests, Tiya wanted to create a society for the families of the missing girls and women so that they could exchange ideas with others affected and commemorate their loved ones.

"I want to create something," Tiya added, "that also includes Two Spirit People and transgender women because they're often considered even more disposable in the settler society than our girls and women already are."

"What do you guys think of Anne Sixkiller's appointment to the position of Secretary of the Interior?" Nick asked the group after a pause. "Will she change anything for you?"

"It's certainly a historic appointment," Tiya replied thoughtfully. "She's the first indigenous woman to hold a cabinet post, and no matter what we think of her, the representation of indigenous and black populations matters."

"It sounds like you have doubts about her," Nick mused.

"Well, as Secretary of the Interior, she also heads the Bureau of Indian Affairs, an agency with which we have historically had a very charged relationship. Among other things, the BIA oversaw the creation of the so-called boarding schools that were located off the reservations and that wreaked havoc on the psyche of our children who were stolen from our families, abused, and re-educated there. The BIA was responsible for the Indian Termination Policy and the Urban Relocation Program: two more initiatives through which we were to be assimilated and made invisible. The reservation land freed up by these policies was to be sold by the government to make it more 'usable.' The BIA was also responsible for the Indian Adoption Project, where up to a third of our children were given white adoptive parents — another treacherous form of assimilation and genocide. In addition, the blood quantum system was forced upon us in order to be able to determine from the outside who could still be considered a tribal member and who could not. Even our financial resources have always been sorely mismanaged by the BIA ..." Tiya let the sentence fade out with a mixture of scorn and contempt.

"You're talking about the BIA," Nick replied. "Sixkiller, however, is Secretary of the Interior."

"The Bureau of Indian Affairs, as I said, is under the Department of the Interior. In the past, the U.S. government had relations with us indigenous people squarely in the War Department. These days, we're on the same level as wildlife and natural resources in this hodgepodge ministry they call the

Department of the Interior."

"I'd rather be put on the same level with all our other-than-human relatives than be assigned to a war department," Uŋči laughed.

"That's true, Grandma." Tiya nodded. Turning to Nick, she said, "The Bureau of Land Management, another part of the Interior Department, is extremely hostile to indigenous organizers who oppose fracking, for example. I wonder if Sixkiller, as Secretary of the Interior, could change anything here at all."

"But at least Anne Sixkiller has publicly backed MMIWG," Mary interjected.

"MMIWG?" asked Nick.

"Missing and Murdered Indigenous Women and Girls," Tiya explained to him with a sideways glance at Phoebe. "Originally, it was public inquiry reports by the Mounties and the Canadian government into the disproportionate number of missing and murdered Indigenous women and girls there. MMIWG has since become an increasingly vocal movement. Here in the U.S., too, our women and girls are much more likely to be victims of violence and murder than members of any other ethnic group. To that extent, it's important that someone at the Cabinet level finally address this bitter issue." She turned to Logan's mother. "But what Anne Sixkiller doesn't understand yet, Mary, is that you can't talk about MMIWG without also touching on resource exploitation. We have to make her understand that fracking, oil and gas extraction, tar sands mining, capitalism, and settler colonialism are complicit in the violence against our women."

Logan, too, had not yet thought enough about these connections. He liked Tiya's passion and political expertise.

"Anne Sixkiller needs to listen to the public she now serves,"

Tiya continued. "She needs to listen to the indigenous organizers who put her in this position. We must be able to hold her accountable at all times, just as we have always done with our leaders. We must not treat Anne Sixkiller as something special. Have you seen the headlines? I don't like these lead stories. 'Anne Sixkiller — for the first time in 500 years, a Native woman holds real power.' That's complete hogwash!"

"Because ...?" inquired Nick. "Didn't you guys gain any influence from her?"

"Sure, in a way we did. But a headline like that implies that we would be nothing without the government and without the American system. And that's simply not true. We hold a form of power that this government will never understand. What distresses me most is the fact that Anne Sixkiller has sided with two indigenous congressmen who want to disenfranchise the *Freedmen*, the descendants of black slaves from tribes in the Southeast."

"Natives kept black people as slaves?" Nick asked incredulously.

"Only five of nearly 600 recognized tribes," Logan enlightened him. "They've been called the *Five Civilized Nations* because they developed a system of government based on the U.S. model, with their own Senate and House of Representatives. They welcomed Christian missionaries and developed their own writing system. And like the whites in the region, they eventually kept black slaves. The descendants of these slaves, the Freedmen, have quite rightly complained that while they are counted as indigenous citizens when tribes report their population numbers to apply for funds, on the other hand they are denied services and tribal membership. So, there is an internal Jim Crow policy going on. Sixkiller siding with these tribes was certainly not a wise decision."

"Indeed," Tiya snorted. "Especially since the tribes have

taken the enslaved Africans with them on the Trail of Tears."

"The Trail of Tears?"

Logan had to stifle a grin as he read utter confusion from Nick's face. How could his adopted Australian brother know about these things?

"The Trail of Tears was the forced relocation of the Five Civilized Tribes from the Southeastern United States to their assigned one-thousand-mile-away reservations in Oklahoma," Logan explained. "At least a quarter, some say up to seventy percent, of the people died of starvation, disease, cold and exhaustion on these treks, which were escorted by the U.S. military."

Nick shook his head. "A brutal world," he mused. "Then as now."

After lunch, Logan watched Tiya walk with Phoebe on the grassland around Uŋčí's log cabin and wondered what they were talking about so intently. He grinned at the two wolfhounds that did not leave his sister's side: a black female and a gray male. They were two intelligent and extremely dangerous animals as soon as they saw themselves or Uŋčí and their property threatened.

When the two women returned to Logan, Nick, Mary, and Uŋčí, Tiya bid them farewell. "I have an appointment with Dr. Kim TallBear for a podcast interview," she explained. "She is a Dakȟóta and an Indigenous Studies professor at the University of Alberta in Canada whom I admire greatly. I have to go back to my apartment in Rapid City for the interview, which will be a video conference."

Logan accompanied Tiya to her car. "Your visit has done my sister a world of good," he said as he held the door open for her.

"Phoebe carries tremendous strength," Tiya replied. "I admire that very much. She will heal one day, Logan."

He nodded. "I hope you're right."

"Isn't it strange?" asked Tiya, her eyes flashing. "In the old days, your tribes were still native to the northern forests of Minnesota and Wisconsin. *Sioux* was considered the French corruption of the Ojibwe-Anishinaabe word for snakes. An unflattering term used by my mother's people for you, their enemies."

She was all smiles and Logan liked the quirky way she flirted with him.

"Dr. David Treuer, an Ojibwe academic I interviewed for my podcast, thinks that in the world's historical consciousness, your people have occupied all the platforms for indigenous coolness," she continued teasingly. "When in fact it was my mother's people who drove you out of the woodlands and onto the Great Plains. So, in the end, it is thanks to us that you were able to evolve into one of the most feared equestrian and warrior peoples in the world."

Logan laughed out loud, enduring her playful taunts.

"We, on the other hand," she admitted with a shrug, "have to be content with one of the back places on the popularity ranks. And this despite the fact that we outnumber you and even have an entry in the *Guinness Book of World Records*."

"You hold an entry in the *Guinness Book of World Records*?" exclaimed Logan. "For what?"

"For the hardest language in the world to learn!" Tiya jutted her chin and propped her arms at her sides. Then she glanced at Mary, who was standing on Uŋčí's porch, watching them. Her expression changed and she lowered her voice. "I, too, know what it means to grow up in an alcoholic family," she confessed, "but in me the resistance was too powerful to align my life with the heart-wrenching hopelessness of so many of my relatives. Something in me found the strength not to follow in the footsteps of that desolation."

Logan looked at her for a long time. Tiya had a directness that left him speechless.

"As a child I swore I would never touch a drop of alcohol in my life. I wanted to live a self-determined, self-empowered life."

"Yes," Logan agreed thoughtfully. "To be a strong, confident, and proud role model, or '*makhá wičhóni ékignakA*' — put down our life on earth and start the journey back to the spirit world." He was struck by the impression that Tiya felt and thought as he did.

"Come visit me before you fly back with Nick," she offered. "Maybe I can show you something in Rapid City that will interest you."

Logan stroked the back of her hand with his thumb, just once, and heard her short, abrupt intake of breath. Then Tiya got into her car and started the engine. She looked up at Logan once more and drove off.

"She's a great woman," Phoebe, who had approached her brother, praised Tiya Redbird. She leaned her head against Logan's shoulder. "She's helped a lot of our people. On and off the reservation."

He put an arm around Phoebe.

"Nick told me," she murmured after a while, "how you saved him that time."

Logan looked at her sharply. "He told you about his kidnapping?"

Phoebe nodded. "And about what happened to him there."

Logan remained silent. He could not believe it. The images of the biker who had worked the then fourteen-year-old like a pneumatic drill made old nausea well up inside him. It had been Nick's muffled screams that had alerted him to the horrific scene. Logan had not been privy to the crime, but he knew one of the kidnappers. He had seen the monster, in his perverse lust, claw his fingernails into Nick's back while raping him violently. Logan had executed the man. Two well-aimed shots from the kidnapper's gun, which he had carelessly discarded earlier. When the dead man's comrades came running into the room to seize the two boys, Logan had aimed the gun at them, too.

At that point, he blacked out. His memory only returned when he found himself alone at a police station. He was told that he and Nick had been found in a state of deep shock — two fourteen-year-olds in a run-down warehouse surrounded by three dead bodies.

It was only thanks to the skilled legal team Nick's father had hired for Logan that his act had been ruled self-defense and he had regained his freedom, first on bail and, after a months-long trial, finally in court.

Logan felt Phoebe pressing against him. He felt the heavy rise and fall of her chest. Then a strangled cry, a long-drawn wail broke through her body. She buried her face in his shoulder and wept uncontrollably. Logan stroked her back gently and continuously. He pulled his sister down to the prairie grasses. Hour after hour, he sat with her and held her in his arms — until the pain of what she had experienced found no more nourishment in her, and his own tears had dried again as well.

Chapter 8

Sydney, Australia: Diamandis Estate

"Marry me," Nick murmured in Tahnee's ear as she arched her back toward him.

"What did you say?" she asked incredulously, meeting the thrusts accentuating his request with equal ardor. Tahnee pushed her head back into the pillows and sighed. Nick made love to her that night with an intensity that took her breath away.

"Marry me," he said a second time.

Tahnee's desire for this man, who years ago had lost his virginity to her, cleared for a moment, and she opened her eyes. "What?" she asked, dumbfounded.

"Marry me," Nick murmured for the third time and Tahnee registered a hint of self-approval on his face. Circling his hips and repeating an intensely pleasurable motion, he must have realized he had her right where he wanted her. He stopped his rhythm, supported the weight of his body with one arm, and brushed her thick hair aside with his freed hand. His lips and teeth slid over her neck. Tahnee felt the corners of Nick's mouth twist into a grin. Like a layer of velvet, his breath brushed across her skin as he whispered, "If you want to come tonight, Carly, you'd better agree to becoming my wife."

That little devil, she thought, as she now heard him purr her old pet name on top of everything. Resistance stirred in her, coupled with her deep love for this man and her appreciation for the impressive degree of self-control he demonstrated. He seemed serious about his proposal. But wasn't it also somehow related to his and Logan's return from South Dakota? What had happened there?

In retaliation for Nick denying her the physical release she craved, she unceremoniously raked her long fingernails into his back. Nick flinched. In a flash, he grabbed her wrists and yanked her hands away from his body. With all his strength he pressed Tahnee into the mattress, clutching her arms like a vise. She let out a cry of pain. Startled, he looked at her and let go. He rolled next to her, put an arm over his face and avoided any eye contact.

"I'm so sorry," Tahnee whispered. She didn't dare touch or hold him.

He kept his head turned away, swung his long legs over the edge of the bed, and sat up. He ran both hands over his face and ruffled his deep brown shoulder-length hair. Then he hung his head and clasped his hands at the nape of his neck, his body bent forward. It was the posture of a defeated man. Tahnee felt as if she might cry.

Three years earlier, when Nick had temporarily broken up with her, Logan had given Tahnee a lot of encouragement during a nightly stroll through Sydney, asking her to be compassionate with Nick and have an inexhaustible amount of patience for him. "He'll find his way back to you," he promised her then, and he'd been right.

Perhaps this would be all it would take tonight: boundless love for this wonderful man beside her and much, much patience.

***

It was well past midnight. In the west wing of the mighty Diamandis estate, which towered over the picturesque scenery of Port Jackson, Logan sat with the master of the house. His adoptive father vigorously pushed back the fine leather-covered swivel chair in which he had been seated and rose.

Logan knew him too well not to notice the shadows of shock and sadness that had flitted across his face.

Deimos Aleksander Diamandis was an impressive man of medium height and striking facial features with sharp, pitch-black eyes around which small crow's feet played. The wrinkles and first gray streaks that ran through his thick, black-brown hair gave the impression of maturity and composure. He wore blue jeans and a white linen shirt with the sleeves rolled up.

Deimos was a media mogul and major player on the international stage. He possessed power and influence on a scale that extended far beyond Australia. For as long as Logan had known him, Deimos, whose grandparents had been Greek and Iranian immigrants, had given the same high priority to his goal of changing the world around him and achieving complete financial independence as he did to his health and fitness. Thus, the body of the forty-five-year-old possessed the form and performance of an athlete a good fifteen years younger.

Parts of the Australian tabloids and gossip magazines had once spread conspiracy theories and reported that Deimos, whose name meant *terror* in ancient Greek, was in league with Satanic circles. The tycoon had been so enraged that he bought up the publishers responsible and had them broken up. However, he did not do this without making sure that the scorched earth his people had left behind would become fertile ground with new job opportunities created for the majority of people who had been deprived of their livelihood. Not once more did Logan see reports of his adoptive father in a negative light.

Slowly, Deimos turned toward the panoramic window, which revealed a breath-taking view of the Sydney skyline at night, and crossed his arms behind his back. Logan followed his movements with his eyes. He realized his father was trying to hide his emotions from him. But Logan's decision stood. He had to leave Australia again and return to the United States. He had to return to a part of himself that he had pushed to the back of his mind for over a decade. He had to return to his biological family, to Tiya, the woman he fell in love with, to his roots, and to his beginnings. Back to the historical land where he had been born. Back to the poverty and trauma of his childhood.

Logan could not have lived with himself if he had continued to turn his back on the crushing challenges awaiting him again on the reservation, even as an adult. He would have despised himself if he had denied Uŋčí, who had never asked anything of him in a quarter century, the request to return to his old homeland. He would have spit on his own reflection in the mirror if he did not move heaven and hell to track down the men who had raped his sister and bring them to justice. Logan had to go back. But for part of what he was about to do, he needed his father's influence and connections.

As if these thoughts had been spoken aloud, Deimos disengaged himself from his position at the window as if in slow motion and returned his son's gaze with silent sorrow. "Both my children have grown up," he began after a while of silence. His voice was dark and motionless like the calm before the storm. "We chose one another as family. You're more than my adopted son, Logan, and you were a daredevil even back then when you pulled Nick out of that hellhole. As a fourteen-year-old, you were already more of a man than most boys will ever be in their entire lives. A man has to make his own decisions and protect his family. Those are things I can understand very well."

Deimos took a long breath. "You and I are cut from the same cloth in many ways. I owe you everything. If you leave us now, you will not go without my full support, as much as I regret your decision. We chose one another as family," he took up the sentiment once more after a short pause, "and as my adopted child you are endowed in every way with the same rights and means as my biological one. No father could be prouder to call a man of your caliber his son."

Logan soaked up the compliment like a dry sponge soaks up water and lowered his eyes.

"But no power on earth," the tycoon continued with a warning tone in his voice, "will be able to dissuade me from protecting my family with the same tenacity and fire as you must now do for the American part of yours. I will tolerate no resistance and no opposition whatsoever when it comes to protecting my family, and thus you, from harm. Do you understand what I am trying to tell you?" The tycoon's eyes bored into his son's and held him as if on a hook. Logan nodded.

"Good. In terms of material resources, you will, of course, continue to have unlimited access to whatever you need. What else do you require?"

"Two contacts."

"Name them."

"Bree McDowell and Hunter Garza."

Deimos narrowed his eyes. "What for?"

"Bree for reporting, Hunter to bring Phoebe's rapist to justice."

Deimos scowled at Logan. "Don't take me for a fool."

Logan was at pains to placate him. "Not my intention, Father."

"Don't try to hide anything from me again!" Deimos warned him so insistently that the fine hairs on the back of Logan's neck stood up. "I demand that you lay your cards on the table with me at all times. I will *not* ask you to do so a second time. What do you need Hunter Garza for?"

Logan exhaled and rose. "The justice system in South Dakota will have no interest in pursuing Phoebe's case. There will be no justice for what was done to her."

Deimos looked at his son long and thoughtfully. When he started to speak again, his voice had dropped an octave and the sounds that escaped his throat reminded Logan of the low-pitched roar of a predatory cat. "Hunter Garza is no ... *hit man*."

Logan bit his tongue. "He has his contacts," he commented matter-of-factly.

"How do *you* know about that?"

Logan strained for a tone of voice that would take the tension out of the conversation with his father. "Your son, Deimos," he quipped with self-restrained pride and a fair bit of self-mockery, pointing to himself, "is a great-grandson of the most outstanding trackers in the Americas. Even a man of your skill can't make every trail useless to me."

Deimos made a gruff hand gesture. Logan, however, noticed the smirk that had flitted across his father's face. The tycoon's posture relaxed. "I'll come back to this subject, Logan. It's not over for you."

The two men exchanged a long look in a silent battle of wills, which the younger man won. With the hint of a nod, Deimos finally conceded defeat. Few people succeeded in doing what his sons and their close bond with him sometimes managed to do: influence the tycoon in a position once taken, or even change his mind. His two children were Deimos's weak spot and the gateway to anything that could curtail his power and influence and undermine his resolutions.

"I will arrange a meeting with you and Hunter Garza," he decided. "But I will attend the meeting," Deimos added in a tone that again allowed no argument.

Logan acquiesced. He accepted his father's presence to humor him. He would have preferred to keep him out of all matters pertaining to the prosecution of his sister's rapists, but as muddled as things had become, Logan had to forgo getting his way. He needed his father as an ally.

"What can Bree do for you?" inquired Deimos, following up on Logan's statement that it was Hunter Garza and Bree McDowell whose contacts he needed.

Logan closed his eyes for a moment. Then he rose and wandered up and down an imaginary line in his father's study. Bree McDowell was an unusually bright mind, and she was brilliantly connected. Not only was she a top lawyer, but she was also his father's press secretary and personal advisor. She could do a hell of a lot for him.

"In my home country, four out of five indigenous women are victims of violence," Logan explained. "The murder rate of our women is ten times higher than the national average. They are more than twice as likely to experience sexual violence as women in other ethnic groups in the U.S.. Almost every family on the rez has one or more stories to tell of female relatives or friends who were raped and murdered. Many of our sisters and daughters disappear unnoticed. They also hardly appear in official crime statistics. Our women are not victims worth reporting. If there are no numbers, then these crimes don't exist."

Deimos had followed his words carefully. "Years ago, during a business trip in Canada, I saw a newspaper article about an underage indigenous girl."

Thoughtfully, he told Logan that he had never forgotten the girl's name, Tina Michelle Fontaine, because her fate had touched him deeply. Abandoned by her mother and finding her father beaten to death, Tina Fontaine's body had been discovered wrapped in bags and plastic sheeting in a river, but her killer had been acquitted in court. The girl's death had not been an isolated incident. More than twelve hundred Canadian indigenous women had been reported missing since the 1980s, the newspaper reported. The fate of the dead had sparked a discussion about the social situation of the First Nations' women in Canada. The government, though, feared the negative headlines and had insisted on calling Tina Fontaine's death a criminal case, denying a social or even racist problem. Experts, however, disagreed. They attributed the high number of victims among indigenous women to several factors: lack of access to education, high school dropout rates, and being forced to earn a living through drugs or prostitution. The shattered relationship of trust between judicial authorities and indigenous people was also held responsible by the experts, as were the historically strained relations between Canadian First Nations and whites. During the forced assimilation attempts of past decades alone, there had been countless cases of violence and abuse against Native people. Traumas that have lingered in indigenous families to this day.

"The situation in the U.S. is no different," Logan countered to his father. "I would even see it as more prevalent and serious. Moreover, before any of our women's charges of rape are taken seriously, they must first prove that they were not drunk or drugged at the time of the crime and therefore complicit in the eyes of the law."

Logan's mother and aunts, he told Deimos, like many other mothers on the reservation, had requested the *morning after pill* for their daughters from doctors so they would have a plan B once their children were raped and if they survived. The assaults on indigenous women were, in their vast majority, committed by outsiders.

"If an offender is to be prosecuted," Logan continued, "the approach and enforceability of the prosecution are dependent on whether the crime was committed on the reservation, and whether a tribal member is a victim or a perpetrator. It's a thicket of overlapping jurisdictions and different laws, creating a lawless space and making the predominantly non-native offenders almost untouchable. And they know it."

Logan thought of the example of one of his cousins. Her rapist, an oil worker from a *Man Camp* near the reservation where she was staying, had neither been apprehended nor prosecuted by the tribal police since rape, like murder, was the responsibility of the federal authorities. Two-thirds of all cases involving the rape and murder of indigenous women, however, were returned to the file by these same federal authorities.

"Near the Man Camps, the casualty rates are particularly high," he recounted. "A bunch of shady characters congregate there. They hire out as workers to the local oil and gas pipelines. These camps are hotbeds of drug trafficking, gambling, prostitution, and sexual violence. The whole thing is given the dark nimbus of glorious Wild West vibrancy." Logan would have liked to bang his fist against the wall. "Our women and girls are not safe around these camps. Neither are the boys anymore. Just recently, the local tribal police picked up a fifteen-year-old who was being passed from trailer to trailer. The tragedy of our women and children, both on reservations and in urban areas, desperately needs high political profile and a strong lobby to finally make a difference."

Deimos heaved a soundless sigh. "You blame racism for these events?"

Logan nodded. "Our women have always been considered invisible and disposable in the eyes of our conquerors, just like the First Nation women here in Australia. Little has changed in that regard to this day. Australian Aboriginal Women also disappear at a disproportionately high rate. Did you know that? If poverty and addiction problems are added to the mix, it makes them particularly easy victims of acts of violence. But lack of resources is also a reason. So is apathy, along with a flawed legal system back in the States and jurisdictional chaos."

Deimos leaned back in his leather work chair and took a deep, slow breath. Logan eyed him. Then his glance fell on the glossy magazine lying open on Deimos's desk. He blinked. *Forbes* had actually ranked his father number five of the seventy most powerful people in the world for the second time?

For years now, the renowned business magazine had listed the Australian in the top twelve. The top four places were generally occupied by the heads of government of China, the U.S., Russia, and Germany. In some years, Jeff Bezos, the Amazon founder, passed Deimos in the rankings. In other years, he had to vie with Bill Gates or the Pope for fifth and sixth place. But never before had his father slipped further than twelfth place in this highly regarded ranking.

With power came responsibility, for himself and for all associated with him. With his father's social position, countless half-secret opportunities and bittersweet temptations found their way to Deimos, sometimes leading to decisions that were on the shady side of his immense power. He possessed such an uncut measure of influence and financial independence that almost every decision, every option became a balancing act between far-sighted and conscientious action on the one hand and the gratification of his dark impulses hanging over him like a sword of Damocles on the other.

To Nick's mother, who had never been able to make much of Logan, Deimos had not been faithful. He had had countless flings with a wide variety of women inside and outside his own ethnicity and social position. If some of the rumors surrounding his father's amorous adventures were true, he had not been shy about putting two of his affairs under massive pressure when they began to work against his interests.

The rumor mill also knew of a high-class prostitute in the style of a modern courtesan. From the time this highly educated seductress incorporated her many years of work experience into a series of successful erotic novels, the tycoon had dispensed with her company. For all the world to read, novel excerpts had revealed that the heroine had spent countless nights with a powerful media mogul in a luxury hotel above the rooftops of Sydney.

One evening, as the two had followed a television report about Harvey Weinstein and the aftermath of the #MeToo movement, the courtesan had dared to ask, in her calm, confident way, how long they would all continue to live in a society where the dignity, lives and concerns of women were so consistently subordinated to the interests of powerful and influential men. The media mogul had owed her an answer. He did not let her know if he had even taken any notice of her question. But the heroine of the erotic novel series later learned that she had sown the seeds of introspection in this powerful man with her casual comment that night.

"I will call Bree in the morning," Deimos now answered his son. "I will instruct her to put all other matters aside, prioritize your concerns in every way possible, and strategize with you and her people."

This was more support for his cause than Logan had dared hope for. He felt satisfaction and relief that his father was backing him so wholeheartedly, and tremendous appreciation welled up in him. However, Logan had never been blind to the darker side of his father. He silently wondered how many times the tycoon had caused a life to be built or destroyed, a story to die or to be promoted.

Deimos's media group distributed more than one hundred

newspapers and several dozen magazines with their associated internet presences in Australia alone. It also had powerful subsidiaries in the U.S. and Europe. He owned pay TV stations and TV news channels on three continents. He also owned market research institutes, a feature film distribution company and majority stakes in one of Australia's most successful rugby clubs, as well as shares in a major London football club. This cross-media setup secured much of Deimos's power and extraordinary influence.

"I want Bree to get in touch with Tiya-Alea Redbird. She's an indigenous activist in Rapid City who is a thorn in a lot of people's side."

"Tiya-Alea Redbird? Tell me about her," Deimos urged his son.

Logan silently cursed. It must have been the small moment, the blink of an eye, that he had needed to decide whether to tell his father Tiya's name tonight that had betrayed him. Deimos possessed excellent instincts. When the tycoon focused his attention on a single person, he could read his counterpart almost as well as a book. Logan had often admired his father's intuitive gift of being able to grasp microexpressions. But he felt no desire to become the subject of those analytical skills tonight. He met Deimos's probing gaze challengingly but silently. No, he thought stubbornly, refusing to avert his eyes, he was interested in Tiya, and not only because she had made a good name for herself as an activist, radio host, and podcaster. The disgust he felt at the thought that his father would have thoroughly checked Tiya's background as a stranger in his son's life, and therefore a potential security risk, was clearly written on his face.

Logan possessed a deep dislike for the dossiers of Hunter Garza, the private investigator who worked for Deimos. The same Hunter Garza he had requested minutes earlier from his father to make further progress in the search for Phoebe's rapists. Deimos had also once ordered this same Hunter Garza to conduct a background check on Tahnee shortly after she and Nick had become a couple, a move that had led to a hard-hitting argument between Nick and Deimos over the right to make his own decisions and have his privacy respected.

Logan's mind wandered from memories of that unusually raucous argument between the two men in which he had tried to mediate, back to Tiya two days ago, the afternoon before his flight back to Australia with Nick. Logan had taken heart and sought out Tiya in her small Rapid City apartment.

"How serious are you about us?" she had asked him standing in the doorway before she had even invited him in, her hands on her hips. "Are you going to take off again after we've had our fun?"

He registered that she had been talking about *our* fun, at least. "I am so serious about you," he replied carefully, "that if it were up to me alone, you would become the mother of my children."

Her eyebrows raised. "Pretty cheap pickup line, huh?" she scoffed, but his instincts told him he had touched something inside her.

As they shed their clothes, he experienced a few moments of uncertainty about how much he could hold himself back once his passion for her took over. He hesitated and tried to take his time making love to her. But when lust finally consumed him, he unceremoniously lifted her onto her desk and positioned her so that he could have entered her in a single movement. Naked and in all her glory, she perched on the tabletop. He couldn't get enough of her full, feminine form and leaned down to kiss her, supporting her lower back with his left hand. Then he pushed her thighs apart and, while massaging the most sensitive part of her body with the pad of his right thumb, plunged two fingers deep inside her. The thrilling abandon with which Tiya enjoyed his caresses drove him out of his mind. She came fast and hard, her fingers clawing into his flesh. As he moved with her again and again that afternoon in the devoted rhythm of deep physical and mental intoxication, he realized that ecstasy like this had been foreign to him until now.

Exhausted, they lay in Tiya's bed until just before dawn, holding each other close.

"We caught my most fertile days," Tiya muttered as Logan finally sat up to get dressed because he had to get back to Uŋčí, Nick, and Phoebe.

"Ah! That explains why you're so insatiable, of course," he teased, kissing her. The thought of possibly having just conceived their first child together with this wonderful woman gave him the long-awaited feeling of finally having come home.

"That Nick wants to marry Tahnee now," Deimos remarked, snapping Logan out of his thoughts, "will probably have something to do with your decision to return to the States. Your leaving will have hit him hard. Tahnee will have to become an even stronger anchor for him and give him even more stability."

Logan nodded. Deimos was an excellent judge of character. "You already know he wants to marry her?"

"I saw the credit card statement for the ring." Deimos shrugged, and Logan couldn't help but grin.

"Nick couldn't have found a better wife for himself," he said, meaning every word. "She'll make him happy, Father. They'll have a good marriage."

Deimos looked inquiringly at his son, and Logan wondered if the tycoon knew how close the Lakȟóta himself had already come to his future sister-in-law in the past.

It was around four in the morning when Logan left his father's study again. The conversation with Deimos lingered with him for a long time. Tired and worn out from the events of the past two weeks and the twenty-six-hour flight back to Australia from South Dakota, he was still unable to find rest or sleep, so he went to the kitchen on the first floor of the Diamandis estate to quench his thirst with a bottle of the premium water the family kept on hand.

It was a mineral water Deimos had bottled in Tasmania and collected as rain in special catchment facilities at a small farm the tycoon had bought a few years ago on the northwest coast of the island 240 kilometers south of the Australian mainland. The CO_2-neutral rain catchment facilities were located near an area designated as a World Heritage Site where the cleanest air in the world had been measured. The rainwater, bottled exclusively in glass, was a product that fell from clouds that had not crossed cities or industrial areas on their long journey across the world's oceans to Australia's southern treasure island. The proceeds from the sale of the premium water went in full to a charity that had been set up by one of Deimos's old university friends and that promoted the construction and implementation of local drinking water projects around the world.

Despite the early hour, Logan found unexpected company in the kitchen. Tahnee sat at the obsidian-gray kitchen island that took up most of the room, spooning chocolate ice cream out of a dessert bowl. The five copper-colored metal light fixtures hanging from the ceiling above the kitchen island dimmed to provide a soft, subdued light. Beneath the casual denim shirt Tahnee must have pilfered from Nick's closet, she appeared to be unclothed. Her right leg was stuck bent between her torso and the countertop, her left dangling lasciviously from the bar stool.

Her long, light brown hair framed a thoughtful-looking face.

Wordlessly, Logan strode past her and headed for the built-in refrigerator in piano lacquer finish that was next to her. He opened it, took out a bottle of the fine water, and let the heavy door close with a "pop." Then, he positioned himself so the kitchen island was between him and Tahnee, and he was facing the young woman. She lifted her head and looked him in the eye.

"Hi," he greeted her.

"Hi." Her voice had a softness that caught his attention.

He took a long, thirsty pull from the water bottle and noticed Tahnee's eyes on him. Logan set the bottle down and his gaze fell on the deep blue gemstone on her right hand. "I see congratulations are in order."

Tenderly, Tahnee stroked her white gold engagement ring with a particularly high-carat, royal blue tanzanite surrounded by twenty-eight small diamonds — one for each of her years of life — that framed both the royal gemstone and the top half of the ring's arc. With raised eyebrows, Logan had stood next to Nick in the jewelry store as his brother had this unusual ring made for Tahnee.

"I can hardly believe Nick actually asked me to marry him tonight," she confirmed. "And at the same time, I feel so much sadness inside me since I found out earlier why you're leaving us."

Logan remained silent.

"I have no words for what was done to your sister," Tahnee murmured. "I so wish there was something I could do to take some of the horror and grief away from you, her, your family ..."

Her gaze searched his eyes. Logan knew Tahnee loved Nick. But he also knew she felt connected to him in a way that Nick, as a white Australian, could not share with her.

"I've known you for five years now," she continued, keeping

her eyes averted, "and I still feel like I only understand part of what really makes you tick and who you actually are ..."

Logan didn't like the direction the conversation was taking, but he understood she was trying to get rid of something that was weighing heavily on her.

"I've ... except for that *one night* back then ..." she paused slightly, "never asked about your past."

Because we'd both better forget that evening, Logan thought.

"To me, you were always Nick's brother and his best friend," she explained. "To me you have always been the adopted son of the powerful Deimos Aleksander Diamandis and, in that role, like a Chosen One. I have envied you the absolute esteem in which he and Nick hold you." She shook her head and laughed. "It's not easy to gain Deimos's respect. Me, he has to accept now because he found no dirt when he checked my past and my family's background. He has to accept me because he can be sure that I am not a gold-digger. And, of course, because he is quite receptive to a certain type of woman. But *real* appreciation looks different. Travis, maybe ... Travis would be one of the few people I could think of, other than the two of you, that Deimos has a soft spot for and respects."

Logan smiled. Tahnee was nobody's fool.

"Of course, I always knew what you did for Nick," she continued. "I always knew that he and Deimos hold you in high regard; I have never had any doubt about what both see in you. But I am also aware of the upheaval your appearance caused back then. And when Nick told me about your two weeks in South Dakota, I realized for the first time how little I still know about you." She paused again.

"I told Nick tonight that I couldn't possibly become his wife unless he learned about the fact that you and I would have started an affair three years ago if you hadn't stopped me."

Logan had started drinking again, and the bottle almost fell out of his hand. "You told him that?" He rolled his eyes and felt his shoulders slump. Resignedly, he shook his head.

"It's the truth after all," Tahnee defended herself.

Yes, it was the truth. And yet it wasn't the whole truth. Three years earlier, Nick had put his relationship with her on hold for a while. Having slept only with the woman to whom he had lost his virginity was no longer enough for him. Perhaps out of spite, Tahnee had spent that time immersed in Sydney's nightlife with her girlfriends weekend after weekend. During one of those trips to the city's hottest clubs, Logan had run into her at the ferry docks at Circular Quay and invited her out for coffee. Until early the next morning, the two had strolled through the streets and across the inner-city beaches of the Australian metropolis, confiding in each other. In retrospect, Logan had learned more about Tahnee that night and revealed more about himself than he would have liked. Respectfully but firmly, he had then disengaged from Tahnee's farewell embrace in the romantic purple hue of dawn that swept up over Port Jackson many hours later, before anything more would have happened between them.

It had been thanks to his self-control, trained from childhood, and the quiet warning voice that had risen within him to protect him from harm, that he had mustered the strength to turn away from her in time. What value would there have been in risking his friendship and attachment to his adopted brother for an affair with a woman whom he liked and appreciated, but with whom he could see no future for himself? The quiet and calm within him, which Unčí had taught him to recognize and respect and to distinguish from the louder voices and his impulsive reactions, were what had gained the upper hand that morning.

"Nick and I had a talk, Logan," Tahnee explained to him,

looking up. Then she lowered her eyes again. "He understood how much I was hurting back then. I told him what you said to me that morning when we parted, and what I've never been able to get out of my head: you said that it was more than just my hurt feelings that made me seek your closeness. That it was the historical trauma of our ancestors that we both carry within us. That it was our mutual understanding of the challenge of living a life with an indigenous heritage. Both, you had said, made it difficult for us to keep the required distance from each other that night."

Logan gave her a long look. In fact, those had essentially been his words. And they were no less true today than they had been then.

"Nick gets it," Tahnee said with a pensive smile. "He really understood. And he and I, we've been able to forgive each other for everything that's happened between us over the years."

Logan felt the tension fall away from him. "Very good. You two belong together, Tahnee. Nick needs a woman like you. Marriage will be good for both of you. I will come back to Sydney for your wedding. But my time here in Australia is up. As much as part of me regrets it, and as much as I've enjoyed the last decade on this continent, I have my old life waiting for me, as well as a new one, in South Dakota."

"There's a woman waiting for you, too, I hear. Nick told me a little about her. Tiya Redbird? He thinks she's got your head pretty turned."

"Absolutely none of his business!" Logan grinned. "But I do hope she's waiting for me, yes."

Tahnee returned his smile. "I'm really happy for you, Logan. We'll still be friends, right?"

Logan listened attentively. The uncertainty in her words surprised him. He stepped around the kitchen island and embraced Tahnee like a big brother embraces his little sister. "Of course we'll still be friends, Carly. Take good care of both of you."

Carly was the familiar form of Tahnee's middle name, Carlynda. It was also considered a boy's name of Gaelic origin and meant *little champion.* Logan knew of this meaning and had not used her old nickname without purpose. He broke away from the embrace, winked at Tahnee, and made his way over to the east wing of the mansion where both his and Nick's rooms were located.

Chapter 9

London, United Kingdom

Three quarters of a year had flown by. Summer had turned into autumn, and the winter, first wet and gray, then powdery white, had turned into a fabulous new spring. It was mid-March and, contrary to the usual chill and dampness that creeps into the bones and wears down man and beast alike at this time of year in Britain, the temperatures were unusually mild. Trees and shrubs were blossoming all over the place and the splendid shades of green that covered the land heralded an extraordinary year.

For former investment banker Marrock Lovell, the ninth of twelve training modules with Professor Kirkpatrick and Zayla was on the schedule. Father and daughter had begun their pilot project in July of last year with fifteen handpicked participants. They had now reached the final third of the year-long training with only seven participants remaining, Travis and Marrock among them.

His students had to work hard for the coveted certification as a hypnosis and regression coach by the renowned professor. He demanded a high level of commitment and perseverance. Just recruiting a sufficient number of volunteers with whom the participants had to practice and document their new knowledge had been a task that several of them had failed at the very beginning of the training.

Marrock had also had difficulty finding people willing to engage with him in the necessary exercises. To mobilize enough volunteers, he had to use a great deal of persuasion, or in some cases money as an incentive, even for the simple smoking cessation and weight loss exercise sessions in the first modules.

Things got considerably more challenging with the October module's regression exercises: These were three- to four-hour hypnosis sessions that the Kirkpatricks called *past-life regressions.* After a theoretical introductory phase, two participants were put under hypnosis by the professor in front of everyone so they could work on the topic in a practical way. Afterwards, Professor Kirkpatrick's students tested their newly acquired knowledge with their training partners. The intensity of the experience gained and the need for exchange of ideas were so great that the professor offered several video conferences at the end of the module so as not to leave his students out in the cold with their questions.

The previous challenges to earn the professor's coveted certificate were not to be underestimated. Now in March, Marrock thought of paying again to round up enough volunteers for the *guided tours of the metaphysical in-between world,* advertised by father and daughter as life changing, that were on the curriculum starting in April. They would be hypnosis sessions with a different emphasis than before. Instead of visiting multiple past lives, as in the regression sessions, they would be guided back to just one.

During a demonstration, the professor used the hypnotized participant's memories of his own death scene as a springboard to take him on a journey to a life between the present and the next. In this state of *in-between lives,* the virtual encounters with those the Kirkpatricks called *spiritual helpers* provided important clues to a person's life path and life purpose.

Marrock had tasted blood and was eager to learn more — on the one hand, to take a closer look at the healing power of this type of hypnosis, but also to illuminate its manipulation possibilities and financial strength. He had to be patient for a while, however, because first the Kirkpatricks took their training group to east London to visit a good friend of the family: Dorothea Nicols.

Dorothea was a resolute and optimistic middle-aged woman. Her flaxen hair and water-blue eyes gave her face an almost fairy-like appearance, while her pale skin spanned the well-fed form of a Rubens figure. In her words and in all her actions, Dorothea possessed a kindness and adorable whole-souled commitment that even went to the heart of Marrock.

On the edge of Epping Forest, she had set up an alternative school for children aged five to twelve in her terraced house. The small academy was located in the immediate vicinity of the Sir Alfred Hitchcock Hotel in Leytonstone, the London neighborhood where the famous filmmaker had been born. The adjacent recreational area, Hollow Pond, invited Dorothea and her schoolchildren to take long walks and, in the warmer months, enjoy idyllic rowboat rides or picnics on the lake shore.

Her *Leytonstone Academy* was Dorothea's attempt to combine her many years of professional experience in the British school system with her interest in metaphysics. It was her ambition, she explained to her guests just after inviting them in and serving them tea and pastries in the living room, to offer children something new and unique. "Something that builds their confidence and self-worth, something that expands their awareness and intuition and, incidentally, helps improve their concentration," she continued. "I am particularly passionate about helping my students develop their natural gifts to their full potential, even though there are rarely more than two dozen children enrolled with me each school year. Still, my little school remains my lifeblood. With every smile I can put on a child's face, with every door I can push open for a young person toward freedom and self-sufficiency, I feel richly rewarded."

Discontentedly, Marrock eyed Zayla's strong affection for her maternal friend. She beamed at her when she spoke, touched her on the arm when she walked by, and spoke of Dorothea's little school with a great deal of warmth and deference. Dorothea quickly became as much of a thorn in his side as Travis, whose connection to Zayla had visibly grown in depth and intensity with each seminar weekend. Treating Travis with tact and respect and exercising strict restraint toward Zayla tested the limits of his self-discipline.

He still recognized in her much of what he wanted in a woman at his side: attractiveness, intriguing abilities, and the social status of her father, the much lauded academic.

But until Zayla reached legal adulthood, he was determined to continue to refrain from any advances. In early summer, the time of the twelfth and final training module, Zayla would turn eighteen. Marrock wanted to hold out for three long months before he dared to tempt fate. He had no idea, however, of the advantageous position he would find himself in for his project on that very day.

The front doorbell rang and Dorothea introduced her guests to three of her students: Emma, age ten, James, age eight, and six-year-old Charlotte. Emma and Charlotte sat down together on Dorothea's sprawling sofa, which was covered in beige linen fabric, while James took a seat across from them on a comfortable dark red upholstered chair. All three children put on the black eye-masks Dorothea had provided.

"These are called *mindfolds*," Dorothea explained. "Their specially shaped foam pads and adjustable Velcro straps guarantee that no light whatsoever can penetrate the goggles, leaving the children's eyes surrounded by absolute darkness."

Dorothea took a stack of flashcards with different animal motifs and objects. She asked the children to identify the motifs on the cards, which she held up one by one. Although the children were wearing their eye-masks, they managed to correctly name each motif without difficulty: owl, dog, dolphin, crayon. Supermarket, book, doll, cupboard. Car, glass, cat, blackboard. The two Kirkpatricks smiled meaningfully to themselves as they observed the amazed faces of their seminar participants.

Marrock noticed that Zayla picked up a raffia basket with a puzzle and placed it on the table in front of Emma. She put two pieces together and smiled at the girl.

"Would you complete the puzzle for me?"

Emma nodded and after a short time, she had assembled the puzzle's fifty pieces.

Growing suspicious, Marrock approached the two of them and asked to be allowed to take the girl's eye-mask off. Emma complied with his request, took the mask off and handed it to him. The banker adjusted the Velcro fasteners and then put the *mindfold* on himself. It was pitch black around him. Without any doubt, these eye masks were opaque. He shook his head. "How is that possible?"

Zayla asked Marrock to pull up any children's page on his phone and present it to James to read. He did as he was told and shook his head again as the boy briskly read to him, without making any major mistakes, the article *Why Civilizations Fall*. Blindfolded.

Then Travis took the initiative. He asked Dorothea if the children would be able to copy a picture he wanted to draw.

Dorothea nodded and laughed. "I'm sure the kids will do a good job of that as well. Feel free to try, Travis."

The Australian took a drawing pad and a pencil from the table and drew the outline of a platypus. He passed the drawing pad to little Charlotte. She giggled and asked what strange animal he had sketched. At the same time, she tried to draw a second platypus on the same piece of paper as Travis's. She succeeded exceptionally well. Travis and Zayla exchanged a long look. A storm of jealousy shook Marrock.

Charlotte raised her head in interest. "You like Zayla," she blurted out.

Travis laughed and turned to her. "Yes, Charlotte," he confessed, "I actually like her a lot."

"Me too," the little girl confirmed. "She's cool."

Zayla grinned. Then her eyes met Marrock's and her smile died. If looks could kill, Travis would be lying dead on the floor. *He hated the Australian.*

"What's a platypus, Travis?" asked Charlotte.

Zayla seemed distracted for a moment by the little girl's question, but by the time she looked at Marrock again, he had regained his composure. Zayla frowned.

"A platypus?" smiled Travis. "Those are animals that exist in my home country. In Australia." He winked at the girl. "Do you know where Australia is?"

The girl shook her head.

"On the other side of the world, isn't it?" asked James.

Travis nodded. "From your point of view, yes. From England, you have to fly a whole day and night on a plane to get there. Or you can go for about thirty days on a passenger ship."

"That's a very long time," Emma said.

"Yes." James nodded.

"Tell us about the platypuses, Travis," Charlotte asked.

Travis swayed his head back and forth, thinking. "Platypuses are very, very strange animals. They're about the size of Dorothea's cat." He pointed to Tiggy, their hostess's jet-black British shorthair beauty snoozing on the back of the sofa. Only the occasional twitch of her ears revealed that the cat was paying attention to the goings-on around her. When spoken to, Tiggy blinked sleepily, eyed Travis with a long look, and then yawned heartily before closing her eyes again and slumbering on.

Travis grinned and tapped his pencil on the picture in front of him. "Platypuses are about the same size as Tiggy," he repeated. "And like Tiggy, they have short fur. However, it's waterproof, thicker, and brown, not black."

"And they have a duck's bill?" asked James, intrigued, as he looked at Travis's drawing.

Travis nodded. "These animals are like a patchwork quilt in a way. They're made up of parts that don't really belong together. They have a beak like a duck, a tail like a beaver, and feet like an otter. Although they lay eggs like reptiles, platypuses are still mammals, just like a cat or a dog."

"That means, Charlotte," Emma explained to the younger girl, pride in her voice, "if Tiggy had kittens, they would get milk from her. Mammals give milk to their babies, and the kittens would drink from Tiggy's teats."

"Yes," Travis agreed. "But platypus mothers, surprisingly, don't have teats, Emma. Yet they give milk to their babies, which is something animals that lay eggs don't normally do. Have you ever seen a hen give milk to its chicks?"

The children laughed.

"Or a mother crocodile to her baby crocodiles?"

"No," the children agreed.

"But there are no crocodiles in England," Emma explained.

Travis slapped the flat of his hand against his forehead. "No, of course there aren't. I forgot all about that. But you know crocodiles from animal shows, I suppose."

The children nodded.

"In any case," Travis continued, "platypuses are aquatic, which means they are water animals, like crocodiles. And platypus babies don't suck the milk they need from their mother's teats like other mammals, but they lick the milk from her fur."

The bystanders made sounds of astonishment.

"How interesting!" exclaimed Zayla, "Aren't platypuses poisonous, too?"

Travis blinked. "Where are you with your thoughts again today, my dear?" he teased.

Zayla blew him a kiss.

"You're right, though," he replied. "Platypuses are not harmless. To humans, their venom can be quite painful even months after an attack. However, the females are non-poisonous. Only the males have a poisonous stinger on their hind legs, presumably to send other males running when they're courting a female."

"Not to hunt?" asked James.

Travis shook his head and looked at the three kids with a grin. "No, because they simply eat the crabs, larvae, and worms they find. They don't need their poison for that. And just like you three Jedi younglings, a platypus doesn't need its eyes either."

"How cool!" exclaimed Emma, James, and Charlotte in unison.

"We see with our inner eye, which we train when we wear the *mindfolds*. How does the platypus do it?" asked Emma.

"A platypus picks up the electrical impulses emitted by its prey," Travis replied. "Its horned beak is full of sensitive electrical sensors. The energy fields it can sense with them are all it needs to successfully hunt its prey. It doesn't need eyes, ears or a nose to do that."

Zayla sat down next to Charlotte on the sofa and compared the girl's drawing to Travis's. Marrock moved to stand behind her. Of course, Charlotte's picture lacked the sophistication of a skilled adult's drawing. But considering her age and taking into account that the little girl had not only worn a *mindfold* but had also been completely unaware of what the Australian would draw for her, she had managed with amazing ease to draw an animal that was exceedingly similar to the one in Travis's picture.

"You did a really great job, Charlotte," Zayla praised, and Charlotte beamed.

The Kirkpatricks and their seminar participants spent another hour with Dorothea and the children, during which, at James's request, they also went out into the garden and played football with the children, whose eyes were still blindfolded. The *mindfolds* did not seem to have any effect on the quality of their movement performance either, and the seminar participants were once again amazed. Eventually, however, the children had had enough. They wanted to go back inside and take off their eye pads.

After a cup of tea and home-baked cookies in Dorothea's living room, Emma blurted out the idea that each of the adults present should describe themselves with three adjectives. Emma then wanted to tell them whether she would agree with the choice of adjectives or choose new ones for each of them. The adults complied with the girl's wish.

Travis started with *psychic, laid back* and *charming,* and after having the word *charming* explained to her, Emma was quite okay with that choice. Zayla followed with *magical, self-deprecating,* and *the odd one out.* Emma frowned. *The odd one out* was no adjective, she admonished. Moreover, she didn't understand the word *self-deprecating.*

"When you make fun of yourself," Zayla explained, smiling. "It's sometimes helpful if you have a lot of skills, like I do, that other people usually find strange."

Emma nodded, but had she really understood, wondered

Marrock, who had followed Zayla's self-description with interest. Zayla, however, left it at that. Apparently, she didn't like to delve deeper into the subject.

Professor Kirkpatrick took over and described himself as *intellectual, down to earth,* and *reserved.* Three more words that had to be explained to Emma and the other two children.

When Marrock's turn came, he answered on impulse, "*Dark, intelligent,* and *undesirable.*" He observed that Zayla frowned and that his words also made Emma sit up and take notice. The little girl approached him and looked him intensely in the eyes. Then she tentatively put her hand on his forearm.

"I don't agree with that at all," she said softly but clearly. "You are loveable and very nice."

Marrock felt a lump in his throat and choked back the tears. But it did not help. The water sprang into his eyes with the force of a broken dam. Emma had completely caught him off guard. In all his life, no one had ever chosen the word *loveable* for him with such sincerity. He could not stop the tears that ran down his cheeks. Full of shame, he turned away from those present and left the house at a sprint. In the garden, behind a hedge of roses, he broke out into mute weeping that agonizingly tried to make itself heard from the deepest darkness of his soul. It was fed by the festering wounds of a torn child's heart. Under the force of the inconsolability that overcame him, he doubled over with nothing to resist the sobs that seized him.

Again, the silent scream sounded, the soundless roaring from the jaws of his black soul. Then he felt someone gently put both hands on his shoulders. He absorbed this small but intense gesture of attention, of compassion, of care like a parched plant absorbs rainwater.

Zayla's touches made each of his cells sing and silenced the cries of terror from his tortured child soul. The closeness of this deeply feeling girl made the darkness within him seem more bearable. The waves of her compassion, which washed over him incessantly like a gentle summer surf, possessed the power to soothe his open wounds. For a few moments, the feeling of being enough spread through him. To be able to breathe deeply. To have arrived.

Zayla. He breathed the name of the girl, both a delusion and a revelation to him, into the warm damp ground beneath him. *Psyche,* he fantasized. Breath of Life and Soul Bird. The king's daughter whose beauty eclipsed even that of Aphrodite. *Persephone,* daughter of Zeus, whom Hades, god of the underworld, had stolen and made queen of the dead. *Mary Magdalene,* companion of Jesus and witness of his resurrection.

Just as quickly as it had fallen upon him, the clouding of consciousness cleared again. The wafting veils of fog in his head receded. With clear eyes and a keen mind, Marrock grasped the full implications of what had just happened: for the first time in nine months, he possessed the unqualified attention and complete acceptance of Kirkpatrick's daughter. He might have rejoiced. During the long three-quarters of a year that lay behind him, he had only succeeded in winning over the professor, not Zayla. He had skilfully managed to convince Matthew Kirkpatrick and the seminar participants of himself and his qualities. His talent for morphing into the exact roles that resonated with the people he hoped would be advantageous for him had won him respect and acceptance within the group. So far, he had only been unable to pull the wool over the eyes of Travis and Zayla. How much the damned Australian would rage when he realized that he had lost his special friend to Marrock on this day!

The banker understood that, of all things, it had been the

moment of his greatest shame that had finally given him access to Kirkpatrick's daughter. She, despite all her previous difficulties in reading him, must have felt his inner turmoil with such force that she could no longer help herself but comfort him in his suffering. Marrock smiled darkly. *This* was the predicament of a highly evolved empath. That Zayla's hands on his body had silenced the cries that raged within him, he regarded as a gift as priceless as it was unexpected.

"Will you take a walk with me?" he asked, wiping the remnants of tears from his eyes with the back of his hand.

Zayla nodded. "I'll just quickly let my father know."

A brief time later, they left Dorothea's house. They crossed the main road and walked along a pathway to Hollow Pond.

"What was wrong?" asked Zayla after a while. "That was an intense reaction to Emma's words. I could feel indescribable turmoil inside you."

She had spoken softly and kept her gaze lowered to the path. Excitement flooded through Marrock. He had been right. She had actually been able to *feel* him. At long last he saw his chance had come to bind Zayla to him and get from her what he needed more and more urgently. But he reminded himself to be careful because he had to advance his plan with cunning and skill.

"Emma reminded me of my two daughters," he replied, "when they were younger."

"How old are they now?" asked Zayla.

"11 and 16 years."

"Do you have pictures of them?"

Marrock pulled his cell phone out of his back pocket. "This is Lydia. She's the younger one, my little sunshine. And this picture-perfect creature here is Melissa."

"They are both incredibly cute," Zayla smiled. "Lydia reminds me a little of Nell, my little friend who was murdered. Your wife has sole custody?"

Marrock nodded. "She did a great job of manipulating the judge and playing my daughters against me. I miss them both dearly. I feel like a failure because I couldn't be more than a paying father to my kids."

"Is that why you said *dark* and *undesirable* when you were supposed to be describing yourself?"

"That may be one reason," Marrock admitted, speculating on her sympathy. "It's not easy for me to barely play a role in my daughters' lives anymore. The few visiting days I have, my ex-wife tries to manipulate. Then the girls are promised new clothes or a new phone if they don't want to see me or don't want to see me for as long as we agreed."

"This is terrible, Marrock. Why is your wife doing this to you? They're your children, too."

He shrugged. "During our divorce, she told me that she wouldn't rest until she squeezed every last penny out of me. My money should put her in a position to never have to go back to work."

"Why didn't you insist on joint custody? You would have been entitled to that."

"We would both have had to live in Brighton to be able to make it work out. I worked for various investment banks in the City of London and Canary Wharf, where I have an apartment. But I only stayed there to sleep. 90-hour weeks are the norm in this job — sometimes even more. It was backbreaking work, but it paid excellent money. My wife didn't want to live in London, so we bought a house in Brighton. My daughters still go to school there. Their friends are in Brighton, their sports clubs ..."

"I hope your wife's house is far enough from my father's," Zayla replied, "because it will remain the site for your training until the summer."

Marrock preferred not to respond to this remark. Zayla silently followed him as he made his way around the lake.

"I would like to see my children more often," he began again after a while.

"It's cruel how your wife uses your daughters to get back at you."

"She was after my money first and foremost, Zayla. Something I realized far too late. Whatever I did about her would only make the situation worse for me and my children."

As the Hollow Pond boathouse came into view, Marrock stopped and cast a longing glance at the scenery. "I've been here a few times with my daughters when they were younger. Too bad the boat rental place hasn't reopened yet."

Zayla looked at him mockingly. "Why? Did you want to go on a rowing trip with me?"

He smiled to himself. Oh, if only she knew!

"Are we going to walk around the lake a little more?" he asked.

Zayla agreed, and Marrock steered the conversation to the day's events, which had impressed him. "How is it that Emma, James, and Charlotte can see despite those dark glasses? I thought at first that they might be cheating and that they could see far more through the *mindfolds* than they would have us believe — until I put them on myself. They can't see a thing."

A smile settled on Zayla's face. "I think Travis summed it up pretty well with the platypus. It's not one hundred percent comparable, but if a platypus can see without its eyes, why shouldn't another creature be able to as well? It only *seems* impossible to us because it does not fit into our world view. Many people consider the illusion that seeing can only work with physical eyes to be the truth. But the children train what is called the *third eye* in Hinduism.

"Of course, critics resist this idea, claiming that the concept of being able to see beyond our 'normal' purely physical vision with the Third Eye is a mystical construct. But just because science lags in explaining so many phenomena does not mean there are no processes outside its paradigms. Dorothea's students are a fine example of how limited the realities are that we accept without question."

"Your father had given us this example of a Hungarian-German in the second module, in which you were not present for one day ..."

"You mean Ignaz Semmelweis? What else did my father tell you?"

Marrock thought. "That he was a doctor in a Viennese hospital in the middle of the 19th century. There were two maternity wards. One was run by doctors and the other by midwives. The death rate of women in childbirth was much higher in the maternity ward run by doctors than in the ward run by midwives. Semmelweis blamed this on hygiene conditions. In particular, the fact that medical students in the doctors' ward also had to learn to open corpses during their training, and with the same bare hands, to which tiny cadaver parts still stuck after the dissection of the dead, they examined the women following delivery and thus infected them."

Zayla rolled her eyes. "Yes. The training of medical students was the only relevant difference between the two wards, which were otherwise run in the same way. I'm sure my father will have told you that there were very few doctors at the time who supported Semmelweis with his theory."

"Indeed. Your father told us that Semmelweis was ridiculed and his findings dismissed as nonsense. Hand hygiene was considered a waste of time."

"Beyond that, however, it was Semmelweis's accusation that

the doctors of all people, the demigods in white, should be responsible for the deaths of women in childbirth. That made them spew poison and bile."

Marrock grinned. He was beginning to enjoy the verbal ping-pong game with Zayla. "Wasn't it also true that Semmelweis's ideas were incompatible with the ideas of the time about how popular diseases and epidemics would arise? Your father told us they were entrenched assumptions that people didn't want to shake at any cost."

"Exactly. And so the term *Semmelweis reflex* is used to describe the automatic rejection of a new piece of information or discovery that contradicts current scientific beliefs."

"The facts are not even examined, and those who adhere to the scientifically unexplainable are opposed."

"Like Ignaz Semmelweis, who was hailed a *savior of mothers* after his death, but who was considered too disruptive during his lifetime."

"Against his will, he was committed to a psychiatric hospital, where he died shortly thereafter."

"It is rumored that they wanted to have him eliminated there," Zayla concluded. After a pause, she continued resignedly, "Unfortunately, not much has changed. Still, people who move outside the accepted scientific knowledge are ridiculed, marginalized, or no longer get teaching positions. Even my father and Dorothea are not always taken seriously or are willfully misunderstood by many people."

She stopped abruptly and turned to the banker. "Dorothea not only teaches children to see without their physical eyes, Marrock, but she teaches them so much more. Through Dorothea, these children develop self-confidence and are open to experiencing the seemingly impossible. They understand who they really are: spiritual beings having a human experience. The younger Dorothea's students are and the less they have already been exposed to ideas that certain things are supposedly impossible, the easier it is for them to fully realize their abilities. For older children and adults, it becomes much more difficult right away.

"My father once had a client who was blind from birth. Under hypnosis, he was still able to see and describe in colorful detail the images that came to mind. The same thing happens when blind people have a near-death experience. When we dream, it is also possible for all of us to see with our eyes closed.

"Even relatives and friends of the families of Emma, James, and Charlotte have difficulty accepting that the children can do something that seems impossible to them. When Emma was younger, an uncle of hers wanted nothing to do with the family because she read to him blindfolded from a children's book. His behavior makes it abundantly clear why so many people have fallen victim to the Inquisition and witch hunts. Fear is, next to love, the strongest force on this planet. What people do not understand, they not only simply reject, but they are also scared of it. And everything they are afraid of, they destroy."

"And what about you?" asked Marrock, looking thoughtfully at Zayla.

She frowned. "What do you mean?"

"How do you deal with all the people who reject you because of the skills you possess?"

Zayla remained silent.

"Who takes care of you except your father?" he added.

"Not that it's any of your business, Marrock, but I absolutely don't need anyone to take care of me. I'm doing just fine on my own."

Marrock realized he had gone a step too far and pulled back. "I have to apologize. I didn't mean it that way. I just remember you telling us all about the hostility you had to endure in school. My understanding at the time was that your school days must have been a lonely time for you. You had mentioned that both boys and girls had rejected and bullied you."

Zayla turned away from him.

"A huge loss for the men in this world if you ask me," he added, waiting tensely to see how she would take this compliment.

With a jerk, she turned back around and stared him belligerently in the face. "You're not the first and you won't be the last man this earthly vessel here will excite." She pointed to herself and dug her index finger into her breastbone. "I am so tired of being perceived for only one of two things: my body or my abilities. I'm made up of more than just my talents, which make me wonder what to do with them every day anyway."

Marrock saw the fire burning in her eyes as she let her resentment run its course. He knew from her stories that she had also been denied the dating experiences of her peers. As soon as she openly showed who she was, every suitor lost interest. Loneliness and isolation, even from her own sex, had remained the price of her otherness.

Marrock looked at her closely. Zayla's eyes were like a deep, dark forest lake on which the raised storm whipped furious waves and let the water slosh over the banks.

"I can contact the souls of deceased people." Zayla suddenly laughed. "Can you imagine the reactions that would cause in other people? I have access to worlds that are beyond our 3-D reality and hidden from most people. I can read people I meet and sense their feelings, provided I engage with them. You are one of the very few exceptions so far. I can hardly read you, and I don't know why that is. I have powers in me that were attributed to witches and sorceresses in the old days. I am capable of remote viewing. I can perceive objects and processes that are beyond what we can grasp with our five senses. Within me are those ancient powers that many women remember when they close their eyes and dare to fully step back into their own power. I am the form and the formless. In me, magic, power, and vulnerability, movement, divinity, and chaos combine to form a whole. I am the non-linear. I am Creatrix and healer. I am a great-granddaughter of Persian magi and a descendant of Celtic high priestesses. I consist of contradictions with a thousand corners and edges. I am the *storm*, Marrock. My father doesn't call me a paranormal powerhouse just for fun. Besides him and Travis, I don't know a third man who isn't afraid, in one way or another, of what is evolving inside me with each new year of life." Every cell in Zayla's body seemed to sparkle and flash. Her pupils had dilated and her gaze danced challengingly toward Marrock's face.

"I'm not afraid of you," he murmured. Dark desire overwhelming him. "When you come of age, Zayla, I will court you. I will be the black knight who slays the dragon to win the love of his Queen of Hearts."

Zayla moved a step further away from him. Marrock remained unperturbed. He cocked his head to the side and regarded the girl like an exotic bird. His eyes tried to feel the depths of her soul, and he triumphed when for a moment he seemed to succeed.

"The affection of a man who wants to carry you to the end of the earth must be something you seek, too," he said, without taking his eyes off her. "Your experiences can't have been so one-sided that, as young and beautiful as you are, you've already given up on love."

Zayla took another step back from him and made a sharp clicking sound with her tongue. "Not love per se, but the thought that ..."

"...that a man might accept you as you are?" completed Marrock out of the blue, and might have patted himself on the back when he realized he had struck a chord. Deftly, he smeared more of the honeyed words that were balm to the wounds of a wounded girl's heart. "That a man can not only desire you, but honor you in every way? That a man can appreciate and respect all that is inside of you? That he can make you grow instead of making you smaller? That he supports you instead of manipulating you and your powers? That he can lay his own powers and abilities at your feet instead of demonizing you for yours?"

Carried away by the dark magic that lay on the small scene, Marrock stepped close to Zayla so she felt his warm breath on her face. He was within reach of the goal of his dreams.

Zayla's cheeks turned red, her lips opened. His fingertips slid over the back of her hand and fluttered up the sides of her body. With his eyes, he forced her to withstand his desire. The passion that gripped him found tinder in the surging heat of her body. She opened to his radiance like a plant to light. Like a lotus blossom, it flashed through his mind, its cellular myriads, stretched by the water and strained to their limits, leaving the blossom no choice but to open and reveal all its splendor. But then Zayla's face contorted and Marrock heard a gurgling scream, as if her guts were being burned out of her. She staggered back and Marrock grabbed her to keep her on her feet.

"A bayonet! It's tearing this man apart!" she screamed.

"What man?" Marrock looked around in confusion.

"A warrior! A man with brown skin and black hair," she moaned. "The soldier's weapon tears ... his organs. He falls into the snow! There's blood everywhere!" Zayla went to her knees under the force of her visions. Marrock caught her by the elbow and supported her.

"What's wrong with you?" For a moment he was honestly concerned.

Zayla fell on all fours and vomited with a violence that brought tears to her eyes. Hesitantly and with a touch of disgust, Marrock stepped behind her and held her dark, waist-length hair out of her face. Reassuringly, he talked to her. When Zayla's wretching produced no more food mush, no more liquid, she moved away from the puddle of vomit and wiped her mouth with the back of her hand. Uncontrollably, she began to sob. Her breathing was frantic and fluttery, and the banker understood that she was in shock. Detaching himself from the theatrics of the scene before him, he looked dispassionately down at the girl. She raised her head and let out another shriek.

"Traitor! Murderer!"

Quick as a flash, Marrock shot forward and closed her mouth with his hand.

Chapter 10

The Lucid Dream II: The Black Hills, South Dakota, USA

*T*wenty-four wolves. A wind-quick and silent hunting pack that has not lost its vigor in the hours-long pursuit of its prey. It is a pack without females. The giant males emerge from the shelter of the trees, one by one, inaudible like ghosts. The gray-yellow eyes of their leader flash as he recognizes the group of men in the valley ahead of them. A low rumble and his hunters fan out to his left and right. Twenty-three massive gray wolves stand side by side in a long line, waiting for their leader's signal to attack.

The alpha, the only animal with jet black fur, is unified with his hunters in mind and heart. The telepathic link to his pack is wide open and his every command sits immediately in their minds. If the leader harbors uncertainty or fear, his hunters are flooded with these feelings as well, risking the pack's downfall. Only a supremely combat- and hunting-experienced alpha with absolute control over himself may dare to use this special bond of the pack.

At a growl from the leader, the line begins to move. The wolves trot down the hillsides, gaining speed. The alpha dashes ahead of them. At a breakneck pace, the pack chases across the grassy ground, taking out the guards in quick succession. Then the wolves pounce on the rest of the sleep-deprived men in camp. Several shots crack. One of the animals rolls over, crashing to the ground. The leader immediately channels the grief from his loss into rage, which he passes on to his hunters through the heart connection. Grief paralyzes their fighting spirit, but anger gives them strength for battle.

After a short time, the hunting is over. Logan wipes the blood from his face and breathes heavily. The sight of the dead fills him with bitter satisfaction. At a sound, he turns his head and his gaze falls on a clearing lit by a small campfire.

Suddenly he sits opposite a man dressed in the leather gaiters of his ancestors. The scars of Wiwáŋyaŋg Wačhípi, the sundance, in which the warrior sacrificed himself, adorn his unclothed torso. He wears his hair in two long, black braids that fall over his shoulders. From his dark eyes, capable of baring a man's soul, he looks thoughtfully at Logan. Is that what you're after, Brother? he asks.

His lips do not move, and yet Logan captures his thoughts. The feeling of an ancient bond overcomes him. Šuŋmánitu Tȟáŋka Sápe, the Black Wolf Chief, runs through his mind.

His counterpart smiles. Ah, you remember. Do you also remember your own name?

The image of a standing elk appears before Logan's eyes.

The Black Wolf Chief nods. Heȟáka Nážiŋ, Standing Elk, you and I were closer than brothers. Each of us would have gone to our death for the other. The Whites murdered you long before they, along with the traitors from our ranks, killed me.

Through the eyes of the Standing Elk, Logan witnesses his young daughter, and with her their entire village, being slaughtered. Then he gets a bullet in the head. Sweat breaks out all over his body.

You had no chance to save your family and our tribe, the Black Wolf Chief murmurs sympathetically. The death of your sister's rapists — is that what you want? he asks again after a pause.

Still Logan does not know how to answer. They are all dead?

You would have your revenge, the Black Wolf Chief evades. But in the world you live in now, revenge would not go unpunished. Once you're caught, you'll never leave a maximum security prison. You will be charged with vigilante justice, and they will condemn you because your skin is brown, not white, and because they are afraid of you. Our people would have lost an important man. But you and I had set for ourselves the goal of rewriting world history. Do you remember?

Logan feels a lump in his throat. What do you suggest?

There are other ways to get even with these pigs, the Black Wolf

Chief echoed the sentiment that Nick had already expressed to Logan as well. Nick! At that moment, the suspicion arises in Logan that he is in his own dream.

Not to mention, the Black Wolf Chief tells him, my hunters only destroyed the bodies of these men — nothing can erase a soul. He points with his head to something behind Logan's back. Logan turns around and the chief is suddenly sitting there on a tree stump. He is now dressed in faded blue jeans, t-shirt, biker boots, and a black leather jacket. A pirate headscarf keeps his waist-length hair out of his face. On his nose he wears sunglasses with lenses so dark that Logan can see himself reflected in them but can no longer make out the expression in his counterpart's eyes.

Why don't you ask your sister yourself what she needs from you? asks the Black Wolf Chief. I don't think it's revenge. Justice, perhaps.

Where is Phoebe? Logan wonders.

A smile plays around the corners of his old friend's mouth. At Mount Rushmore. Call her and she will come to us.

Logan frowns. Then he opens his mouth. Phoebe! he calls softly. Phoebe?

And indeed: she stands in front of the two men and the leader greets her with a warm embrace.

You know each other?

The Black Wolf Chief chuckles. Don't you know who she is?

My sister, Logan mumbles, immediately realizing how simple-minded his answer is.

Phoebe, however, nods. I was also the sister of the Standing Elk. Haven't you ever wondered, brother, why we still have such a close relationship today, even though you left the reservation when I was still a little child?

No, Logan has not thought about this until now. He has registered the close relationship with Phoebe, but never questioned it. Then another connection becomes clear to him. Who is the sandy-haired woman? he asks his sister the same question he already confronted

Uŋčí with.

He hears the Black Wolf Chief make a mocking sound. You and I, Brother, were foolish enough to love this woman who brought death to our people.

That's harsh, Phoebe remarks. It was not her fault!

A matter of perspective, perhaps, the Black Wolf Chief admits.

I met her at Mount Rushmore, Phoebe tells them. The non-material, spiritual force in her is even more pronounced now than it was then. Uŋčí says that her younger daughter must find her way back to this land.

Logan holds his sister's gaze, but he doesn't understand the meaning of her words. Turning to the Black Wolf Chief, he asks: Will you return to us?

A smirk flits across the face of the man who was once closer to him than any other person. The day will come, Brother, the Black Wolf Chief says, when we will meet again.

A gunshot crackles. Logan wheels around. He stands in front of a cave in the middle of deep black mountains and rushes into it. In front of him, on the rocky floor, lies a dead man. Blood oozes from his forehead, runs down his face and collects in a pool above his collarbone. Logan sees Nick aiming for another man's head, but Hunter Garza, their father's right-hand man, beats him to it. A second shot cracks.

Logan woke from his sleep.

Chapter 11

London, United Kingdom

Dressed only in tennis shorts and a spaghetti strap top, Zayla sat on the récamiere in her father's living room in London's South Kensington neighborhood with a mug of Darjeeling tea in her hand. The windows on both floors were wide open, but not a breeze moved. Sweat beaded down Zayla's neck and back, soaking the cushion she leaned against. She rose and fetched a linen sheet from the bedroom, which she laid across the récamiere. Her path led her past the small roof terrace on which the sun blazed down mercilessly. The thermometer on the door read 39 degrees Celsius. It had been a good ten degrees lower in the shade that morning, and Zayla hated the unusually high temperature for Britain.

Back in the living room, she turned on the ceiling fan and breathed a sigh of relief when she felt a slight rush of air. She looked out the window and fixed her gaze upon the shimmering asphalt below her. A few blocks away, her favorite fish-and-chips shop had unceremoniously posted a sign in the door yesterday, *"So sorry. We're closed today. It's simply too hot to work."*

Weather experts predicted that the extreme temperatures of the current heat wave would soon replace the conventional summer temperatures, that the hot spells would be longer and more intense, and that it would become hotter and hotter in cities like London. Zayla wanted to ask her father to leave the metropolis for the summer and return to Brighton. The house that belonged to her late grandparents was there. It was more spacious and more comfortable, and close to the sea, away from the urban heat. The air was cleaner, breathing was easier, and

Zayla could avoid the crowds more easily. If it had been up to her alone, she and her father would have left the hustle and bustle of London long ago and just lived in Brighton, surrounded by the many happy memories at her grandparents' home.

She sat back on the récamiere and thought about her father's seminar modules on hypnosis and regression coaching, which she held with him in Brighton. Besides Travis and Marrock, the only other members of the training group were Sandra, an Austrian alternative practitioner, two psychologists with their own practices in Scotland and the United States, and a lively teacher from Ireland. In two weeks, at the end of June and one day before Zayla's eighteenth birthday, the final exams were due.

As recently as March, in Dorothea Nicols's living room in Leytonstone, London, little Emma had laid her hand on Marrock's arm and spoken with fervent conviction that she thought he was *lovable and very kind*. Just what had the little girl seen in this man that still remained hidden from Zayla and Travis? The two friends still could not read him comprehensively. But in Dorothea's garden, the thunderous waves of pain from his tortured child soul had broken through the protective shield around him and swept over Zayla like a tsunami. She thought of her subsequent walk with the banker around Hollow Pond. He had shown her nothing but courtesy and respect since then, despite the hysterical scene she had made in front of him when the images of the murder of the man with brown skin and long black hair had come crashing down on her. With stoic composure, he had accepted her outburst. The scenes of that memorable day now seemed almost surreal to Zayla, as if her nerves and overactive imagination had played tricks on her. Full of doubts about herself and her abilities, Zayla decided to confide in her father about the events at Hollow Pond after all. At dinner, Professor Kirkpatrick listened intently to his daughter.

"Is it possible, child," he inquired cautiously, "that the images of this murder arose from a combination of deep-seated fears and your special abilities?"

Zayla was silent for a long time in response to this question, which had struck her to the core. Then she asked in a brittle voice, "Are you saying, Papa, that even you no longer trust the things I can perceive?"

The professor took her in his arms and hugged her tightly. "Of course not! But you possess a badly wounded heart." He stroked her head. "I love you very much, Zayla, and I wish I could have kept away from you all the torment you have already experienced in your young life. Don't you feel that the part of you that wants to protect you from new pain might, for better or worse, have played a trick on you at Hollow Pond?"

Zayla didn't know the answer to that. "Where do you get this assurance, Papa, that Marrock is a good person?"

"He gives me no reason to doubt him at all." Her father stroked her cheek. "He has behaved impeccably toward all of us, including you, from the beginning. He is approachable, reliable, and has a sharp mind. He is excellent with other people and is a natural in the discipline of hypnotherapy. I don't understand where your distrust comes from. Is it Travis who put that idea into your head?"

"He has nothing to do with this!" boomed Zayla. "Travis is the only friend I have, Papa. Don't talk down to me about him, please!"

"That is not my intention at all, dear. I have the highest regard for Travis. But I don't understand why the two of you are so adamant about refusing to give Marrock a fair chance. If I didn't know any better, I might fall prey to the idea that Travis is jealous of him." The professor gave her a kiss on the forehead. "Marrock is one of the few people who can accept you in your charming uniqueness, Zayla, remember that. He has great respect for you. Nothing would make me happier than to know you are in good hands someday."

It was not the first time her father had made such a wish. Zayla bit her lip and fought back the tears.

Two weeks later, during the final exams of the twelfth seminar weekend in Brighton, Sandra, the alternative practitioner, led one of the professor's doctoral students, who had volunteered to be a test subject, on a peaceful relaxation journey. Mark was lying on the couch at Zayla's grandparents' house in Brighton wrapped in a thin wool blanket, as the heat wave that had swept the United Kingdom had already subsided. The seminar participants sat in a semicircle around the two of them.

Sandra filled the first half hour of the regression with the relaxation suggestions that had become second nature to them all. She instructed Mark to sink deeper and deeper into his imaginary worlds, to relax his body and mind, and made sure that his breathing rhythm became increasingly steady and calm. Within a short time, Mark was sitting in his protective shield of self-chosen blue light and mentally anchored to a safe place to which he could return at any time if an event under hypnosis made him uncomfortable or frightened.

At his first stop, Sandra took him back to a pleasant childhood memory, and then asked him to absorb the positive energies from that scene and take them with him on his journey through time. At his second stop, she took him back to the months he had lived in his mother's body. It was at this point that the first difficulties arose. Mark was unable to perceive how his mother had felt about her pregnancy with him. Zayla sensed Sandra's uncertainty. Nervously, the alternative practitioner tried to skip the last step and lead the doctoral student further back into a past life.

"Go to a life that is of special significance to your present one." She snapped her fingers once. "You find yourself there *now*. When you look down at yourself, can you see what you are wearing on your feet or how you are dressed?"

Silence.

"When you look around, are you able to see anything?"

"A town ..."

"Is it a big town?"

Silence.

"Do you know what this town is called?"

"Brighton."

Sandra looked up. She seemed to realize that something was wrong here. Professor Kirkpatrick gave the signal to take him deeper. She nodded. Then she tried to put the doctoral student into an even deeper state of relaxation with further suggestions and made a second attempt.

"What can you see?"

"A light ... it comes from above ... like a funnel that spreads downward."

Sandra threw her arms up in the air. This was not an answer that fit a past life regression. The session was not going according to script. She gave the signal for help, and without hesitation, Marrock jumped to her side.

"What color is this light?" he asked Mark, sitting down next to her.

"White ... It's golden at the edges."

"What else can you perceive?"

"Clouds ... white clouds."

"What do these clouds mean to you?"

Silence.

"How do you feel about them?"

"They have a calming effect on me."

"Why?"

"There is a light ..."

"Is there a message that the light would like to share with you?"

"I'm supposed to trust."

"Who?"

"Me." Mark swallowed, and then he began to cry unrestrainedly.

"What exactly is the light trying to tell you?" asked Marrock, pressing a handkerchief into his hand.

"I'm not supposed to look at my past, it doesn't benefit me." Mark blew his nose.

"What are you supposed to do instead?"

"Be aware of my power."

"Does it suggest a way for you to do that?"

"I will find the answers. It won't be long now."

"What does that mean?"

"I don't need to know that yet."

"How do you feel when you hear an answer such as this?"

"Quite satisfied."

"Where is the light now?"

"It's evenly distributed around me."

"Can you contact the light?"

Mark sobbed. His body shook uncontrollably. "I can touch it!" he pressed out softly.

"What happens to you when you touch the light?"

"It flickers."

"What does it mean to you that it flickers?"

"It wants to help me."

"Do you recognize the light?"

"It reminds me of something very ... old ..."

Mark's voice broke and tears streamed down his face.

Marrock held his hand for a moment, and when the tremor in Mark's body had subsided, he asked, "What does 'something very old' mean? Can you describe it in more detail?"

"A very deep wisdom that has been there before."

"Does it have a name?"

"No."

"When you look in a mirror, can you perceive yourself? What color are you?"

"Blue. A deep, dark blue." Mark swallowed again.

"What's happening right now?"

"The light contracts, and then it becomes big again. It's in flux, in motion."

"Do you want to come back, or would you rather interact with the light a little more?"

"Well, I am curious to find out what it wants ..."

"Then ask the light to make itself known to you."

"It's not time yet, though ..."

"Do you understand what it means by that?"

"No."

"Ask for an explanation."

"It only shows itself to me when it's time."

"Is it still the right time to get your questions out now?"

"Yes."

"Then ask this light all the questions that move you and give yourself all the time in the world to do so."

Zayla felt the deep peace of the two men during the next few minutes. Tears rolled steadily down not only Mark's cheeks, but Marrock's as well. After a while Mark signaled that he had asked his questions and that he was ready to continue.

"Now ask the light to give you back the feeling of this incredible love," Marrock said, "so that you will have enough strength until the existence of the light is explained to you."

Slowly the banker led the young man out of hypnosis. Mark opened his eyes and Marrock, full of euphoria, asked, "Did you feel this extraordinary power that was here in the room?"

Even Zayla's eyes were watering, so overwhelmed was she by the energy that had flooded the room.

"It was so strong! Awesome!" exclaimed Mark. "I was shocked at first at how the mind is constantly there and watches from afar. When I reported on the town, I thought, what are you talking about here?" He laughed. "It all went so incredibly deep!"

"What else did you feel in the presence of the light?" asked Zayla's father.

"As if I were the light itself, but from within. It really shook me. It was incredibly intense."

"Yes," mused the professor. "I know this energy. It is a form of love that is unknown to us on the human level. It is impossible to put it into words."

"I had no choice but to cry along, either." Marrock shook his head. "It was indescribable. I'd say there's no need to do any past-life regressions with Mark, would you, Matthew? After all, he took off into the in-between life right away."

Professor Kirkpatrick nodded. Zayla didn't quite concur with this analysis and was surprised that her father didn't disagree. But she said nothing. She was too impressed by the way Marrock had conducted the session and by how much he had been taken by the feeling of unconditional love.

The next day, the small group celebrated the passing of the six remaining participants' training as hypnosis and regression coaches and Zayla's eighteenth birthday. Then, with heartfelt warmth, Travis and the others said goodbye to her and her father and returned to their respective homes.

Although Zayla kept video chatting with Travis, her feeling of loneliness grew immeasurably from that day on. The longing for the closeness of a person with whom she could exchange ideas, on whom she could lean and to whom she could show and expose herself in all her differences, increasingly took hold of her. The more she gave herself over to the melancholy and her dull longing, the more her abilities seemed to fall asleep. Zayla welcomed this uncommon numb state.

Marrock, who was the only one living in London like the Kirkpatricks themselves, saw that this was his time. Just as he had told Zayla he would, he slipped into the role of knight and dragon slayer for his dark queen and began to court her openly. Countless times over the next few weeks, he invited her to dinner, to the movies, to museums, or to theater performances. One evening, he took her to his favorite Chinese restaurant on a boat in Millwall Inner Dock, and then took her for a stroll through futuristic Canary Wharf. Marrock's upscale and stylish apartment, which the former investment banker had rented near his old workplace, was also located here.

The surrounding Docklands had once belonged to the Port of London and had been the hub of world maritime trade for centuries. Canary Wharf was built on the site of the West India Docks and owed its name to trade with the Canary Islands. The now ultra-modern district was considered one of the world's most important financial centers and rivaled the City of London.

"A merciless battleground," mused Marrock, pointing to the skyscrapers of Canary Wharf that towered like titans above the old waterfront's scenery, which was as wistful as it was trendsetting. "Here, the game is played for high stakes and at a breakneck pace. For the most successful players, the scent of blood is like an aphrodisiac."

Zayla stopped short at Marrock's bluntness and the darkness behind his words.

As they crossed the bridge from centrally located Cabot Square to the old West India Quay, he pointed to one boat that was a hotel, and then to a second that was used as a wellness center and party venue. Next to it was a third boat that served as a church.

"As a church?" marveled Zayla.

Marrock chuckled. "In the bars across the street, my dear, you could commit every sin under the sun and then cross the street here and find forgiveness on this boat."

With an approving glance at the high stilettos into which Zayla had squeezed her feet, he held the door open to a cab and took her to St. Katharine Docks, four kilometers away, the first mooring for private boats outside the highly secured Canary Wharf. He told Zayla he was co-owner of a small yacht that had docked here, so he was able to spend the evening on deck with her.

When she shivered despite the balmy summer air, he wrapped her in a wool blanket and made her hot chocolate in the galley. He served her the drink with such a heart-warming smile that a pulling pain in her loins, along with the heat that followed, replaced the chill that had gone to her bones. She noticed Marrock's eyes following her fingers as they stroked the ceramic rim of the mug she held in both hands. The banker was glued to her lips as she sipped the fluffy milk froth. She felt a blush settling on her face, but she held his gaze.

"Pain we feel completely," he said, "is dissolved."

Zayla looked at him questioningly.

"Pain that is not fully felt lives on in the body. Did you know that?"

Zayla nodded. "Yes. It can manifest anywhere. That's also why the intelligent body system my father is developing to communicate under hypnosis with all the parts of our body that are bothering us is so incredibly helpful."

"Once we feel the pain fully and move it through the body, you have access to an ally, or so they say." Marrock looked at her for a long moment. "But what if it's been driven out of men to feel? What if aggression is not allowed? Anger? Despair? Grief?"

"My father says that anger is the bodyguard of sadness, and that anger and aggression are a man's ways of acting out grief and sorrow."

"There is no room in this world for a man's grief," Marrock said, lowering his eyes. "And certainly not for a white man's grief."

Zayla was hit with the complexities of this charge like a thunderbolt.

"Nothing a man does is ever enough," he sneered. Zayla heard a pain in those words that she couldn't define.

"Providers and protectors have become less important today," she murmured, faltering.

He nodded. "The rise of women leaves men in a world of uncertainty."

He stroked her face with his index and middle fingers and Zayla quivered.

"Don't get me wrong — patriarchy, its ownership, property rights over women, vilification and abuse are not achievements I would want to celebrate. But men are more than the aggressors and rapists that women's movements make them out to be."

"No woman would claim *every* man to be a rapist," she whispered, closing her eyes for a moment.

"You call us to find a new form of intimacy with you," he continued, ignoring her interjection. "But if I gave you a choice between another white water like yourself and a rock that holds and guides the water, which would you choose?"

Zayla shook her head. "We call on men to be mindful of women and to see us, *not* to become like women."

"Which would you choose?" repeated Marrock.

"The rock," Zayla replied.

"Why?"

"Because the opposing forces complement each other and offer perfection. The yin and the yang. The light and the dark. The air and the earth. The white water and the rock."

His eyes burned into hers. He stroked her cheek again. "That's right."

Zayla's pulse was pounding. In Marrock's words was the promise of being the yang that completed the yin. From his gaze sparkled the self-assurance of a seasoned lover, the confidence of a man for whom it was easy to realize the girlish dreams of an eighteen-year-old.

He can see into my soul, Zayla sighed inwardly, ignoring the soft voice that warned her of the next step. For the first time in her life, she experienced how it felt to be admired and embraced by a man, and she gave herself to this long-awaited feeling body and soul. It was a moment when everything else lost meaning. Zayla bathed in what she thought was bliss, and the thin, small warning voice inside her head didn't stand a chance. She jumped into the depths hoping to be held afloat, but instead sank to the stony bottom.

Nearly six months after that magical evening on his yacht, Marrock leaned over Zayla in the bedroom of his Canary Wharf apartment and smiled somberly. He looked down at her and tapped his index and middle fingers against her lips. "Shhhh. Don't cry again, little one."

His words were as cold as the ice halls of the heartless Snow

Queen from Hans Christian Andersen's winter's tale. He positioned Zayla's body so that he could have unhindered access to her one more time. "Why do you put on such a show, my love?" he whispered in her ear as tears ran down her cheeks. His fingers slid over her bare skin. "Have I made love to you even once in five months without your body being ready for me?"

He clicked his tongue and let out a disbelieving snort. As if seeking confirmation of the smugness that dripped from those words, he slid the fingertips of one hand between her legs. He found the moisture there, which seemed to him proof enough, and nibbled at her neck. His fingers trailed up her body and ran over Zayla's mouth, where he clung like a honeypot. He pressed a thumb between her palate and tongue, smearing the blood-red lipstick he'd bought her. With his middle and index fingers, he rubbed the tears out of her eyes.

"Don't cry, little one," he repeated. He pulled out his thumb and kissed her. "Have you ever felt pain?" He tongued her lips. "Have you ever once been uncomfortable with when and how I wanted you?"

"Perhaps," he mused when Zayla owed him an answer, "you did feel pain once. For a moment, at least, when I finally took your virginity that summer."

Tears poured out of Zayla's eyes. Even on that memorable day on his yacht, there was no pain that she remembered. Marrock had pulled out all the stops to make it a pleasant experience for her. Untouched and inexperienced as Zayla had been that summer, she had nevertheless made the request that the banker also introduce her to his shadowy world, which had been so utterly alien to her at the time. She had read the hesitation on his face when she confronted him with this request, but also the eagerness. The weeping that now tore from Zayla's throat as the banker reached for her was an expression of a hurt that fed on the misery of having run after a mirage and stumbled blindly into an abyss, despite all her own warnings.

Marrock's fingers brushed over her breasts. "Since we've been together," he asked softly, "have you ever once said *no* to me and actually meant it?"

Zayla turned her face away and felt disgust with herself.

"Are you going to say no today?" he taunted. His warm breath brushed over her skin, flooding her with goosebumps. "As ripe as your body is for me once again, do you really want me to stop?"

Without waiting for an answer, he entered her with a single movement. Zayla gasped for breath. She could not shake off the poisonous nectar of the words with which he covered her as passion overtook him. She hated the humiliations she endured as they kept the beast in him happy. She despised her body's addiction to the short-term satiation from his, and what part of her still thought was, affection. But the incessant rapes of her soul caused tears to stream down her face like flash floods. Her sobs finally choked in the pillows Marrock had pressed her into, turning into little sounds of pleasure as the experienced lover set a rhythm that drove them both safely over the cliff.

After Marrock rolled over next to her and finally fell asleep, Zayla stayed awake for a long time. She tormented herself with scorn and contempt. Had she really expected that a man, the cynic in her revolted, could love and care for her? She, from whom people turned away because she instilled fear in them? What was the use of attributes like *stunningly beautiful* and *feast for the eyes,* she continued to mentally beat herself up, when everyone shunned the paranormal powerhouse that lay behind that façade? What good was it for her to possess a desirable body if she could not be loved for the being that dwelled within it?

She would have given a kingdom for being simple and unobtrusive in exchange for being firmly rooted in a human community, deeply loved, and cared for by those around her. With each time she allowed Marrock to use her, while her soul sat beside her and wept, she felt more defiled than before. In silent despair, she cried out in those moments for her mother's arms and love.

Mother! Why have you left me?

If you cannot separate yourself from him, then your suffering is still not great enough, had been the sad words of her maternal friend when Zayla had confided in Dorothea Nicols in an hour of greatest need.

Zayla cried without making a sound so as not to wake Marrock. She had kept her eyes closed and played into the hands of the devil.

Marrock's honeyed promises of love and acceptance had been so overwhelming to the part of her that thirsted for affection that she had rashly given room to the longing to be held by a man in all her uniqueness. Zayla had hoped that illusion could replace reality. In reversal of the Camelot legends, however, which told of a Sir Marrock, a knight of the Round Table who had to live temporarily as a werewolf because of his wife's malediction, the banker was far removed in temperament from the knight and rather resembled the beast in those legends. She should never have offered her wounds to a wolf with the request for healing.

In desperation, she wished her father would be less enthusiastic about Marrock and finally find a reason to turn away from the banker. But Marrock's presence in his home had always encouraged Professor Kirkpatrick. He praised his intellect, his integrity, his eloquence, and his talent for the work of a hypnotherapist. He had encouraged Marrock to study psychology to perfect his skills and saw the former banker as an exceptional talent and a worthy successor to work in his practice.

Her father increasingly denied Zayla the ability to follow in his footsteps on her own. *Too young, too inexperienced, too sensitive* — those were the words she had heard him say when she eavesdropped on a conversation with him and Marrock one evening.

For Zayla, her world had collapsed. Why didn't her father help her instead of driving her further into the arms of this man? Why couldn't he see the unholy alliance his daughter had entered into? Why couldn't he see how tangled she was in the web that Marrock had so skillfully spun around her? Why had he lost faith in her and was now relying on a stranger instead of his only child? Was it not, after all, due to herself? Hadn't it been she who had holed herself up in her room for days on end and had been impossible to talk to, even for her father? Hadn't the bouts of depression from which she suffered become so frequent that appointments were canceled and her father's clients had to be sent home and rebooked?

Invoices had repeatedly disappeared, incoming payments had been posted incorrectly, and e-mails had been deleted. Zayla had not been able to resolve any of these events to her or her father's satisfaction.

At *John Sandoe's*, the charming independent bookstore just around the corner from her home in South Kensington, Zayla purchased an Asian cookbook a week later that excited her. Marrock was an enthusiastic fan of Japanese and Chinese cuisine, so she bought everything she needed for a romantic dinner for two for the banker's forty-third birthday in a few days.

When Marrock returned to his stylish Canary Wharf apartment on his birthday, Zayla had set the table, lit candles and created a romantic atmosphere with essential oils and incense. Dinner was steaming on the stove. He pulled Zayla close and gave her a kiss on the forehead. "Can I take a shower before dinner?"

Zayla nodded.

Shortly after, he sat down at the table with her. Zayla smelled the shower gel on him that she liked so much and smiled. For appetizers, she served him homemade *avocado maki* and *nigiri sushi* with salmon. Mandarin pancakes with duck and a delicate *hoisin sauce* followed. Marrock made an initial disparaging remark and Zayla took pains to ignore it.

For dessert, she placed a piece of homemade matcha cake in front of him. Once again, the banker voiced his displeasure. "Not such a good idea to mix Chinese with Japanese dishes," he grumbled.

The remark stung Zayla.

Just that morning, he hadn't liked the frame of the photograph that showed the couple on the beach in Brighton. She had spent a lot of effort and time making the vintage picture frame herself from kraft and clay paper, log sticks and parcel string.

"You don't have to try so hard to please me," he had said to her. "It doesn't make you very attractive."

Zayla swallowed, and once again tears rolled down her cheeks. Crying had become her default response to everything the banker used to hurt her.

Marrock closed his eyes. "Not this drama again, please. We've had enough of your hysteria lately. Sometimes I think I made a mistake getting involved with you after all. You're so damn young. Way too inexperienced. You don't know who you are. Why don't you try to act more like a woman, little girl?"

To Zayla's sobs, Marrock responded with anger.

"Oh, fuck it! It's *my* birthday! Are you always thinking of yourself?" He threw his silverware back on the plate.

Zayla's attempts to choke down her tears failed. Then the pent-up anger of the past weeks burst out of her and she raised her fists. Desperate, she lunged at the banker. He immediately defended himself and hit her in the face with the back of his hand. Zayla staggered.

"You asshole!"

Marrock snorted. "Watch who you're insulting here! Who went after whom first? You think I'm just going to stand by while you hit me?"

Zayla scrambled to her feet and reached for a kitchen knife on the dining room table. For a split second, Marrock looked startled, then stunned. Outraged. And finally, he laughed out loud.

"This is such a pitiful sight you're giving me here!"

He had the audacity to take a series of pictures of her with his smartphone: hair disheveled, mascara smudges under reddened eyes, kitchen knife in hand. Zayla felt exposed and on display. Enraged, she hurled the knife into the sink. Marrock was filming.

Cursing, she tried to get to the apartment door to leave him. He stopped the video and blocked her way.

"Let me go!" she shrieked.

Marrock pressed his back against the door and pushed Zayla away from him. He dragged her back into the living room and threw her onto the couch. With an iron grip, he held her down and sat next to her.

"I want to get out of here, Marrock! Let me go!"

His hands clutched her face like a vise. "How are you going to find another man who isn't creeped out by your abilities, love?" He kissed her. "No one but me can handle you. You'd be alone for the rest of your life — a lonely old woman, shunned by everyone. Is that what you want?" He wiped the mascara from her cheeks with his thumbs. "Don't you know how much I love you? I alone can give you a life that will make you a respectable woman in this society."

"Are you crazy?" Panic spread through Zayla.

Marrock looked at her with wide eyes and changed his tactics. "You still know far too little about me," he sighed, ruffling his full, dark hair with one hand. "You're not giving me a chance to explain myself to you. You can't just walk away when things get tough! My childhood was a horror show! I have my faults, I know that well, but compared to your outbursts, I feel like a saint."

The doorbell rang. Marrock froze. The doorbell rang a second time. The banker scowled at Zayla, then took a deep breath and opened the door.

"Gentlemen," he calmly greeted the two policemen who were standing in the doorway in front of him.

"Mr. Lovell?"

Marrock nodded. "The same."

"Your neighbors heard a woman screaming at your apartment."

"Feel free to come in." With a welcoming gesture, the banker pushed open the door. "We have just suffered one of my fiancée's now thankfully rare seizures," he told them. "She hears voices in her head, you know. Then she's plagued by paranoia and hallucinations. Occasionally, she loses control of herself, too. It's not an easy situation, and it is not always possible to avoid some noise. But I love her, and I want to marry her, so I stand by her. She is already in psychiatric treatment. Her father and I try to support her as much as we can in everyday life. But today, unfortunately, something flipped a switch in her head and she blindly lunged at me. That must be what startled my neighbors."

Zayla was in a daze.

One of the officers stayed by the door, talking to Marrock, while the other made his way into the living room and took a long look at her. "Madam?"

Zayla looked the policeman in the eye.

"Do you understand what happened?" he asked.

Zayla nodded.

"Do you need a doctor?"

She shook her head.

The policeman regarded her closely. Zayla felt the waves of his compassion and sympathy. Before he averted his eyes from her, she saw in them flashes of what she so often encountered in men before they realized what they were dealing with: desire.

"Who is your psychologist or psychiatrist, Madam?"

Zayla scrunched her eyebrows together. "I … My father is a psychology professor."

The policeman nodded. "Call your father and ask him to come here."

When Professor Kirkpatrick arrived, the police officers exchanged a few words with him and then left Marrock's apartment.

Zayla lay curled up on the couch. Marrock had put a blanket over her and prepared an herbal tea with honey, which she did not touch. Feeling powerless, she dozed off. She had perceived the arrival of her father only through a fog of drowsiness. Leaden fatigue settled over her like a protective cloak, shutting off all her feelings. She was grateful for the emptiness in which she floated and closed her eyes.

She feels her father's warm, tender hand stroking her shoulders with worry. Child, she hears him say, what has happened to you? She nestles her cheek against the back of his hand and then embraces him with the arms of a five-year-old. Firmly she presses her small child's body against her father.

Papa! Help me!

Her shouting is suffocated in the grip of the wet tube that wraps itself slippery and gleaming around her neck like the Maledictus Nagini that carries a part of the black soul of the Dark Lord. Behind her father looms the silhouette of the soul sucker that will rob her of light and life, stopping only when she has become a bloodless shell of herself.

Matthew, the vampire addresses her father, putting his hand on his shoulder. Let your daughter sleep, she is exhausted. I want to show you something.

He leads the professor back to the kitchen. Zayla sees her body lying on the couch, but a part of her that is not her body is able to follow the two men. She sees the soul sucker showing her father the footage he took of her when she came at him, kitchen knife in hand.

What is wrong with my child, her father asks, rubbing his eyes in despair. What in God's name has happened to her?

The vampire offers the professor a chair. I think it has to do with her abilities, Zayla hears him say. They overwhelm her. She is depressed, cries a lot, sleeps badly. She gets hysterical when you call her on forgetting something. Like your emails, your clients' appointments ... Things like that happen all the time even here at home. Just yesterday morning she didn't remember where she was. She talks in her sleep, and according to that, which I can understand, she misses her mother.

Nazneen, her father stammers. Oh God, I miss my wife every day.

The soul sucker puts a hand on his shoulder. I love your daughter, he says, looking at her father. I love her very much. Ever since I first saw her, I wanted her to be the woman by my side, Matthew.

The man's voice sounds pleading, with a slight tremor. I love your daughter. Would I have your blessing if I asked her to become my wife?

Her father sighs. You want to marry her, despite this downward spiral she's currently living in? What if her depression gets worse? Will you be able to endure that?

Marrock smiles. In the phases when her mind is clear, she gives me more joy and satisfaction than I could ever have wished for. We'll bring in specialists from around the world if necessary, Matthew. We will make Zayla well again.

Her father nods. If anyone can do it, it's surely you. I never thought she would find a man who could accept her differences so well, Marrock. Never would I have dared to hope that a man could even love her for it.

My answer must be yes. If my only child wants you, I will give you both my blessing.

Zayla fell into a leaden sleep. When she awoke again, she heard the soft rhythmic sounds of Maurice Ravel's Bolero. One hundred sixty-nine repetitions of rhythm and melody, it flashed through her mind, still half asleep.

She noticed it was still dark. A storm swirled furiously around the houses and rain pelted against the windows of the apartment. Lightning struck and thunderclaps cracked.

Zayla raised her head. Marrock's living room was lit by a single candle that stood on the table in front of her. In a black leather chair across from her sat the banker, his long, muscular legs in faded jeans, spread wide. His hands rested in his lap. His feet and torso, steeled by regular weight training, were unclothed. Marrock's gaze rested on her with the same bleak ferocity as that of a mantis on its prey. He clenched the fingers of one hand into a fist and stretched it out again. Once. Twice.

Three times. What had she expected? That he would tolerate her embarrassing him like this?

She rose and slipped into the bathroom. When she returned to the banker, she had washed, shaven and carefully combed her hair. She stood before him, naked, and defenseless. An approving grin twitched around the corners of Marrock's mouth. Zayla shivered, goose bumps prickling across her skin, all over her body.

A slight tilt of the banker's head was enough, and she sank to her knees before him. With this gesture of submission, he initiated the descent into a deep black underworld. It was a descent in which he would spare her no more humiliation that night. To escape the pain, she had learned to submit to the monster in him in his darkest moments in every possible way.

When she came — not because she felt a single spark of desire, but because his disgusting tentacles and pitch-black eroticism dominated her body even against her will — she began to gag. Drunk with lust and in a state of soulless ecstasy, the banker rode her like a stud riding a mare. It was a cruel game of total dominance and brutal submission in which Zayla had long since given herself up.

While the master of deception and mirages played her savior before the eyes of the world, he sucked the life force out of Zayla behind closed doors. Without Zayla realizing what had happened to her, this man had taken everything she needed to live: her body, her mind, her only friendship with another human being, her ability to love and feel, her closeness to her father and her connection with the light and life.

In the garden of her maternal friend Dorothea last March, Zayla had succeeded, through the power of her touch alone, in soothing the ravings and pains in the banker's dark soul. When she had laid her hands on Marrock's back while he cowered on the floor, she had been overwhelmed by the waves of peace and gratitude that had spread through him. But since her nearness no longer silenced the voices of the children who lay buried alive in Marrock, the lover of the first weeks, who had been devoted to her and exceedingly tender, had become a prince of darkness.

Chapter 12

Avalon Beach, North of Sydney, Australia

Named after the sacred island of Celtic mythology considered the resting place of King Arthur, Avalon Beach lay in the dark of night below closed sidewalk cafés and streetwear, art and surf stores on the Pacific coast north of Sydney. Bordered on both short sides by sandstone cliffs and backed by mighty foredunes, Avalon was part of a thirty-kilometer chain of sandy beaches stretching from Manly in the south to Palm Beach in the north. The saltwater pool that had been carved into the rocks at one end of the bay served as a meeting place for visitors who were less fond of surfing than of swimming in the open air, but who liked to avoid the hazards of the Pacific.

In the protective cloak of night, six women found themselves on the beach at Avalon. In a circle of mats, blankets, and picnic baskets, they sat, stood, and lay giggling together. Each had placed a lantern in front of her, but none of the six candles had been lit yet. The women joked but spoke to one another in hushed tones. A loud laugh or a bright shout would have made the shelter their small sisterhood had created in the early hours of the morning in Avalon collapse like a house of cards.

Zayla brushed a strand of hair from her face and gazed longingly out at the sea, near which she felt more at home than anywhere in the world. She glanced at her cell phone. Two hours to go before the sun would cast its first rays over the thundering surf from the head of the beach. How much the Portuguese Magellan had underestimated the violence of the Pacific, which he christened *the peaceful sea!*

When her cousin Tahnee had told her about the plans for her bachelorette party, Zayla had been pleasantly surprised. She had expected the usual British-Australian hen nights, with dancing, loud music, male strippers, and lots of alcohol.

There had indeed been dancing along with music and alcohol. But neither Zayla nor Tiya, Logan's wife with whom he had traveled from the United States to attend his brother's wedding, had touched a single drop, so the alcohol consumption of the other women had also remained moderate. Moreover, Tahnee had announced that she wanted to use the early morning hours on Avalon Beach for a ritual that was very close to her heart, so her companions had to remain in control of their cognitive abilities if they did not want to disappoint her.

Just then, Zayla heard Tiya say that her own wedding to Logan two months earlier had been a quiet, unspectacular affair. "Until the arrival of the Europeans, our wedding ceremonies were often nothing more than a public recognition that a man and a woman wanted to live together," she told Tahnee's guests. Adding with a laugh, "To the dismay of the missionaries of the time, the divorces of my people in the old days were just as uncomplicated!"

Zayla had learned from Tahnee that no one in the Diamandis family had been able to persuade Logan and Tiya to hold belated celebrations in Australia, and that Tahnee and Nick had expressed disappointment that they had not been invited to the couple's wedding. Whether Nick and Logan's father, the tycoon and head of the family, felt the same way, Zayla didn't know.

She watched Tahnee rise now, reach for a pack of matches, and light the first lantern. Smiling, her cousin thanked her friends for partying the night away with her in Sydney's hottest nightclubs with so much fun and good cheer, and that they were now ready to end this special day in her life on Avalon Beach in an equally special way.

Tahnee unearthed a photo on her phone and let it make the rounds. Zayla, who was sitting next to her cousin, first caught a glimpse of the picture Tahnee was passing around and was startled.

On the left side of the photograph, she saw the face of a young woman with long dark hair and a countenance like velvet and silk from which warm, intelligent eyes flashed. On the right side of the photograph, however, it seemed as if Zayla were staring into the face of a monster. The skin of the person in this photograph was extensively burned and scarred, the face swollen and disfigured beyond recognition.

"This is Turia Pitt," Tahnee told them. "She's a Tahitian-born Australian. The picture on the left shows her just before the start of an ultramarathon that would take her one hundred kilometers through the rugged mountains of the Kimberley. The right picture was taken after this marathon, which changed her life completely."

Zayla's eyebrows shot up. The same woman in both pictures? How was that possible?

"Turia Pitt is a marathon runner, engineer and activist," Tahnee continued. "Because she used to be very attractive, she also worked as a model. During her ultramarathon, she was caught in a bush fire in the Kimberley and trapped. She was literally cooked. Can you imagine? One of her doctors reported that he had never seen a person survive with such severe burns. Turia Pitt spent half a year in the hospital. She underwent a couple hundred surgeries, and three times doctors lost and resuscitated her on the operating table. After the wave of fire swept over her in the Kimberley, she could no longer walk, speak, or move her arms. She later described how the day she was able to wipe her own buttocks for the first time again was like an Olympic victory." Tahnee took a dramatic pause. "The fear of the painful daily dressing changes in the hospital woke her up again and again, sweat pouring from her forehead. Day after day, week after week, she cried out with the other burn victims in the ward during this excruciating procedure. But despite all the devastating prognoses, she began walking again just one year after her accident. Four years later, she completed her first Ironman in Australia and a second in Hawaii."

The women were amazed.

"Thousands have since been motivated by her inspiring story at her public appearances. Turia Pitt graced the cover of *Australian Women's Weekly* and became *Australian Woman of the Year*. What also moved me was that her boyfriend and later husband never let her down. When asked if he had ever toyed with the idea of turning his back on Turia, he replied with something quite wonderful. He said, 'I am married to her soul and character. She is the only woman with whom I can realize my dreams.' Isn't that a great statement? I hope Nick will one day say something similar about me.

"Turia and her husband ardently wished to become parents, but Turia's doctors warned her against pregnancy. However, she miraculously became the mother of two healthy sons.

"At first, Turia struggled a lot with her fate following the accident. But then she realized that we are all infinitely more than just our bodies. She said she learned that self-confidence has nothing to do with what you can see or how beautiful a body is, but everything to do with the mindset and thought process a person maintains. That outlook impressed me as well."

Zayla felt a twinge at Tahnee's words. Indeed, an attractive body was no guarantee of self-confidence, especially if the person who lived in it was convinced that she was worthless.

"The reason I chose Turia Pitt as my personal hero for tonight," Tahnee concluded her report, "is because of this woman's attitude and will to make the impossible possible and to have not only survived against all odds, but to have been virtually reborn. Since her accident, she once said, her life has become more valuable and more worth living than ever before. I think that's an attitude we should all take to heart."

Her listeners murmured words of approval at the gripping biography that had just been presented to them.

"Marlee, would you like to tell us about your personal heroine?" asked Tahnee of her kindergarten friend, whom Zayla had met on many occasions, for before her mother's death, she and her parents had regularly visited her Australian relatives. Marlee was a witty and insightful person Zayla admired. She was the granddaughter of a Yolngu First Nation didgeridoo builder from Arnhem Land in the Northern Territory and lived in the Blue Mountains with her partner, a white Australian.

Marlee nodded. She stood up, lit the second lantern, and introduced her audience to the woman who had impressed her more than any other. "Judy Atkinson is my choice for this evening," she told them. "Judy is a Jiman and Bundjalung First Nation woman with Anglo-Celtic and German ancestry. She is a professor emerita and wrote a book on *trauma trails* and restoring the *songlines.* In my ancestral worldview, people are connected to the land, which is the source of life. Songlines represent an oral archive that records the stories of all earthly and non-earthly beings. Songlines transcend language barriers. Their melody and rhythm identify landmarks. Those who know these songs can navigate anywhere no matter what language they speak. A songline expert can tell how many times a river has been crossed or a mountain range climbed, and he can calculate how far he has progressed on his journey. To the initiated, songlines are like a map. They can travel huge distances without getting lost."

Marlee paused for a moment and took a sip of water. Then she continued, "Professor Judy Atkinson has done a masterful job of connecting the traumas of colonization and the wounds of violence and displacement with an ancient healing ritual as well as recreating songlines from trauma trails. She also describes the deep listening and understanding, without any judgment, that Ngangikurungkurr First Nation Women in the Northern Territory call *dadirri*. Its only goal is to truly understand the other person. Used correctly, it is a profound form of healing. I wish so much for you, Tahnee, that our little group here will be for all time the women who can genuinely listen to you in your pain but also in your joy, and who will see you and carry you whenever you need it."

She smiled and Zayla saw how much these words touched her cousin. She felt that Marlee would have shared even more with the other women if her own feelings had not overwhelmed her and her voice had failed.

After all five had acknowledged Marlee's words, Tahnee asked, "Would you continue, Ava?" Ava was the daughter of an Australian with Swiss ancestry and a mother whose parents were from Myanmar. She knelt forward and lit the third lantern.

"The woman I have chosen," Ava began, "is Wai Wai Nu, a Myanmar-born Muslima. Wai Wai Nu is the daughter of Rohingya parents. Rohingya are Sunni Muslims and one of the most persecuted minorities in the world. At the age of eighteen, Wai Wai Nu was thrown into prison. Her 'crime' was being the daughter of a political activist. For seven years, she and her parents endured harsh conditions in one of

Myanmar's most notorious prisons. Her brother had been separated from the family. Today, she lives in the U.S. and has founded two non-governmental organizations. One focuses on peace-making in Myanmar, and the other is a network of female lawyers that provides legal assistance to women in need. She once countered the accusation that in living in the U.S., she had escaped Myanmar's difficult conditions, by saying, 'I am not free. Our society is not free. My country is not free. The situation for Rohingya girls and women is indescribable. I see it as my responsibility to help restore human dignity, respect, and freedom.'"

Ava sat down and Zayla reflected on what a privileged position she found herself in.

Kalinda, daughter of Indian ancestors and a third-generation Australian, nodded to the women, rose, and lit the fourth lantern. "My heroine is Indira Gandhi," she began. "In case you are wondering, no, she was not related to the great Mahatma Gandhi. Indira was a shrewd and, in due course, ruthless power politician. What I admire about her is that she was, above all else, a fearless woman. She fought for unity and for India's independence from British colonial rule. For me, Indira Ghandi is proof that women in India can play a political role. But her example unfortunately also shows how much family cir-cumstances determined whether a woman could make a political career in 20th century India. Had Indira's father not belonged to one of the most distinguished and highly respected Hindu groups in the country, she would certainly have been denied access to educational institutions at home and abroad. Like all other Indian women at that time, she would have had to submit to social restrictions. Had she had even a single brother, Indira would probably never have risen to become India's prime minister. In my grandparents' country, rocked by religious conflict, she was eventually assassinated by her own bodyguards, who were Sikh and not Hindu like herself."

In Zayla's mind, these words echoed the stories that an Indian friend of her parents had shared at a dinner at the Kirkpatrick home when Zayla was a child. She had already been sent to bed but had slipped out of her room, pausing in the shadow of the balustrade. With her head leaning against the wooden rib railing on the top step of the staircase that led from the dining room to the floor where her bedroom was located, she listened horrified as Dr. Kaur — a Sikh like Indira Ghandi's bodyguards — told of her grandfather, who had been thrown into a blast furnace and burned by angry Hindus at the steel mill where he had worked. How angry Hindus had snatched children from Sikh families after Indira Gandhi's assassination, raped the women, and murdered them along with their husbands. Dr. Kaur railed that these massacres were among the darkest chapters in Indian history, and she cast great doubt on the narrative that it was Sikh bodyguards who had killed Hindu Prime Minister Indira Gandhi. No other time had Zayla seen her parents' normally gentle friend as upset as she was that evening.

Zayla watched as Kalinda handed Tiya, Logan's wife, the box of matches after her remarks. The Anishinaabe woman thanked her and lit the fifth candle. Zayla gazed at Tiya, admiring the elegance of her movements, the attentive expression of her eyes, and her powerful presence.

Tiya took a deep breath and told the audience about her hero, Dr. Kim TallBear, a Dakȟóta who worked as a professor of Indigenous Studies at the University of Alberta in Canada. "I host a podcast with two friends," she shared, "that focuses on Indigenous perspectives and concerns. A few months ago, we interviewed Professor Kim TallBear. There are certainly many ways to understand the world, but I particularly like Kim's perspective. One of the things she talked to us about is how the issue of indigenous women and sexuality only comes up in the context of violence. A friend of hers, fed up with this, created an erotic writing course just for indigenous women in response to this grievance. Due to centuries of colonization, many of us grew up in very sexually repressive households. The generations of my grandparents and great-grandparents were forcibly separated from their families and raised in residential or boarding schools that had more in common with internment camps. Here they were shamed and mistreated for their origins, their skin color, their traditions, and their sexuality.

"Professor Kim TallBear points out that the monogamy model imposed on us by the conquerors went hand in hand with the Christian religion, patriarchy, European notions of private property, and the dissolution of our tribal lands. Only Indian men, never women, had been able to lay claim to property under this social model, and thus to the last fragments of our own lands. If a man was married and had children, the size of his land holdings also increased. Like the land, wives and children were now considered the property of our men. This was different in our ancient societies. So it was primarily heterosexual white men who determined and controlled what could and could not be considered a good and functional relationship in our societies after our conquest.

"From Kim's point of view, forced monogamy and lifelong marriage are a cornerstone of unhappiness in most couple relationships. We joked a lot with her about this thesis. What's wrong, she countered, with raising children with friends or relatives rather than with a romantic partner? Ultimately, the only thing that matters for a child is a good network of relationships that is supported by openness and human warmth — just as it was traditionally the case among our tribes.

"Kim advocates opening society to what she calls *ethical non-monogamy*. This means building multiple healthy and supportive relationships that are not about possessing another's desire, wishes, or body. Kim herself lives *ethically polyamorous*. Honesty and responsibility are indispensable foundations for such a life.

"Kim, like me, grew up in an extended family structure where couples don't play such an overriding role and where it doesn't matter if someone is divorced or never married. She argues that the couple as the anchor of the Western nuclear family is generally not a wise family model, because once a couple separates, everything else usually goes down the drain. Extended family structures, I agree, are a better concept, because if one family member gets into a crisis, others are immediately on hand to help them back on their feet.

"For me, it has become so incredibly important," Tiya added in conclusion, "that my people question the structures of colonization imposed on us, that we remember our own traditions again and try to live them, as far as this is still possible after the centuries of genocide and violent assimilation. And to you, Tahnee, I wish with all my heart that you will be happy as the wife of a white man and that Nick, whom I had the pleasure of meeting and who is a genuinely kind person, will be able to appreciate your indigenous heritage. That your husband will let you live that heritage and that you will pass it on to your children with pride, as part of their biography."

Zayla had followed Tiya's explanations with fascination. Logan's wife was a gifted speaker who could move much in her listeners. The stories of the heroines of Tiya, Kalinda, Ava, Marlee, and Tahnee had sparked in Zayla memories of a formidable feminine force that sensed, in the sisterhood on the beach of Avalon, the breeding ground for its revival.

She was now the last woman to introduce Tahnee's guests to the female icon who had impressed her most so far. Her pulse beat faster. In the line of heroines that the other women had taken as their role models of female transformational power, Zayla's own choice seemed strange and alienating: She had resonated highly with Elizabeth Blake, a direct-voice-medium who had lived in Ohio, in the U.S., in the second half of the 19th century. Elizabeth Blake had belonged to the Methodist Church and, despite her deep religiosity, had been expelled from the church for her mediumistic work. Nevertheless, more than two hundred thousand people had attended the séances of this unique medium throughout her life. Elizabeth Blake had been so popular that Sir Arthur Conan Doyle, the author of the Sherlock Holmes stories, had publicly claimed that she was one of the most talented mediums of the time.

Zayla lit the sixth lantern and hesitated. When, after a few deep breaths she finally composed herself and began to speak, a gust of wind whipped through the circle of women. Zayla's head flew to the side. She looked in the direction of the natural swimming pool that lay a scant kilometer to her left. "Father," she breathed.

The other women looked at her in surprise.

"What's wrong with him?" asked Tahnee, concerned. "What can you see, Zayla?"

"Father..." Zayla repeated, her eyes boring into the night.

The women watched as a shadow detached itself from the darkness in the direction of the rock pool, moving at a steady pace toward the small group. With mixed feelings, half a dozen pairs of eyes gazed at the arrival. The shadow seemed to be alone. Could a single person pose a danger to them all?

"Logan ..." Tiya murmured when the figure had come close

enough so that its outline could be discerned.

Her husband stepped into the circle of six women and greeted first Tiya and then Tahnee with his eyes. "I'm looking for your cousin," Logan turned to Tahnee.

His gaze fell on Zayla, who was standing next to her and had taken a step forward. The world came to a halt for a moment.

"Kimímela," Logan murmured as their eyes met.

The surprise he felt at that moment and the wide, soft, open flow of his heart flooded through Zayla as he looked at her. Kimímela was a word she knew. But from where? It had not been a mere exclamation of amazement, but a ... *name*. Had it really been a name? The name for a ... butterfly? Zayla felt hot and cold at the same time.

She sees the delicate creature sitting on her forearm. It bears white markings on the brown side of its left wing and black markings on the yellow side of its right. The man standing in front of her, who has begun to wash her body with the water of the river, pauses as his gaze falls on the winged messenger.

Ah, little brother, the warrior greets the male butterfly, smaller than the female of his species. Her husband's words ring out, without forming, only in Zayla's mind. In your honor, she hears him say, my wife will bear a name that will belong only to her and me. It will remind us of this day, little brother Kimímela, when my wife and I have long since returned to the spirit world.

In Zayla's mind, new images were now breaking through with a violence that almost brought her down. They were scenes of destruction, of boundless hatred and inhuman suffering. Zayla's heart hammered in her chest. She barely dared to breathe and fought tears. The images of the Aboriginal family's lives she had shared with Travis on the beach in Brighton last summer mingled with those of the murder of the Native American warrior that had sent her into sheer panic when Marrock first tried to touch her after their walk together at London's Hollow Pond last spring.

Then, the gruesome images of this murder were overlaid by the scene by the river that filled her with deep love. She experienced the ecstasy of the sandy-haired woman whom the warrior, who had given her the pet name butterfly, Kimímela, introduced to the realm of physical love with tenderness and respect. It was the snapshot of a natural and sacred act that appeared before Zayla's inner eye, an event as spiritual as it was sensual, the purity of which flooded her with bitterness when she compared it to the shamelessness of a slut to which Marrock had reduced her.

The banker had been hospitalized along with half a dozen others injured after the terrorist attack by a lone assailant in central London a few days earlier. Zayla was under no illusion about the price she would pay for her and her father flying to Australia for Tahnee and Nick's wedding while leaving Marrock to his moping on his own in London. Fifteen missed calls and twenty-two messages showed on her cell phone for today alone.

Zayla sighed. Her last bleeding was overdue for almost two weeks. She would have liked to drown herself here on Avalon Beach. She had no strength left.

She noticed Tiya giving her a long look. Zayla took in her confusion and her hint of discomfort and closed her eyes. She greatly admired and appreciated the Anishinaabe woman. Nothing was further from her mind than to vie with this great woman for her own husband's attention.

"Travis is with your father," Logan murmured. His eyes still hadn't left hers. "He asked me to come get you."

Zayla's gaze flared. The will to live flashed through her. "What happened to him?"

"I'm supposed to take you to him," Logan repeated, but that was all he told her.

Chapter 13

Sydney, Australia

The jet-black Porsche Taycan rolled onto the driveway of the Diamandis estate, and Logan turned off the engine. He struggled with the impulse to pull Zayla into his arms and calm the troubled girl. The ailing professor was in good hands, and Logan didn't think his daughter needed to worry about him. Ever since their encounter on Avalon Beach an hour ago, her proximity contained something disconcertingly familiar to him. He shut his eyes and listened to the humming of his nerves running on overdrive like the buzzing in a hornet's nest. Then he lifted his lids and met Zayla's gaze. He interpreted the embarrassment he read there as confirmation that she felt the excitement raging through him like a torrent of white water. He let her smile affect him and realized that the ruthlessness with which he wanted to protect her sprang from an ancient programming. Then shame overtook him. *Tiya!*

Moodily, he removed the key and got out of the car. He heard Zayla climb out of the vehicle after him.

"Oh, my goodness!" she exclaimed. He turned his head and saw that she was spinning around. With outstretched arms, she stroked the air as if her movements could make the invisible tangible. Memories of the sandy-haired girl from his dream that night in Uŋčí's log cabin arose in him.

"Do you see that, too?" whispered Zayla.

"What?" asked Logan, shaking his head.

"Gossamer threads," respect and awe resonated in her words, "in royal blue, purple and white. A pulsating web of energy that lies over the entire property. It is picture perfect and tremendously powerful."

Travis had told Logan of Zayla's extraordinary abilities and how the young woman had been forced into the role of an outsider by them — even more than Travis. The longer Logan's eyes rested on Zayla, the better he understood why. In her absorption in a world that only she could perceive, she was amazingly like his grandmother.

Uŋčí's powers had fascinated him from childhood. Like Zayla's, her gifts often caused discomfort in other people, too. All the earthly and non-earthly things Uŋčí knew and could see, hear, and feel had led her to a self-imposed life of relative seclusion. Unlike the people in Zayla's and Travis's environment, the Lakȟóta paid the greatest respect to a person through whom the mysterious forces of the universe worked. Only a few understood how to meet such a person with lightness and humor though. He himself belonged to this small circle, as did his sister and his wife. His mother, however, had taken refuge in the shadow of her own mother. Often, Logan had caught the daggers she threw at Uŋčí in the form of glances; he could read on her face the feeling of inferiority she felt with his grandmother.

Logan led Zayla to one of the guest rooms on the first floor of his adoptive father's house. In the hallway, Travis was already rushing toward them. He embraced his friend and stopped her from racing into the room where her father lay.

"We were sitting with Matthew," he explained, "while Tahnee was out with you girls. My partner Carl, your uncle Yarran, Deimos, Nick, Logan, and me. Your father dismissed his discomfort as jet lag, but all of a sudden, he collapsed. Deimos immediately had a medic drummed out of bed. The doc was able to stabilize Matthew. He wants to run some more tests tomorrow."

Travis cracked the door to Professor Kirkpatrick's room and

Zayla slipped inside. "He's asleep now," he said.

She nodded and carefully sat down on the edge of her father's bed. Tears rolled down her cheeks. Travis stepped behind her and placed his hands on her shoulders. She leaned her head against his chest, and he gently stroked her dark, silky hair, which fell in waves down to her hips.

At the sight of the deep intimacy between the two, Logan felt a twinge. "I can't lose my father, too!" he heard Zayla sob quietly. "I don't have the strength anymore, Travis. I want to stop feeling. I want someone to finally pull the plug and take me off the playing field."

Travis knit his brows in anguish. Logan also registered the boundless desperation behind her words.

"Forgive me for not fighting harder for our friendship," she pleaded with Travis.

He pressed her against him. "This cursed soul sucker is poison for you, Zayla. You *must* separate yourself from him."

The intimacy of the exchange made Logan uncomfortable. This conversation was not meant for his ears. Travis and Zayla seemed to have forgotten that he was still standing in the room with them. But before he could turn around and leave them alone with the sick professor, he heard approaching footsteps. He turned his head and met his father's coal-black eyes.

Deimos pressed a hand on his shoulder in greeting and appraised Zayla through the open door with an intensity that made Logan take notice. Instinctively, he straightened to full height and shifted his weight back onto both legs. Deimos brushed him with a critical glance and the corners of his mouth twitched. Disapproval, Logan thought, but also a warning.

With the facial expression of a man accustomed to acting quickly and, if necessary, regardless of the sensitivities of others, Deimos entered the room. "Good morning, Miss

Kirkpatrick." His sonorous voice had taken on such a velvety timbre that it shook Logan inside. "Your father is already on the mend. You don't have to worry anymore."

Zayla's head flew around, and she stared at the master of the house. "You are a man of power," she exclaimed.

Deimos laughed harshly.

"Descendant of a priestly caste of the ancient Persian Empire. Just like my mother's family."

Logan saw his father's eyebrows draw together.

"*Mageia,*" Zayla whispered, nibbling her fingers. "The ancient power of *Magian,* branded as witchcraft by Greeks and Romans and at the same time honored as spiritual and intellectual enlightenment."

There was something ethereal about the scene unfolding in front of Logan. His father's eyes were glued to the girl like the adhesive pads of a wild vine, and Zayla never turned her face away from him either. Instead of being intimidated, she seemed to blossom under his probing gaze. The heap of misery that had just sat at the professor's bedside had become a sublime apparition. For a few moments, she stood in the room like a queen.

"When I was a child, my mother used to read Plato's *myth of Êr to* me."

Deimos's reaction to Zayla's words sounded dark and alluring. His eyelids drooped as he replied, "His story about the fate of souls in the afterlife. Did your mother consider the *myth of Êr* as originating from a source of Zarathustra?"

"She and my father have always understood Zarathustra as a teacher of this great Greek philosopher."

Deimos cast an approving glance at the restlessly tossing professor and waved his daughter, Travis, and Logan out of the room. "We'd better let him sleep, Miss Kirkpatrick. If you'd like," he offered her outside the door, "I'll have another guest room made up for you."

"Thank you, but that won't be necessary. Travis told me that my father will have a doctor's appointment in the morning?"

Deimos nodded. "If you don't want to stay with him until then, my driver can pick you up at your aunt's house in time for you to accompany your father. First, though, Miss Kirkpatrick, there is something I would like to show you."

He gestured toward the library room on the second floor and invited Zayla to follow him. Wordlessly, Logan and Travis joined them. In the light-filled room, which boasted a breathtaking panoramic view of a natural, lush green park, the tycoon reached for a thin single volume bound in black leather. "The key to your father's complete recovery lies in an ancient time."

Zayla took the book and Logan noted the terror that ran through her as she opened it. The pages slipped from her fingers and landed with a thud on the floor.

"You are the former Templar!" Zayla's trembling hands searched behind her for a firm grip. "The dark mage who was burned with the daughter of the High Priestess." Her voice was now only a whisper.

Deimos grabbed her faster than Logan or Travis could have reacted. "Who else do you recognize in me?" he asked. The grip of his fingers left pressure marks on her wrists, although he let Zayla slide gently into one of the library chairs.

"A Druid scholar." Her voice sounded brittle. "An ancient Greek mystic. And ... the *Colonel.* It can't be!"

"You have remarkable abilities." Deimos's eyes danced like a dervish across Zayla's face, and Logan was covered in full-body goose bumps. Never before had he seen his father so entranced.

"Travis?" Zayla turned her head in the young Aboriginal's direction. "The two men you recognized in the scenes we shared on Brighton beach — were they ...?"

Travis lowered his eyes. He gestured toward father and son and just sighed.

Logan's eyebrows shot up.

"But the warrior who came upon his old boyhood friend on the Great Plains after the massacre of his people," Travis explained, "I have not yet recognized."

Zayla rubbed her temples. "Maybe he's the man who was killed just before the Canadian border," she murmured, "the leader with the fighting knife in the shape of a black wolf's head."

Logan cut through the air with the flat of his hand. "Oh, for fuck's sake! Have all three of you lost your minds?"

Zayla's gaze jerked over to him and he saw that he had hurt her. "What exactly happened to my father?" Her eyes drifted back to Deimos.

Creeping seconds passed before the tycoon replied. "You know it." The indefinable smile that played around his lips made Logan's hair stand on end.

Zayla propped her head in both hands and closed her eyes. "A black magic attack," she said at last.

The tycoon nodded. "We need holy water." He turned to his son and held up a vial with a cork. "Take Travis with you, Logan. Find a Catholic church. You will find holy water there in the entryway."

Logan hesitated, and Deimos narrowed his eyes. "Who else but you two can I entrust with such a matter?" he cajoled him. "Nick is on his way here with Tiya and Tahnee. My people would just get ideas. Hunter Garza is my first choice for many things, but not for this."

Logan pressed his lips together. "You will owe me a

detailed explanation."

Deimos agreed and reached for a mirror box the size of a shoebox that lay on one of the huge bookshelves rising to the ceiling. Then he turned to Zayla. "*Remember.*"

Zayla heaved a sigh and a tremor overtook her, her teeth chattering. "We also need incense and a burner," she said after she had regained control of her body, "a small rag doll for the attacker ... a ritual text invoking the guardians of the four directions," she looked to the box Deimos held in his hands, "a mirror box with spellbinding pentagrams inside. The Lord's Prayer."

"An item sacred to Zayla's father and four black-dipped candles," Travis concluded her list.

Deimos's eyes shot over to him approvingly and he urged the two men to leave.

Logan made a sound that indicated he understood but could muster no enthusiasm for the assignment his father had given them.

Travis nudged him with his elbow. "Let's go, man."

Reluctantly, Logan started moving. "Do you believe in this nonsense?" he asked his former protégé on the way to the driveway, where he had parked his sports car. At the same time, he pulled up a map of Sydney on his cell phone.

"Not a matter of faith for me," Travis replied. "It just *is*. In an ancient incarnation, your father and Zayla once masterfully controlled the dark and light powers. They burned at the stake together for it."

Logan snorted and rolled his eyes. Then, he pointed his chin at the map on the cell phone. "St. Mary's Cathedral. On the way there, you'll tell me everything you know about your little friend."

"My *little friend*?"

"Isn't she younger than you?" Logan put as much innocence into his voice as he could.

Travis got into the car with him. "What do you want to know?"

"You didn't realize she was Tahnee's and Carl's cousin when you applied for the training seminars with her father?" Logan shifted gears and the two nearly flew off the Diamandis estate.

"Where from? When Florence pointed me to Zayla's father's website back then, she didn't tell me about the professor being her brother."

"What reason could she have had?"

"Zayla once said that her father only wanted to train students who had no personal relationship with him or his family. If he had known that I knew his sister, he most likely would have weeded out my application from the beginning."

"The girl has your skills?"

"What's your problem with her, man? The *girl*?"

Logan shrugged. The more distance he could put between himself and Travis's friend, the better. "Well, okay then, does *Zayla* have your skills?"

"Hers are more pronounced than mine," he got to hear in response, and it didn't surprise him. "I've never met a person like Zayla. Not only are we both highly intuitive and empathic, but we can also contact souls who have shed their human shells again in this 3-D world."

The disclaimers of Australian media flashed through Logan's mind, which warned Aboriginals and Torres Strait Islanders against it as soon as an upcoming feature contained names, voices, or images of deceased people. He wondered if Travis's skills would have become a stigma in Australian First Nations communities as well. Logan found it unfortunate that Deimos's tracking dogs still hadn't located his friend's father. And he glumly admitted to himself that his own understanding of

Australia's indigenous peoples remained spotty at best, even after twelve years in the country.

"The information that reaches me comes primarily through my own spirit guides," Travis told him, "or through what a person radiates. Occasionally also through dreams or a being from another dimension. Just like me, Zayla is clairvoyant, clairaudient, and clairsentient. Sometimes she manages to do remote viewing. A few times, I have experienced that she had more intense, direct access to things that were hidden from me. On the other hand, she can't always control her abilities as well as I can. My downloads are more consistent and easier to recall. With her, they often come and go as they please, but they are more powerful and fascinatingly accurate. After the first seminar weekend over a year ago, we shared scenes from three lives together on the beach in Brighton."

Logan slammed on the brakes. He pulled the car into a vacant parking space on the side of the road and turned off the engine. Irritated, he banged the steering wheel. "That's what you told me about a while back! But you also said you were unsure exactly who you saw then. So now you not only think Zayla was the mother of the girl through whose eyes you saw the Aboriginal family escape, but you suddenly also think I was that girl's father?"

Travis looked at him coolly. "You bet. Your path and mine have crossed more than once, man. Entertaining, by the way, watching you and Deimos become real top dogs in Zayla's presence earlier."

Logan clenched his teeth. The grin he saw flit across his friend's face annoyed him.

"Did you recognize her right away in Avalon?" asked Travis.

Logan shook his head. "A scene popped up that ..." He broke off. He couldn't tell Travis about the force of the images that had assaulted him on Avalon Beach and kept him in constant tension during the trip with Zayla to the Diamandis estate. The feeling of guilt gnawed at him again. "Couldn't she be one of those esoteric and pseudo-mystic women after all?" he asked, struggling to cling to something he could use against her. "One of those hippie women and crystal wearers who cherry pick elements from foreign cultures that appeal to them? One of those people who appropriate and market things that aren't their own?"

Travis looked at him, dumbfounded. "What? No! What makes you think that?"

"*Pretendians* — there are many. They're all weirdos who, when it suits them, even pretend to belong to fake tribes. Given the choice, I'd rather deal with a hardcore racist than some wannabe Native any day. I was nine years old when one of those hippie women came to our reservation and claimed to be the incarnation of the White Buffalo Calf Woman."

Travis whistled between his teeth. "Your people's divine messenger? What arrogance!"

"These people think they have recognized meaning and utility in rituals and customs that they do not understand. Their own culture no longer offers them any sense of meaning, and such windbags and profile neurotics then plug this hole with other people's feathers."

"I don't understand why you would associate Zayla, of all people, with them."

"Did *you* then tell her about my great-great-grandfather? How did she know about the Black Wolf Chief?"

Travis shook his head. "She participated in a regression with her father where she saw herself as one of the three wives of a man that the U.S. Army tracked to just outside the Canadian border, then caught and killed him."

"That's impossible, Travis. Do you hear me?" Logan clenched his teeth so hard he tasted blood.

Travis looked off into the distance and sighed. "It sent chills down my spine when Zayla addressed Deimos as the Colonel, a Magian, and a former Templar. I was such a damn fool not to have realized who he actually was much earlier myself. Black magic! I wouldn't be surprised if that fucker they left in London was behind it."

"The guy you called a soul sucker earlier?"

Travis nodded.

"How does such a man fit in with the professor's claim to want to train only trustworthy students?"

"Not at all. Zayla's father fails to see through him. This devil is a master manipulator, and the professor is unfortunately taken in by him."

"Doesn't the devil avoid holy water?" Logan contorted his face into a grin at his tired attempt at a joke and pulled out the vial Deimos had thrust into his hand. "Maybe you should rub some of that holy water in that Mephistopheles' nose after we get it out of St. Mary's Cathedral. It's possible he'll let go of your little friend then."

"She's *not* your enemy, you know."

"No," Logan admitted, "but she's a sandy-haired ghost from a bygone era. I'd better leave such a genie in her bottle — despite the three wishes she might grant me."

Travis threw his arms in the air. "What a lousy comparison!"

When the two men reached the seat of the Archbishop of Sydney in the middle of the Australian metropolis, Logan parked his Porsche in the underground garage next door. The Roman Catholic St. Mary's Cathedral was the largest of its kind on the continent. Its neo-Gothic architecture was reminiscent of the gigantic European churches of the Middle Ages. The closer the two of them got to the structure with its tall, tapering spires, the more uneasy Logan became. It was as if he were walking straight into a mausoleum. An invisible cloak seemed to wrap itself around his head and neck, constricting his throat.

Feeling like his legs might give way beneath him at any moment, he battled to conceal his trepidation as he stepped through the main entrance of the cathedral. In front of him stretched the long corridor of the nave, at the end of which first a magnificent stained-glass window and then the main altar caught the visitor's eye. The stained-glass window showed the Mother of the Christian God and her Son on a throne surrounded by holy women on Mary's left and figures of male saints on Jesus' right.

"The Crowning of Mary," Travis came to a stop beside him.

Logan's eyes followed the vaulted ceilings of the nave and the pillars of the side aisles. He guessed they were made of the same golden-yellow sandstone as the exterior walls, which had weathered to a golden-brown outside. He observed that Travis dipped his fingertips into a pool of water but avoided striking the sign of the cross. He asked Logan for the small vial Deimos had given them and filled it to the brim. Carefully, he closed it again, muttered something about the sign of the cross blocking the Third Eye in the act of baptism, and pressed the vial back into Logan's hand.

Logan accepts it as his gaze falls on the group of children sitting in the front pews. Some of them have pale red spots on their faces that itch and turn into little nodules. Others rub festering blisters and pustules on their arms and legs. Healthy children have also had to take their places among the sick ones. The anguished boys and girls are forced by priests and nuns to remain seated on their benches. A single photographer captures the oppressive scene on film.

Logan looks up at the north window of St. Mary's Cathedral. He sees a nun push a girl through it. Motionless, the child remains on the ground. Her playmate, who has witnessed the murder, freezes to stone. Tears roll down the cheeks of the Virgin Mary at the sight of the two children. The water collects in the reddish-brown baptismal font, which becomes a bathtub in a washroom. Two nuns put a girl in it, then throw several garter snakes into the bath water. Immediately the yellow-black snakes flee from the heat of the water onto the cooler human body. The child cries out in horror and tries to escape, but mercilessly the women push her back into the tub.

As Logan looks around, a priest approaches the boys' dormitory. He holds a can of Vaseline in his hand and pulls a child less than six years old out of the room. In the dormitory, the other boys press their faces into the pillows, afraid of the horror that could befall them and their sisters at any moment.

Logan falls to his knees. He lifts his head and stares at Jesus hanging on the cross. Blood beads from his body.

He feels a hand on his shoulder and turns his face toward the man crouched before him. The Black Wolf Chief's dark eyes rest on Logan as if the infinity of the universe is drawing him in. Again, the leader is clad entirely in black leather. With a casual sideways movement of his head, he shakes his waist-length hair out of his face. The Black Wolf Chief points to the desecrated body of Jesus on the cross. If Christians had followed the teachings of their own god, he says, there would have been no genocide. They used the Son of the Christian God to rule and to kill in his name. He carried a message of love and respect to the world. It was for all people. Even for the least among them. For this message he was nailed to the cross. For whoever tries to bring truth and love into your world, brother, challenges lies and darkness in the same breath. But the shadow cannot bear the light, and so religion and the Church itself became traitors to this man. They perverted his teachings.

What can I do? Logan asks, tears rolling down his face like torrents.

The Black Wolf Chief taps him gently against the chest. Follow your heart, brother, and act in the spirit of the greatest of our old leaders: Know yourself. Know your friends. Know the enemy. And lead the way!

Logan blinked. The Black Wolf Chief had described the legendary *Tȟašúŋke Witkó* — Crazy Horse — under whose leadership the U.S. Army had been routed at Little Big Horn.

The face from his vision gave way to Travis's worried countenance. He had crouched in front of his friend kneeling on the floor and was looking at him with a serious expression.

"Who did you see?"

Logan picked himself up and wiped the tears from his eyes. "My relative and old brother-friend, the Black Wolf Chief. The suffering endured by the countless children stolen from our families — in the death camps they called boarding schools."

The pain that settled on Travis's face was an eloquent sign of the force with which Logan's words had struck him. He held his friend by the arm and, despite his inner turmoil, drew on a well of peace that surprised Logan.

"Eshua Bolton."

Logan looked at him uncomprehendingly.

"A Murruwarri man from what is now known as New South Wales and Queensland. I heard him speak."

Logan settled into one of the back pews. The man he had chosen as younger brother was an old soul, and he guessed, even before Travis started to speak again, that he wanted to put hope alongside Logan's anger and despair.

"Eshua is a sound healer." Travis sat down next to him. "He told us that the horrific memories of the massacres, the rapes, the stolen generations, the desecration of sacred places, the erasure of our languages, our songs, our cultures, had driven him to numb himself with drugs and alcohol. He said he was well on his way to killing himself because he couldn't stand the pain anymore until the moment he literally had to choose death or life. He chose to live and began to study psychology. Eshua tried to dissolve the anger and sadness inside him. He studied until he was exhausted.

"One day he realized that *nothing* is really lost. He understood that on another level, *everything, really everything,* is remembered. From that moment on, he told us, he no longer had to blame anyone for the loss of his culture. No one had to apologize to him anymore. The moment he turned inward, he regained everything he thought he had lost. He says that each of us has access to what is remembered on the spiritual plain. Since then, he has arrived at a place in his life where retaliation and anger no longer have a place.

"He says if you go back far enough, everyone has indigenous roots. Again and again, peoples came from outside and took over the land of the original inhabitants, their ceremonies, their culture, their way of doing or not doing something. Even the British, Eshua says, once possessed an ancient earth culture. But the Romans occupied Britain and crushed the spiritual traditions of the Celtic tribes. Later, the British — and all other European colonial powers along with them — spread their own ancient trauma across the world.

"Eshua's words have touched my soul, Logan. Like him, you made a different choice a long time ago. Since we first met in Manly Beach, I have looked up to you and followed your example. Nothing was more life-threatening, you once said to me, than being *Lakȟóta* in your old homeland. Let me come with you and Tiya. At least for a while. As your friend. As a black ally. As someone who needs to learn, see the world, find his way, and heal his own wounds. How I would love to see Uŋčí again, and Phoebe, who was just a little girl the last time I saw her.

"The martial arts school you ran here with Nick and Stom — can't a similar project become a focal point for your youth on the reservation?"

Logan felt slain by Travis's words, and at the same time, as if he had been given a whole new set of ideas. "A martial arts school…" he muttered to himself, letting the sentence hang in the air. That was an interesting thought. "Tiya's had a crush on you from the start, little brother. I suspect she'd be thrilled to have you with us. Let me talk to her first, and I'll give you my answer later."

Upon their return to the Diamandis estate, Logan asked his friend to deliver the holy water to Deimos in his place. He had seen Nick's car parked in the driveway and read Tiya's message on his cell phone. Without detour, he made his way to his quarters in the east wing of the house, where his wife was waiting for him.

He sat down beside her on his sprawling king-size bed and pulled her into his arms. Perhaps he should have asked her how the evening had gone with the other women in Avalon Beach, but he wanted to keep the sandy-haired genie locked in her bottle and remained silent. Nor did he feel like giving an account of the little mission Deimos had sent him on. He did not want to give explanations or arouse suspicion, but he had to admit to himself that it was too late for that. When he had looked Zayla in the eyes for the first time in Avalon, the name *Kimímila* had burst out of him out of nowhere. That moment alone had been reason enough for Tiya to become suspicious.

What a fool he was.

With one hand he stroked Tiya's face. For him, she was the most desirable woman in the world. His fingers slid over her neck, her breasts, down to her belly, which still barely suggested pregnancy, and he smiled.

Grateful that she also refrained from asking questions, he lost himself with her in a rush of the senses. The happiness and satiety that seeped into his every cell as he later held her in his arms intoxicated him. "I love you, Tiya," he murmured. "More than you can imagine."

An expression of deep satisfaction was on her face, and she pressed herself against him. He would never jeopardize his relationship with this woman, never jeopardize the well-being of his new family. He could not understand why his wild determination to do the only right thing was joined by a soft cosmic laughter.

Chapter 14

Mystery Bay, New South Wales, Australia

Zayla had looked in vain for stores in Mystery Bay. Situated 350 kilometers south of Sydney, the town of just two hundred souls was a delight with its spectacular rock formations, picturesque bays and sandy beaches. Its two other assets were its natural camping area and the crime story after which it was named. Adjacent to Eurobodalla National Park, a wedding venue also sprawled over a 130,000-square-meter site that had access to a couple of private beaches. The bride and groom's guests had taken up quarters in the cottages and vacation homes on and around the site.

After a lively party, Tahnee and Nick said goodbye to their guests in the early evening and left for their honeymoon in Queensland. Zayla, who had been immensely affected by the many people and the hustle and bustle of the wedding party, pressed her fingers to her forehead and temples.

"That bad?" asked Tahnee as she said goodbye to her cousin.

"You know how it is with me," Zayla replied with feigned nonchalance. "Empaths perceive far too much around them. I had hoped I could filter my impressions better. Unfortunately, I didn't do so well. Instead, my head is now buzzing." She smiled.

Tahnee dug a headache pill out of her purse and handed it to Zayla. Nick called out to his wife, and Tahnee gave her cousin a big hug.

"Have a wonderful time," Zayla said.

"By the way," Tahnee whispered in her ear. "Nick didn't agree to K'gari in Queensland until I told him about the uniqueness of this longest sand island in the world. His choice would have been the Caribbean or the Cyclades. But thanks to my detailed description of a wedding night on the edge of a rainforest that thrives on sand dunes two hundred meters above sea level, he reconsidered his list of favorites after all." She put her head back and laughed. Then she stroked Zayla's cheek. "You need another man, cousin! Preferably someone not so much older than you. How about a younger partner who doesn't take life so seriously and can make you smile again?"

Zayla flinched. Did her misery show so clearly? "Please don't worry about me," she waved off.

Aunt Florence stepped toward the cousins and hugged Tahnee tightly. Her daughter smiled at this unusual outburst of emotion. Without pathos, she broke free from her mother's embrace and ran across the grassy grounds and under the circling rotor blades of the helicopter to Nick, who helped her to her seat. The bride and groom waved to the cheering crowd of guests and flew north with their bodyguards.

Tahnee had told Zayla about the heated arguments that had broken out between Deimos and his sons on the subject of personal security. Zayla could understand the tycoon's position all too well. If her own child had once fallen victim to a kidnapping, she would behave the same way. She put her hand on her belly. Only with Marrock's spawn here, she might have applauded when it disappeared, she mused bitterly, immediately castigating herself with contempt for this thought.

She linked arms with her aunt, who was tearfully watching the bride and groom's helicopter, and pulled her toward the festival grounds. Already from afar, at the edge of the eucalyptus trees of the Eurobodalla National Park, she saw her father standing with her Uncle Yarran. She guided her aunt to them, engaging her in a long conversation about her art gallery and the past years on the Red Continent. The sonorous bass with typical Australian intonation, which Zayla heard even before she could turn her head and identify its owner with her eyes, made her body hum like a crystal glass, its edge being rubbed with a wet finger.

"You seem to be doing much better tonight, Professor!"

She saw that Nick's father had joined her family with Travis and Carl in tow. True power is passive, she thought as she watched Deimos. True power required no force, no intimidation, perhaps not even manipulation. A truly powerful man controlled the world by his presence alone — and, if necessary, by the word he knew how to wield like a fighter his weapons. There was no trace of the dark power of the Templar, the Magian, the ancient Greek mystic, or the Druid scholar of three evenings before. Deimos was like a shapeshifter. The face the tycoon presented to the world was completely different from the one he had shown Zayla at her father's sickbed.

"Fortunately, yes," Professor Kirkpatrick replied. "Thanks to the remarkable doctor you had sent to me, Mr. Diamandis."

Deimos smiled meaningfully, probably remembering what had actually relieved the professor of his suffering, and his gaze settled on Zayla. Under its tremendous weight, she lowered her eyes and caught a spot below Deimos's collarbone. The edge of a tattoo peeked out. Was it the beginning of something written?

The tycoon's skin possessed neither the pale whiteness of her father nor the ebony tone of her uncle Yarran, but a dark bronze hue. His eyes were jet black, as was his thick hair, which was streaked with a few gray strands. The Australian's Iranian-Greek ancestry stood out clearly on the outside. He had discarded his tuxedo jacket in the warm summer night and wore a pale silk shirt, sleeves rolled up, with dark gray trousers, attire that did little to conceal his athletic body and muscular arms.

The scholar's pale skin and slightly stooped posture made her father appear older next to Deimos. The tycoon and Uncle Yarran, on the other hand, appeared younger than they were. Both seemed to be bursting with strength and virility.

Aunt Florence, too, was still an attractive woman. Zayla sensed the melancholy that had settled on Tahnee's mother since she stood between her niece and her ex-husband, whom she still loved. To Zayla's delight, Florence's despondency did not seem to have escaped Deimos's notice, for he paid her compliments so bold that they visibly attracted the attention of Uncle Yarran. Deimos's words put a glow on her aunt's face that she would not lose again that evening, and Zayla silently thanked him for paying her such attention — even though she understood that his gallantry was, in a roundabout way, equally directed at herself.

After some time, the tycoon switched places with her aunt and moved to Zayla's side. She breathed his scent of moss and cedar deep into her lungs, and the heat of his body made her burn up like a smoldering comet.

"Look!" Deimos extended his right arm and pointed to a bird of prey with dark gray wings and white tail feathers that soared above the treetops of Eurobodalla National Park. His left hand rested on Zayla's back, and he gently turned her in the direction where he had spotted the animal. "White-bellied sea eagles mate for life," he explained.

And only she, Zayla hoped, heard his breath catch as it tempted her to play with fire and nestle her body against his touch.

Travis gave her a surprised look. He seemingly had not missed the highly charged moment.

"Do you know the myth about Mystery Bay, Professor?" asked Deimos, his fingers stroking Zayla's back. Then he withdrew his hand and longing flooded her.

"So far, no, but I'm dying to know more, Mr. Diamandis."

"Deimos," suggested the tycoon. "If it's all right with you, Professor."

Matthew Kirkpatrick nodded. "Of course."

The two men shook hands.

Deimos told of the British geologist Lamont Young and his shady German assistant Maximilian Schneider, who had been sent in 1880 to the Montreal Goldfield, which was less than twenty kilometers south of where the small group now stood. "Young's and Schneider's job was to report back on what the gold discovery was all about," Deimos recounted. "They arrived at the gold fields and returned to their camp at Bermagui, but then all trace of them was lost. Witnesses saw their boat sail north with three other men. But their crew was never seen again either. The boat was later found on a rocky reef with Young's and Schneider's belongings inside. Despite countless investigations and even more speculation as to what might have happened to the two and their crew, attempts are still being made today to unravel the mystery of Mystery Bay and explain the disappearance of the men. However, many questions remain unanswered: For example, the boat was found in a place where it could not possibly have drifted on its own. So, if there was an accident and it happened at sea, how could the boat navigate through the rocks without a crew?

"Also discovered were supplies and a revolver bullet. A pair of glasses lay on one of the seats. None of it had gotten wet, so the boat could not have been flooded by seawater. The bullet casing was found nearby on the beach. But neither the crew nor the two geologists were known to carry weapons. There were also boulders in the boat. Holes had been cut in the walls from the inside. What for? Where had the anchor and the sail gone? And if the men had indeed been murdered, why were there no signs of a struggle?"

"What a fascinating story that gave its name to this beautiful place here."

Zayla turned her head and saw a pretty blonde woman with an athletic figure walking with her partner toward the small group. Deimos introduced the couple as guests of his son. The young woman was a university friend of Nick's named Michaela. At the same moment, Bree, Deimos's assistant, appeared and took the tycoon aside. He excused himself and promised to return.

Michaela revealed that she recognized Zayla's uncle and cousin from the media. She and her partner were full of praise for Carl's performance at the past *Rip Curl Pro* at Bells Beach in the state of Victoria, where they had been among the spectators. As avid amateur surfers, they offered great respect for his victory in one of the world's most important competitions for professional surfers. On the sidelines of the *Rip Curl Pro,* Carl had expressed solidarity with the protests against racially motivated police violence in a well-received interview.

"The death of the African-American Jay Duke is truly tragic," Michaela commented, recalling that interview. "The police violence cannot be justified by anything. But you still have to be allowed to say that Duke did not have a clean slate, but had a criminal record that reads like something out of a gangster movie: aggravated robbery, resisting law enforcement, drug abuse ..."

"Are you suggesting that he deserved to die?" Carl's eyes narrowed to slits. Travis tugged gently at his arm. Carl, however, shook him off like an annoying fly. Zayla felt Travis's sense of humiliation, and it cut her to the heart.

"No," Michaela replied calmly. "Of course Jay Duke did not deserve to die. And it was altogether wrong for a police officer to hold him in a chokehold for minutes so that he couldn't breathe. But he wasn't entirely innocent. He was under the influence of methamphetamines when he was arrested and could have caused trouble for police."

Carl became indignant. "Whether Duke was high on meth is by no means clearly established. Anyway, we have enough of our own Jay Duke moments here in Australia, but unfortunately not the media attention these cases attract in the U.S. 43 million African Americans there, only 800,000 First Nation people here. We have no Obamas, no Beyoncé, no Michael Jordan and no Oprah Winfrey. The words of our black stars count for little compared to those of the Americans. People like you, Michaela, need to finally open your eyes and realize the deep-rooted racist structures we still live in around the world."

Michaela sighed and turned to Carl's father. "Yarran, you are an excellent journalist. Doesn't it strike you as odd, on the other hand, that right-wing militias were discovered in the protest movements, hoping to spark a civil war in the United States? Or that neo-Nazis were called upon to attack blacks in order to start a race war? Besides, what police officer would allow a passer-by to film him at close range abusing a black detainee? Doesn't this all reek of deliberate incitement to racial unrest?"

"Even if you insist on seeing it that way, the basic problem remains the same," Yarran replied coolly. "Systemic racism — in the police, in the job market, in health care, combined with a legal system that is more likely to track down blacks than whites, more likely to classify their actions as crimes, and more likely to punish them harshly for them, even for banalities like not paying parking tickets, because, after all, they often don't have the money to do so. As for Jay Duke himself, Michaela, as a well-educated woman, you should have learned what *framing* means."

Yarran paused meaningfully and looked down at the young woman. "A story, Michaela," he overemphasized her name again, "is given a new frame of meaning. With the help of omitting all the content that does not fit into the new narrative, the reader or the audience is manipulated. Duke is reduced to a criminal in the reports you have read, the rest of his life completely blanked out. The protest movements are reinterpreted into organizations that worship a criminal. The real goal, which is to raise awareness of racism, is thus taken out of focus."

Michaela seemed unconvinced. Zayla admired the calm and the clarity with which both her uncle and Michaela stood up for their respective convictions. She sensed how deeply assured they both were of their positions. Zayla herself was too little interested in politics to be able to decide on which side of the debate she should have fallen.

"These movements are just being used," argued Michaela. "Their masterminds are not at all concerned with equal rights or self-empowerment for a black population. On the contrary, they are being instrumentalized across the board."

Carl's eyes bored irritably into the young woman's and he began a new line of argument. "African Americans make up twelve percent of the adult population in the United States, but they make up *thirty-three* percent of the U.S. prison population. Did you know that?" he asked, upset. "Here in New South Wales, one in four prison inmates is Aboriginal, but we only account for fifteen percent of the crimes." Zayla noticed Travis making another effort to influence Carl. His whispered suggestion that controversial topics of conversation had better be left out of Nick and Tahnee's wedding reception infuriated Carl enough that he snapped at him, "Just because you don't have the balls to stand up for your own political beliefs and your own heritage doesn't mean you have to try to silence me, too!"

Zayla saw Travis flinch. He hung his head, turned away from his partner, and walked away. Zayla followed him.

"You two would be a more suitable couple anyway," Carl goaded them. "Too bad for you, cousin. If you were a man, you might be some serious competition for me."

Zayla ignored him, but she heard both her uncle and her father express their displeasure at this altercation. Far away from her family and hidden from the prying eyes of other guests, she embraced Travis.

"Carl has a point, I'm afraid," he sighed. "I'm one of those people pleasers who can't confront others very well. Even when it comes to issues that are important to me."

Zayla stroked his dark, curly hair. "I don't agree with that opinion at all. Carl has more of a doer and aggressor in him than you, that's certainly true. You're more sensitive and don't act out your aggressiveness as much as he does. But you have clear positions, which you also represent. Just maybe not always publicly. And you formulate them more carefully."

He gave her a kiss on the forehead. "I don't want to waste my life thinking that everything that doesn't go my way has only to do with the fact that I'm half Aboriginal. I have no desire to feel oppressed and subjugated 24/7 because I'm black. There's no power or self-empowerment in that kind of attitude."

Travis suddenly lifted his head as Michael Jackson's *They Don't Care About Us* rang out from the dance floor. "How appropriate!" he grinned, his body immediately moving to the beat of the music. He grabbed Zayla by the hand. "Dance with me!"

Zayla hesitated, but then she let herself be carried away by his enthusiasm for the music. She released her inhibitions, let him pull her onto the dance floor and lost sight of her surroundings.

When Michael Jackson's protest song was followed by

Beyoncé's *Naughty Girl*, Travis pulled her closer to him. As if in a trance, she went along with his movements, which he dictated with light pressure, his hands firmly placed on her hips. He was a good dancer and Zayla enjoyed the sensuality of the moment. She delighted in the security Travis offered her as a friend, not a lover, allowing her to play with a hidden part of her femininity, and admired the grace with which he moved to the beat of the music. Beyoncé sang of female lust and sexual conquest. Zayla surrendered to the rhythms of Arabic music, funk, and reggae, and danced herself into a frenzy of deep emotion with Travis.

To the sounds of Christina Aguilera's *Get Mine Get Yours,* her hymn to fulfilled sensual love without obligations, and Beyoncé's *Beautiful Liar,* Travis, who adored both singers, was at his dancing best. The spectacle they offered over the course of a whole chain of rhythmically erotic pop, soul and contemporary R&B songs was only realized by them when they caught the gazes of the bystanders, who were glued to them like prey animals to Australia's carnivores.

"Shit!" exclaimed Travis. "I guess we caused a little bit of a stir."

Zayla spotted Carl at the edge of the dance floor. His eyes gleamed with the anger of the betrayed. Ashamed, she disengaged from Travis's arms and ran away. On her way to the bathrooms, where she hoped to lock herself in and hide from the world for a while, she bumped into, of all people, Logan's wife.

"My goodness, girl!" Tiya smiled at her. "What dancers you two are. I thought you were a shy and reserved one. But this ... my gosh!"

Zayla muttered something about having drunk too much, and Tiya laughed good-naturedly.

"You certainly don't have a drop of alcohol in you."

Zayla felt herself gaining color, and Tiya made no move to

release her from her embarrassment but eyed her closely. "By the way, my husband swears he can't remember what he said to you on Avalon Beach. Do you remember?"

Zayla froze. "Tiya, I …" She ran her hands through her disheveled hair. "I …" She faltered again. "I can't control what I see. I can't control what I hear and feel. I can't control whether it's unpleasant for others. I can't even control whether it's unpleasant for myself. All I can do is ask whether someone wants to know about what I perceive or not."

Tiya looked at her uncomprehendingly. "Zayla, what do you want to tell me?"

Zayla swallowed, then took heart and said, "You didn't ask Logan about that night in Avalon. You didn't ask him about what he said to me there either. You want an answer from *me* and not from him at all."

She saw acknowledgement flash in Tiya's eyes, and a smirk settled on her face. "Are you going to tell me the truth, then?"

Zayla heaved a sigh. "If you give me enough time to do it and your husband doesn't interrupt us."

"Deimos and Bree are having a conversation with Logan." Tiya pointed with one hand in the approximate direction where the three were standing. "I'm not quite sure what it's about, but it seems to be going on longer. Shall we sit down a little away from the others?"

Zayla agreed, and the two women left the bathroom. Tiya pointed to one of the garden swings at the edge of the wedding grounds from which one could look out over the sea. She started to move, but Zayla held her by the arm.

"Tiya, you must know that I make no claim whatsoever that what I see and feel is a reality that you or any other person can relate to."

Tiya looked at her intently.

"If you really want to hear what I have to say," Zayla continued, "then you have to understand that I'm only going to reproduce what I receive in terms of images and feelings. I'm not going to add anything to it, but I'm not going to sugar coat anything either."

"Now you're making me curious," Tiya admitted, pulling Zayla behind her.

At the cliffs, they settled on the largest and most comfortable of the three all-white garden swings. Zayla looked out to sea and heaved another sigh. What had she gotten herself into?

Finally, she pulled herself together and calmly told Logan's wife about the regression with her father and the killing of the Black Wolf Chief just before the Canadian border. Zayla let Tiya partake in her lucid dream at Mount Rushmore and the scene on the North American Great Plains that she had shared with Travis in Brighton. Finally, with her eyes closed and her head glowing, she even hinted at the images that had risen within her on Avalon Beach when she had first met Logan.

"My gosh," Tiya stared at her. "You even saw the Black Wolf Chief, Phoebe and Uŋčí?"

"Phoebe and Uŋčí? Are those the names of the girl and grandmother at Mount Rushmore? Their names didn't appear in my lucid dream."

Tiya seemed stunned. "These are deep and very old connections you share with them," she said.

"Tiya, I swear to you by all that I hold sacred: it is not my intention to come between you and your husband."

Tiya laughed out loud. "I believe you. But even if you wanted to go for him, you wouldn't stand a chance, little one. Logan loves me. I have no doubt in my mind that he would never give up on me or his unborn child."

"Oh!" Zayla looked up. "You're pregnant, too? Congratulations!"

"Pregnant, *too*? Are you ...?"

Zayla gritted her teeth and made a dismissive gesture. "That's a story that doesn't belong here."

Tiya eyed her closely. "Logan seems to be connected with a memory of what your soul embodied for him in a past time. It was impossible to ignore back on Avalon Beach. Your connection is too old to disregard. So, it would help me a lot, Zayla, if we didn't have to see you again. And Logan, too, I'm sure."

These last two remarks cut Zayla right in the heart. She liked Tiya very much and would have loved to have a person like her as a friend. But as if guided by an invisible hand, the two women had been pitted against each other in one fell swoop as supposed competitors for the same man. Zayla shook her head. The old social programming ran deep.

"I thank you for your honesty." Tiya rose and stroked her belly. "But you're in my way, unfortunately. I hope you can understand that."

Zayla felt a lump in her throat and her stomach clenched. There was no malice in Tiya's words, no hostility in her eyes. Yet her message was clear: Zayla did not belong. She might carry memories from another time that connected her to Logan, Phoebe, and Uŋčí, but she didn't belong with them. No matter how Zayla spun it, her abilities pushed her further and further into the role of outsider. She felt like a leper.

"I still wish you well." Tiya nodded to her once more. Then she strode away, leaving the young Englishwoman alone with her thoughts.

Zayla pulled her legs up and rocked her body back and forth, without stopping, like a perpetual motion machine. She listened to the soft squeak of the garden swing and dozed off, her head on her knees. The balmy wind blowing from the sea across the huge wedding grounds dried her tears.

When she registered the buzzing of her cell phone, she was surprised to discover that it was already well past midnight. Had no one missed her for all those hours? She winced as she realized that Marrock had tried to reach her another dozen times. Giving in to anger and despair, she hurled the phone over the cliff, down into the sea. For a few moments, she bathed in a sense of freedom and detachment. She was 17,000 kilometers away from London. On the other side of the world and at a different time, she would have been safe from him here with no cell phone and no air travel. She could have started a new life in Australia.

"Miss Kirkpatrick!"

Zayla looked up and recognized Bree McDowell, Deimos's personal assistant.

"I've been looking all over for you. Did you just throw your cell phone into the ocean?"

Zayla shook her head.

Bree frowned and held out her own phone. "He wants to talk to you."

Her heart stopped for a beat.

"Zayla," she heard a familiar voice say on the other end of the line. The reverence this man put into the two syllables that made up her name went through her like a bolt of lightning.

"Forgive me this thief-in-the-night game. Will you follow Bree?"

Zayla closed her eyes and forced herself to breathe. She pushed the phone back into Bree's hand. "Where is he?"

Wordlessly, Bree led her a little further along the cliffs to the place where a steep wooden staircase led down to one of the private beaches. In the distance, she recognized the outlines of three people.

"The other two men are his bodyguards," Bree explained to her. "They will make sure that you two are safe here and that your privacy is protected."

Zayla's eyes rested on the tycoon, who stood like a pillar of salt in the surf and kept his gaze fixed on the sea. She descended the wooden stairs to the beach and her long, dark hair fluttered in the wind.

Deimos was wearing the same clothes as a few hours earlier. He had rolled up his trouser legs and left his shoes and socks in the sand. When she had come within inches of him, he turned and laughed softly to himself. "I've been waiting for this moment my whole life. The images I've had since I was a boy of the former Templar's mate, and of the sandy-haired woman driven mad on the snow-blown northern Plains, have haunted me night after night into my dreams." He sighed, "You weren't even born when I started looking for you."

"Only my body is still so young," Zayla defended. "My soul is as old as yours."

Deimos stroked her face tenderly with his fingertips. "You are only just regaining your old strength, love of so many of my lives, while I am almost running out of time again. You have not yet regained complete access to your true self."

Knowing that she had dwindled to a shadow of herself, she lowered her eyes. She picked up on the leaden grief that Deimos felt at the loss of her great power, and a sense of longing and deep connection with him came over her.

"It seems to me that you are coated in a thick black slime," he said, his hands rummaging through her hair, "in which you are stuck like a bird in an oil slick. What was it that could put such a magnificent creature as you in this deplorable condition?"

Zayla leaned her head against his chest and began to cry, unrestrained and without shame. Deimos stroked her head, her neck, her back. Like a father with his daughter, he held her in his arms until her tears had ebbed away, wordlessly and without making promises. Since she had no handkerchief with her, she turned her back on him after a while and freed herself in the salt water from the snot that had run down her nose. Then she turned back to him. "How do I look?"

Deimos laughed. "What do you want me to say?"

Zayla slapped his upper arm. "Whether the makeup is dripping down my face, for example. Or whether I still have snot hanging from my nose." She was surprised herself at the remarkable familiarity she felt with him. The complete absence of shame or the need to put herself in the right light inspired and liberated her.

Deimos looked at her with feigned horror. "You're lucky, my love, that it's the middle of the night." He gestured toward the sky. "As soon as the moon peeks out from behind this cloud cover, I'll take a closer look at your face just in case."

He pulled her with him into the sand and they sat down facing each other. Deimos had his legs drawn up and his arms rested on his knees. Decorum forced Zayla to bend her legs sideways and cross them. For a moment she toyed with the idea of abandoning all propriety and presenting herself to this man in a deeply provocative manner that he could only understand as an invitation. The desire to give herself to him shook her.

"Tell me what happened to you."

Zayla was grateful for Deimos's diversion, and in the same way she would have talked to her best friend about the past year, she told him about Marrock. About the images of the murder at Hollow Pond that had risen in her mind when the banker had first touched her there. Of how much she and her father had become entangled in his web. She told him that she didn't share Travis's assessment that Marrock might be responsible for the black magic attack on her father, and that she was carrying the banker's child. Deimos hissed between his teeth, and Zayla felt how much that last sentence had hit him.

"Logan's and my soul were once Travis's parents," it still burst out of her and tears sprang to her eyes again. But this time, she swallowed them back. "Travis lived in the avatar of a girl whose parents would have given their lives not to lose their children to the European conquerors."

"The Stolen Generations?"

Zayla nodded.

"Was Logan the Native warrior you saw killed at Hollow Pond?"

Zayla shook her head. "I believe it was the death of his relative, the Black Wolf Chief, but from a different perspective than the one I saw when my father did the regression with me back then. In it, I had also seen the Colonel ..." She looked at Deimos for a long time. "I wished for his death then. Is that the reason you adopted Logan? Because the Colonel was hunting the Black Wolf Chief? Because *you* had brought guilt upon yourself?"

Deimos shook his head. "It was war. The Colonel was only doing his duty. The Black Wolf Chief was his enemy, but he did not hate him. On the contrary. He held him in high regard."

"Duty, you mean? I don't know ... The Colonel could have refused."

Deimos snorted softly. "That was not an option. Not as a soldier. Not in war. It's more relevant now for me to know what made *you* get involved with his killer, of all people."

Zayla froze, grasping the truth in front of her. "Marrock?"

"Who else? You didn't realize that? You described the murder yourself. Did this guy make you so dull that you couldn't put one and one together?"

Zayla struggled to her feet. "Oh God!" she cried out into the night. "Oh God! How is this possible?" She grabbed her stomach, feeling as if she had the devil's spawn inside her.

Deimos's gaze followed her gesture. "We can find you an excellent gynaecologist in Sydney," he suggested.

"Oh God!" cried Zayla again, shaking. "I don't want it! But I can't kill it either!" She ruffled her hair. "Deimos, I don't trust my father anymore."

Zayla's thoughts were all over the place. She couldn't believe she was saying out loud what she hadn't even admitted to herself yet.

"Marrock controls him almost completely. Instead of me, now even he proofreads and edits his research results ... They think I'm a nervous wreck. Both of them. He almost deprived me of my friendship with Travis, too."

Deimos pulled her close and stroked her cheek with the back of his hand. "Life in the bodies of the Australian First Nations family, is it the only life you remember with my son?"

Zayla shook her head. "When Travis sent Logan to Avalon Beach to take me to my father, he called me Kimímela there ..."

"Butterfly."

Zayla looked at him in wonder.

"I learned a few fragments of *Lakȟóta* from my son. A bloody complicated language," he answered her unspoken question with a laugh.

Zayla blinked. "Logan saw in me at Avalon Beach the sandy-haired woman you also recognized, but he is not the Black Wolf Chief. The warrior in my vision who made the sandy-haired girl his wife was definitely not the Black Wolf Chief. Logan is his biological great-grandson, but Logan's soul did not live in the body of the Black Wolf Chief. I am sure of that. How could the sandy-haired woman have been the wife of both men, Deimos? And what was she to the Colonel?"

"The Colonel wanted you and could not have you," Deimos

replied calmly, smiling at her. "The former Templar and Mage loved the daughter of the High Priestess, but his happiness with you was short-lived. I want you, but you are still too young, too girlish. You are still only an adolescent."

Zayla felt a twinge.

"You will first have to wade out of the mud, Queen of my heart, in which you have gone swimming. Besides, I counted on many things, but not on competing for you with one of my sons."

"What are you talking about?"

"Your connection to Logan is strong. There's no denying that." The smile Deimos gave Zayla was a beautiful, open one that went to her heart and, to her surprise, was free of jealousy. "My son has made his choice. He married Tiya because he loves her. He will not give in to the feelings he has for you. Not only so as not to jeopardize his marriage, but also because he is struggling to find his identity as *Lakȟóta.*

"The twelve years here in Australia have enriched his life as much as they have diluted his identity of origin. That he became my son was an indispensable experience for him to broaden his own horizons, to raise the reference line from which he can now operate upon his return to the reservation. That his time here could be an important piece of the puzzle on his way back to himself and his true greatness, I suspected even when I took him under my wing as a fourteen-year-old. But the years with us here in Australia have also made him an outsider in his old homeland. And an object of envy. Logan has become a wanderer between many worlds. Here lies his vulnerability as much as his strength and his uniqueness."

Zayla heard the deep respect that was in Deimos's words. He loved and cherished his adopted son very much.

"But the world whose call he feels most strongly right now, and to which he wants to return, is in the U.S., and it is with his family of origin. What he wants is a woman from the culture he was born into. A woman who understands what it means to be of American-Indigenous descent. No non-native woman could ever do that for him."

He looked at her for a long time and Zayla leaned against his body. He gently stroked her shoulders and back. She felt the slime and poison water with which Marrock had defiled her drain away. For a moment, she stood freed from the web of steel silk threads in which the banker held her captive.

"Before the ugly funnel-web spider catches its prey again," Deimos murmured sadly, as if he could read her thoughts, and kissed her on the forehead.

Zayla shook her head. "Sleep with me," she whispered, surprised by her own courage and fired by the urge to absorb all of this man's energy. The only one who would have succeeded in washing her clean of Marrock in any way imaginable.

Deimos hissed like a cornered cobra. "Zayla!" That one word sounded like a prayer. "I will help you with whatever I can provide." He pulled her close to him. "But I'm not going to sleep with you tonight." His words were harsh and passionate at the same time. "I want back the daughter of the high priestess I once knew," he declared solemnly. "I want a woman, not a girl. I want the queen in my bed, not the wounded deer. I want the goddess in all her glory, free of the killer's imprints. I want the prudent, confident huntress who won't let anyone keep her down." He lifted her chin and looked into her eyes for what felt like an eternity. "For that privilege, I am willing to wait and pay a very high price." He stroked her cheeks. "Find your way back to your old power, Zayla. Break free from this sticky web the killer has spun around you. And above all, decide what you want to do with your child. I will support you as best I can. When you have detached yourself from the murderer and finally stand before me as a woman and no longer as a girl, I will lay my heart and with it the whole world at your feet."

Deimos's words both moved and hurt Zayla. They stirred memories of an ancient power within her. They gave her the impetus to pick herself up and once again take care of her wounds herself. But his words also dripped hot wax on her open flesh. Zayla tormented herself with the realization that the tycoon saw something in her that she might not have had access to after the six months she had let Marrock trample all over her.

I want the queen in my bed and not the wounded deer. This sentence whipped her heart across the beach like the tentacles of a giant octopus. Deimos was on fire for her. With every fiber of her body, she could feel how much he desired her. And yet the tycoon had rejected her.

I want the queen in my bed, not the wounded deer.

The inner critic struck her with its full contempt. You are not good enough for him!

Embrace this pain, daughter, she suddenly heard her mother's gentle admonition in her head. *It is the only way.*

Chapter 15

London, United Kingdom

The first tuft of her thick, waist-length hair fell to the floor. The hairdresser behind her sighed and set for the second strands. Then the third fell, sliding down the black neo-cape that kept Zayla's street clothes free of hair and water residue, and dropped into her lap. She shook out the cape and the strands landed on the light gray tiles of the salon.

The young Englishwoman sat at a hairdressing table with a faux-leather chair and a gold-framed baroque mirror on the wall. In it, she observed that not only the face of the shopkeeper who cut her hair but also the faces of her employees contorted in horror. It seemed incomprehensible to them that their customer would want to part with such a beautiful head of hair, which the hairdressers had showered with praise since the moment she entered the salon, in this shockingly radical way. They had no idea that each tuft of hair that fell to the floor freed Zayla from the heavy burden of always catching eyes, but never really being seen.

When the salon owner brought over the electric hair clippers from the men's department and shaved her head, Zayla heard their groans and put on an ironic smile. She tapped the latest issue of a popular women's magazine next to her with her index finger.

"An article here recounts how actress Maggie Gyllenhaal was condescendingly told that, at 37 at the time, she was too old to be cast in the role of a 55-year-old man's mistress. Unbelievable, really. Out of this dehumanizing division of women into two categories — *fuckable* and *unfuckable* — my baldness will become the expression of another category: *unfuckwithable women.* Women who are at complete peace with themselves and who no amount of belittling or drama in the world can reach. That's where I want to go. And this," she pointed to her shorn head, "is just the beginning!"

The hairdressers looked at her disconcertedly and Zayla fell silent. The path to her described goal was long and her role as a bald rebel, she knew, was only a temporary second step there. The first had consisted of flushing Deimos's private cell phone number, which his assistant had slipped to her while still in Mystery Bay, down the toilet at Sydney airport. "I'll show you the *wounded deer,*" she had muttered stubbornly to herself as the paper had been caught by the whirlpool of water and dragged down into the sewer. But her inner voice whispered to her that she was just acting defiantly. In truth, she mused on the twenty-one-hour flight back to London, Deimos had done her a service that gold could not buy. He had provided a salutary impetus, placing her development to her full potential above the yearnings that had flooded them both in Mystery Bay. What man would have done this in a similar situation?

When you stand before me as a woman and no longer as a girl, I will lay my heart and with it the whole world at your feet.

What she construed as a rejection had, in reality, been a declaration of love. Deimos was willing to wait for her to re-emerge without succumbing in advance to the young Circe who had stood before him in Mystery Bay, alluring but unfinished. For the privilege of having the essence of the woman he had loved and adored in many incarnations back in his bed, he said, he was willing to pay a high price. She had felt the enormous strength it had cost him to renounce her, and yet she had inwardly stamped her feet. A desire caught fire in Zayla to one day meet the tycoon at eye level. But for such a goal, she first had to go inward, falling back on herself. The child she was carrying was an additional burden on her new path, and she didn't know how to get rid of the killer's spawn without destroying the new life.

Marrock was still in St. Thomas' Hospital after the knife attack by a lone assailant on London Bridge more than a week ago. When Zayla and her father visited him that afternoon, he bared his teeth at the sight of her nearly bald head. "My God, you're ugly!" he snapped after her father had left the room briefly, and Zayla smiled smugly. She sat down on the bed with him, grabbed his hand and scratched his skin with her fingernails, leaving red welts.

"Can't you get it up when you see me like this?" she whispered sweetly, facing the door. Any moment now, her father would return with coffee mugs for the three of them.

Marrock seethed.

"Oh, calm down," she murmured. "I'm sure my father has a few more students you can have fun with instead of me." She thought back to the moment when the Kirkpatricks had first visited the banker on the very day they returned from Australia. Her father had urged her to take that step, letting her go ahead alone at first so as not to disturb the young couple's 'reunion.' Upon Zayla's entry into Marrock's hospital room, an attractive brunette had jumped back from his bed as if bitten by a tarantula.

As they left the hospital after their second visit today, they encountered a middle-aged woman at the main entrance with two young girls holding hands. Zayla stared at the two as they passed. Marrock had shown her photos of his children at Hollow Pond, and she had a good memory for faces. Suspiciously, she asked her father to go ahead and scurried back to Marrock's hospital room. Heart pounding, she pressed her ear to the door and heard a woman's and two children's voices. She didn't understand every word but enough to conclude that it must indeed be Marrock's family.

The door opened a crack, and at the same moment Zayla jumped to the side, pulled her hoodie over her ears, and strolled with feigned nonchalance down the hall to the exit, she heard a woman say, "You need to come back home, Marrock. The girls miss you."

Zayla was in a daze.

Outside the hospital, her father looked at her thoughtfully and stroked her shaved head. "Was that really necessary?" he asked. So far, he had held back from commenting on her new appearance.

"Papa!" Zayla gently rebuked him. "What do you care if I have hair on my head or not? Marrock has made fools of us. Don't you realize that? Why can't you see it? Right now, his wife and children are sitting with him. And he may even be responsible for you collapsing in Australia."

"What are you talking about, child? What nonsense!" Her father pulled her close. "I was hoping your condition would finally improve. Of course Marrock's children are coming to see him. It was bad enough that we flew to Tahnee's wedding without him and left him in the hospital in London. Surely it's only right that his family should visit him. Do you really expect the kids to come over without their mother? I'm afraid he was right about you, dear. Your nerves, your extreme way of feeling, your hypersensitivity — it's all getting to you more than you realize. Mum's death... "

The way her father spoke to her gravely alarmed Zayla. It took all her strength not to panic. The only person she knew who was still safely on her side lived 17,000 kilometers away from her. Travis was planning to follow Logan and his wife to the U.S. for a while, and although this decision would reduce the physical distance between him and Zayla, the feeling of having to do without her best friend gnawed at her more and more.

In Mystery Bay, Deimos had offered to stand by her side with whatever she needed. And yet, after his rejection, she was reluctant to turn to him in a state of helplessness. She had never felt more upended than in that moment when the tycoon had compared her to a 'wounded deer.' She stood up. *Deimos also recognized the goddess in you, you twit!*

If she had expressed her desire to surrender to him from a position of strength rather than with her self-worth in the gutter, he would have given her the moon and the stars. This was a realization as powerful as it was tormenting, and it only propelled her on her new path.

"Let's go home first, Papa," she said, striving to present a calm and collected version of herself to her father. "I'm going to lie down for a bit. Maybe I'll feel better tonight."

The next day, as Professor Kirkpatrick went to his lectures at the university, Zayla looked in his study for the documents relating to her father's trust fund for her. After locating them, she threw some of her favorite clothes into a suitcase, hid it in her room, and headed for Marrock's apartment, to which she had a key.

As she charged his high-end tablet, which she had found with a dead battery between two sofa cushions, unease spread through her. She hoped the password was the same one she had seen Marrock enter on his phone time and time again: when she would sit next to him on the couch, she was able to see the letters as they flashed briefly across the screen, but she had kept that knowledge to herself.

Indeed! Both devices could be unlocked with the same password. Zayla didn't dare click through Marrock's files for fear it would give her away if they were saved under the day's current date after being accessed. Instead, she opened his browser and froze when, among the most recently visited pages, appeared the website of a couple who considered themselves practitioners and followers of *Satanic Black Magic*. The two had written several books on Satanism, remote viewing, and remote influencing and occasionally helped track down murderers. Zayla saw that the couple's books also contained powerful black magic curses and various suggestions to ensure the preservation of the satanically strongest. A chill ran down her spine.

Then her eyes fell on a video file with the name 'Selene.' In ominous foreboding, she forced herself to double-click.

An hourglass-shaped blonde squeezed into a bright red minidress with a bellybutton-deep neckline and sky-high fuck-me heels stalked through Marrock's apartment. She stopped in front of a photo of him holding Zayla in his arms and stroked her fingers over the homemade frame. "Is this that little lunatic you were telling me about?" she taunted.

Zayla heard Marrock's voice reply off screen. "A pretty but naïve girl with Borderline Disorder who is beginning to bore me."

The blonde smiled, pushed up her dress under which she apparently wore no underwear, and lasciviously leaned forward, resting her forearms on the bed. "How fortunate that you hadn't deleted your old fuck buddies from your contacts yet."

Zayla heard the opening of a zipper and the falling of clothes. Then a naked Marrock with the habitus of a Roman god of war strode into view. He grabbed the rear end offered to him with both hands and thrust into the blonde with such brute force that Zayla winced.

She threw the tablet into the corner and rushed out of the apartment. She wandered aimlessly around Canary Wharf, staring tearfully at its three skyscrapers: One Canada Square straight ahead, the HSBC Tower on her left, and the Citigroup Centre on her right.

At one point early in their relationship, Marrock had pulled her into the small park in front of One Canada Square and asked her to look up. The three towers rose into the sky around them like titans. It had been an awe-inspiring sight. Small and inconspicuous she had felt in the midst of these massive monuments that were emblematic of all that the Canary Wharf financial center represented.

"Standing here gives you a good sense of the true power of this place," Marrock had whispered to her, moving close behind her, and wrapping his arms possessively around her body. "Looking at the towers from this perspective gives you the feeling of standing in the middle of something meaningful. Something to which you are but a small cog in the machine, and which could crush you as easily as an ant." His hands had wandered lustfully down and up her body.

The banker had taken her to his home and, for the second time in their relationship, seduced her downward into a pitch-black erotic underworld. It was a descent that had filled Zayla with shame yet arousal, which deeply upset her.

She sighed. Fixing her gaze on Canary Wharf's skyscrapers, she vowed before her dead mother and her unseen helpers to give the banker's child up for adoption, to do everything she could to keep her father and herself safe from this man, and to destroy the Black Wolf Chief's killer.

On the way to the Tube station, however, she was overcome by her first doubts. With the exception of the video, she had only found circumstantial evidence, not proof. Her father thought highly of the banker and treated Zayla like a nervous patient. So what was the likelihood that he, who thought black magic was just a sham anyway, would believe her?

Her declarations that it had been due to an ancient ritual that had contributed to his recovery in Australia would be dismissed by her father as fantasy, and countless arguments would be found for Marrock's innocence. And the banker's wife and children? The two phrases Zayla had picked up at St. Thomas' Hospital — *You need to come back home, Marrock. The girls miss you* — were not enough to prove that the banker was leading a double life.

At Canary Wharf Station, Zayla changed from the westbound platform, from where she would have taken the Tube home, to the eastbound platform. Four stations down the line, she changed again for Leytonstone. From there, she walked quickly to Dorothea Nicols' house.

"Zayla!" cried Dorothea delightedly, but obviously surprised, and hugged the girl tightly. "How good it is to see you. What brings you to me?"

She invited Zayla into the living room and handed her a cup of tea. After some small talk, Zayla finally launched straight into what was on her mind. "Can I stay with you for a while, Doro?"

Dorothea frowned. "Are you in trouble with your father, child?"

Zayla shook her head. "No, but I need some distance from him and from Marrock to regain my composure. May I please stay with you for a few days? I don't know where else to go."

Dorothea nodded. "You are always welcome here, love. And I know you are of age, but please tell your father where you are anyway."

Zayla thanked her and headed back home to get her suitcase. Her father was still in a lecture. She left him a voice message asking him to leave her alone at Dorothea's for a while and to keep her whereabouts secret from Marrock at all costs. She was fine, she assured him, but needed distance from the banker. As she had expected, her father called her back shortly thereafter.

"Zayla, what's wrong with you? Why are you running away?"

"I can't be with Marrock any longer," she replied, feeling close to tears once again. "*Papa!*" She put all her despair about the situation she found herself in into that one word. "Papa ..." she whispered as she started to speak a second time. "Why don't you trust me anymore?"

"Zayla, child." She heard the dismay in her father's voice. "Of course I trust you. You are my heart and soul, you know that."

"Then why does Marrock get to read your research and not me? Why do you tell him I'm too young and inexperienced to follow in your footsteps? I have so much more skill and knowledge than he does — in all the areas that count and matter to you!"

"So that's what this is about? You're jealous?" Zayla noticed his disappointment and a hint of disdain.

"I'm not jealous, Papa." She tried to force herself to be calm, but she couldn't. Her voice was shaking, her heart pounding, tears were pouring from her eyes, and sweat was breaking out. "I don't understand why you're depriving me of everything we've built together since Mum died," she cried, sensing that while she was moving her father, she was also reinforcing his view that she had withered away to a shadow of herself.

Images of old mental hospitals appeared before her. Insane asylums, where those who had evaded the so-called age of reason had been incarcerated under inhumane conditions: delinquents and the unemployed, vagrants, the politically conspicuous, prostitutes, the physically handicapped, and the mentally ill and depressed alike.

"Marrock is the killer of the man the U.S. Army caught near the Canadian border, Papa! And he is in contact with black magicians. I found the evidence of it on his tablet!"

She heard a heavy sigh on the other end of the line. In her wildest dreams, she could not have imagined that her father, of all people, whom she loved so dearly and who had accompanied her all her life, supported her, admired her abilities and encouraged her, would deny his daughter the power of reason.

"Papa, I love you," she sobbed. "Please give me some time to calm down. And please don't tell Marrock where I am."

She hung up, turned off her cell phone, and cried herself to sleep.

Two days later, when Zayla returned to Dorothea's house after a long walk around Hollow Pond and Leyton Flats, she noticed her maternal friend had a visitor. Her inner alarm bells rang. Cautiously, she opened the front door and heard the voices of her father and Marrock, who had apparently been released from the hospital. The two men were sitting with Dorothea in the living room.

"I'm afraid that if Zayla's condition doesn't improve, we'll have to suggest self-admission to a psychiatric ward," she heard her father lament. "It breaks my heart, but my beloved child is only living in delusions."

"Yes," Marrock agreed. "She got it into her head that I was responsible for Matthew's breakdown in Australia, Dorothea. It's really beyond belief. She probably found the website of two black magicians on my tablet and drew her erroneous conclusions from it. The fact is that I have seen an interview with this couple, a BBC report on people with psychic abilities. Yes, I did research these two to get a better idea. But with their outrageous notions and narcissistic self-dramatizations, it is impossible to take them seriously. Completely misguided people. Two total failures. Still, they certainly made the TV ratings soar."

He paused dramatically, and Zayla sensed by the tone, rhythm, and cadence of his voice that he was lying. It surprised her how quickly her intuitive powers had returned. Was it because she had begun to stand up for herself instead of just rolling over? Was her soul applauding her for the path she had now taken, therefore unlocking all her channels of reception again? Or were there energies at work here that the killer's unseen aides would have to bow to — ones that had initially protected Marrock from her and Travis's intuitive grasp but were now pulling away as Zayla reunited with her ancient powers? Either way, she welcomed the resurgence of her abilities from the bottom of her heart.

"Sometimes Zayla struggles with clouding of consciousness," she heard Marrock say. "At such times, she thinks I'm a monster trying to drain her of her life force. Then she's like a cuddly kitten again, looking for attention. I love her, Dorothea, despite everything. Matthew knows that. Once her rational mind takes over, she's an incredibly impressive person and a charming young woman."

The hairs on the back of Zayla's neck stood up like the hackles on a cat in the mood to attack.

"When my ex-wife came to visit me in the hospital with my kids, Zayla must have lost it. She told Matthew I wasn't even divorced. Utter nonsense. Matthew has already seen my divorce certificate. I insisted on it."

"Well," Dorothea replied thoughtfully, "just leave Zayla with me for a few more days. I will try to influence her and send her back home. We should try to help her together. Staying in a psychiatric hospital can't be a solution to her problems, Matthew. Think about what this child has already been through."

"Doro," Zayla's father said, and she heard the desperation in his voice, "my daughter is my life, but I don't know how to help her anymore."

Dorothea turned to Marrock. "Zayla is full of panic regarding you. She came by a few months ago and poured her heart out to me. I had believed that the problem lay with you alone, but now I see that assessment can't be entirely correct. Perhaps her mother's death hit her harder than any of us thought. Perhaps it is this bottomless grief and disorientation that is speaking."

"I fear," said her father, "that it is also this shaky condition of having to live constantly in two worlds that makes it impossible for her to live a normal life. Her abilities are both a gift and a curse. There is an excellent colleague of mine working in a London clinic. Maybe she can help Zayla. She no longer listens to me but digs herself deeper and deeper into a view of this world that has nothing in common with reality. It breaks my heart." he repeated.

Zayla had heard enough and quietly retreated toward the front door. When she accidentally bumped into Dorothea's tray table in the hallway, she heard the three of them pause, and then Marrock curse.

"Zayla? Zayla!"

She whirled around and ran as if her life depended on it. She didn't dare go to the nearest Tube station for fear this would be the first place Marrock and her father would look. Instead, she boarded one of the red double-decker buses that was driving down the main street. All she had with her was her backpack, her purse, and a credit card. She booked a place to stay at a hostel in Kings Cross where she shared a room with four other women.

Shortly after checking in, she restlessly ran back out into the street and called Dorothea from her phone. "How could you betray me like that?" she scolded. "I trusted you, Doro!"

"Zayla, it was not my intention at all to disappoint you. Your father is terribly worried about you. I couldn't just turn him away."

"But you could listen to Marrock's stories about me and believe them, too! Don't you realize that he's only out to make me look like I've lost my mind?"

"You shouldn't have run away," Dorothea rebuked gently.

From that moment on, Zayla understood that she was on her own. She could expect help neither from Dorothea nor from her father. Both had succumbed to Marrock's charm and tall tales. Zayla's body became as hard as steel. Either she managed to keep her head above water now, or she went under. The cold anger that raged through her strengthened her resolve. She took a deep breath and let a silent battle cry travel through each of her cells.

"Doro, I need my things," she said frostily. "But I'm not coming back to Leytonstone for them. I ask you to give them to the cab driver I will send you."

"Don't you think you're overreacting, child?"

"You don't understand Marrock. You don't, and neither does my father. He will not keep his hands off me until there is nothing left of me. Since my decision to separate from him and step back into my own power, all my abilities that had fallen asleep are beginning to return. They are more powerful than ever before. I can read people again, Doro! Even Marrock. And in his presence, my blood freezes in my veins."

It was incomprehensible to her how she could have ever let herself be captured by him. What had made her so blind to the true nature of this man? But she felt very clearly that she could not yet oppose a soul sucker like him. Not until she succeeded in completely neutralizing the poison with which he had paralyzed her. Not until she had gotten rid of his spawn. Not until she found her way back to the center of her ancient powers.

"He's manipulating you, Dorothea, just as he manipulated Papa and me. I don't know how to protect him and his work from Marrock. Look after him if you can, please. My job is to land on my own two feet first before I can possibly do anything for my father."

Zayla ended the call and removed the SIM card from her phone. She felt like she was on a long-haul flight where the oxygen masks had fallen from the ceiling because of the drop in pressure. Zayla would have had to put them on herself first before she could help her father.

She walked down the street and bought a prepaid card from one of the few providers that didn't require her to register her contact information. She wanted to remain undetected as long as possible.

At times, she doubted herself again. But then she realized that she felt more relaxed and cheerful. She felt the tough, wafting absorbent cotton wool that had clogged so many of her channels of reception continue to dissipate. Zayla registered that not only were her metaphysical abilities returning, but so were her thinking and judgment skills, and the first of her body's trauma debris was in the process of being removed. She was on a new path and her soul was jubilant. In this situation, where she would live from hand to mouth and had to learn to trust herself and the world again, she enjoyed to the fullest the powers that now carried her. Her decision to leave Marrock and her father as well as to become independent of Deimos's support seemed to have a liberating effect on her entire nervous system.

She stood on the forecourt of King's Cross St. Pancras Tube Station, which was overflowing with people. Despite the stuffy car exhaust around her, she sucked the air deep into her lungs.

It was quite amazing what Deimos's words had triggered in her. She appreciated the clarity with which he had shown her who she really was and felt relief at having escaped Marrock's grasp for the time being. But the thought of her father pained Zayla greatly, as did the possibility that Marrock might make him pay for letting her slip away. But what was she to do? If the banker learned of her pregnancy, he would try even harder to chain her to him. Her father would also drive her back into his arms.

Child, you need a man and a family of your own to hold you and give you security when I am gone. He meant well, but he didn't understand what a master of the black arts the two of them had gotten involved with.

Over the next few weeks, Zayla changed her accommodations several times. In the fourth hostel, close to the British Museum, she encountered a middle-aged woman at the reception desk one morning who asked to be allowed to post a flyer for women in need. Zayla, who was about to check out of the hostel to cover her tracks, paused. She looked at the stranger intently. Something in her eyes seemed familiar. But no images or information emerged that would have helped her place her. Nevertheless, Zayla had the overwhelming feeling that fate was speaking to her. The decision, however, was hers. Continue straight ahead or change direction?

"I'm Hope," the woman with a fiery red head of curls introduced herself and offered Zayla a flyer. "We organize open meetings for women in need," she said, her eyes twitching over Zayla's belly. "For pregnant women. For rape victims. For victims of narcissistic abuse." She spoke with a Scottish accent and met Zayla's surprised gaze with a smile. How did Hope know she was carrying a child? Her pregnancy was far from obvious to an outsider.

"*Hope's Safe Haven,*" Zayla read on the flyer she had accepted.

"A place where we meet regularly," Hope explained. "It's a small apartment that we rent. It's a safe albeit temporary haven for women in need and for sharing with each other. We also refer people for further help, and we host regular evening talks. I am the founder of Hope's Safe Haven, as you have probably guessed. Many good souls work for me, all as volunteers. What we can pay them often doesn't even cover their expenses, but they still come — from all over. Psychologists, social workers, doctors, therapists, alternative practitioners, healers, priests, shamans. They come because they find their work with us meaningful and because we hold a space that nurtures the souls of *all* women. All we ask is that you register in advance because space is limited. This is our phone number."

Hope pointed to the flyer. The address given next to the phone number was in north London. The nearest Tube station was Holloway Road, very close to Emirates Stadium, home of one of England's most successful football clubs: Arsenal F.C.. A strange place for an institution that was supposed to serve as a refuge for women, Zayla thought.

The first evening of conversation, which she attended with a pounding heart, took place two days later on the top floor of a building above a busy computer shop. In a round of beanbags and colorful wool blankets, Zayla sat in close quarters with eight other women and three cats who belonged to Hope: Porsche, an intelligent and immaculately groomed Persian cat; Alex, a feral street stray; and Smoky, a jet black and cuddly British shorthair. All three had taken to being near Zayla in no time and stayed there purring with pleasure for most of the evening.

After a small tea ceremony designed to welcome the women and support the inner serenity of those arriving, Zayla listened to Hope's response to a participant's question about the difference between a pathological narcissist and a player.

"Well," Hope began thoughtfully, "unlike a player, a narcissist may well succumb for a while to the belief that he has found his ideal mate in you, Ruby. At the beginning of a new relationship, you are like a drug to a narcissist. You provide him with admiration, validation, and recognition. This is what we call 'narcissistic supply.' When it comes to a malignant and particularly dangerous narcissist, characteristics of the *dark triad* come into play: narcissism is joined by Machiavellianism and psychopathy. Sometimes sadism is added. Malignant narcissists are shapeshifters, superior manipulators and extremely toxic people who know exactly how to behave in order to entangle their victims in a sticky web of lies, isolation, gaslighting and brutal devaluation.

"They are masters at nurturing hopes and desires in you that they would never fulfill. With virtuosity, they manage to toy with your deepest longings. They set the stage for their emotional abuse in a particularly deceitful way: They soften your boundaries ever so slightly, so that in the end, like an alcoholic, you tolerate large toxic amounts of their behavior that would kill a non-alcoholic instantly. Some grandiose narcissists keep themselves in top shape and are great lovers. But not because they are particularly empathetic. Make no mistake about it: empathy and love cannot be felt by any narcissist in the world. To his partner, sex with a grandiose narcissist may seem special because he has learned what he has to do to come across that way to her. In truth, however, you are nothing but a masturbation object for him."

Zayla winced. The cats around her blinked and perked up

their ears.

"Surely there are not only male narcissists," she heard one of the other women ask.

Hope shook her head. "No, any person can be such a monster, of course. Narcissists are not limited to one gender, nor are they limited to a life partner or a spouse. Your boss can be a narcissist. A girlfriend. Members of your family. There are also varying degrees of narcissism. Malignant narcissists, however, are the worst. They are like soul vampires, leaving their victims as drained and washed up as the Dementors from the Harry Potter books. Like a vampire, by the way, a narcissist can't see his own reflection."

Zayla looked up. "Because what he projects to the outside world is so far from the real him, whom he couldn't bear to face in the mirror?"

Hope nodded appreciatively. "That's right, Zayla. Narcissists categorically separate themselves from the origins of their own deep-rooted childhood pain. They wouldn't be able to face their sensory numbing darkness. The image they have of themselves, their entire identity, would literally crumble into dust."

"What do malignant narcissists look for in partners, Hope?" asked Zayla, already guessing what the answer would be.

"The easiest victims for narcissists are people whose self-worth is already in the gutter, or who crave external validation through the splendor of a grandiose narcissist at their side. And, of course, codependents and empaths."

She gave Zayla a sympathetic look.

"Codependents, after all, learned as children to run around with their Red Cross kit and fix every problem," she continued. "They know they always have themselves to blame and are masters at excusing even the most intolerable behavior of others."

"In general, highly empathetic and sensitive people are his ideal prey?" asked a woman with short gray hair sitting across from Zayla, who heaved a heavy sigh. Hope answered in the affirmative. "By the way, no psychologist, no matter how skilled, will ever really be able to reach a malignant narcissist," she went on to explain. "The only chance you have as a victim is to radically detach from a narcissist and try to heal the trauma. Because as long as you keep in touch, he will bleed you dry."

"Don't all people have narcissistic traits?" asked Zayla thoughtfully.

"Of course. And they are also necessary for all of us. But it becomes problematic when the narcissism is so dominant that empathy and respect for others are lost. A true narcissist cannot feel remorse. He doesn't even know what it means to have a guilty conscience. This is also what makes them so dangerous. Unfortunately, we live in a world full of narcissists, many of whom we also admire and encourage. Just take a look at politics or social media.

"A malignant narcissist, however, whether male or female, rapes the souls of their partners and devalues every counterpart. It is an experience that one would not want to wish on their worst enemy. I have faced what it means to live with such a person. 'My' narcissist flattered me with an incredible intensity and wooed me by every trick in the book. He believed in his own magnificence completely and promised me a breathtaking life full of magic and enchantment as no other man before or after him. But while he smoothly assured me that he would move heaven and earth for me, he left me out on a limb. None of his promises ever amounted to anything."

When Zayla returned to her hostel and went to bed after the long and upsetting evening, she fell into a fitful sleep and dreamed of a slimy shadow hanging from the ceiling above her.

Spiritual narcissism, sounds the croaking voice of the shadow that drops from the ceiling and lands on her bed, pretends holiness that does not exist. It was once your strategy, too, not to want to face your shadow, daughter of Avalon. The pride of being ostensibly more evolved prevented the unclouded view of yourself.

Genuine spirituality makes us more empathetic and sensitive. A spiritual narcissist, however, in the role of a priestess and healer, will with somnambulistic certainty seek out the weak points of every human being and use them mercilessly against all who dare to question them. Just as you did, daughter of the Isle of Apples.

Zayla recognized the grimace of Marrock above her, which drenched her in sweat, rousing her from sleep. A scream escaped her throat and woke her roommates.

"What were you dreaming?" asked one of the women, a backpacker from South Africa, beckoning the other two, an Australian and a Dutch woman, to join her.

"A nightmare," Zayla replied with a gasp, reaching for her water bottle.

"Dreams are lies," muttered the Australian.

"Oh, well," the Dutchwoman replied skeptically, "maybe not lies. But the subconscious is trying to process the things you've dealt with during the day."

"Were you scared yesterday?" the South African woman asked.

Zayla shook her head. Dreams were so infinitely more and multi-layered than what these three women believed them to be. "No, but a lot of realizations fell like scales from my eyes yesterday. And my nightmare just gave me a few more pieces of the puzzle."

"Then why did you scream?"

"Because it felt like there was a monster in human form standing over me."

***

Christmas was approaching and Zayla began to offer hypnosis sessions — covertly and without advertising herself much. Although, without exception, she refused to work with people she didn't like, more and more people came to her through word of mouth alone. She held sessions for smoking cessation as well as for weight loss, but regressions to past lives also enjoyed amazing popularity. At the same time, she was increasingly able to convey messages from the in-between worlds to the people around her when they asked for them. Zayla had no set rates, but gratefully accepted what a client could or would give her. Some paid her hostel bills or invited her to dinner. Others pressed a bundle of notes into her hand, so she was neither hungry nor homeless and hardly had to touch her trust fund during the months she toured London without a fixed abode.

One day before Christmas, she wrote an e-mail to her father. She pretended to be in Northern Ireland and asked him not to worry about her. She would be fine. Her father's reply was not long in coming. He wrote that he had been worried sick and she should be sure to get in touch with him. That evening, she called him from her new cell phone, but withheld the number.

"*Zayla.*" Her father's voice sounded brittle. "Please come back. Why won't you answer any of my calls?"

"I have a different number now, Dad, so I don't even get your calls." Zayla fingered the small SIM card in her hand. "If you want to talk to me, just send me an email at my new address. I'll call you every now and then, all right? Are you still working with Marrock?"

The long pause answered her question, and Zayla's stomach clenched.

"Papa, if you really want me to come back home, you need to get Marrock out of your life." She heard a stifled sound in the background and bit her tongue. "Is he with you? Merry Christmas, Papa," she said, and hung up.

The hostel was only one-third occupied over Christmas. Zayla retreated to her room, which she currently occupied alone, and once again cried herself to sleep.

***

The following summer, Zayla was three weeks away from giving birth to her child. She plugged in her old cell phone's SIM card for the first time since running away from home and saw 84 missed messages: from her father, from Marrock, but also from Travis and Tahnee. Her cousin's messages troubled her the most. She glanced at the clock. It was just before 8 p.m. in Australia. She hit speed dial and called Tahnee.

"Zayla!" her cousin shouted into the phone on the other end. "Oh God, you're alive! We were so worried about you! My goodness, your father and Travis are almost out of their minds. Deimos has called in a private investigator, but so far even he hasn't been able to find you. Where the heck have you been?"

"Tahnee, I'm not ready to tell anyone."

"Your father thinks you're paranoid."

"If you had experienced what I experienced, you would be paranoid, too. I'm going to call my father again sometime soon, and then Travis, too, and explain to both of them that I'm fine, considering the circumstances. What about Nick?" she changed the subject. "You had left me several messages saying he was having nightmares and throwing up all the time, but that no doctor could help him?"

"That's right. We've been to a dozen doctors by now. I was hoping you or uncle Matthew could do something for him."

"Have you asked my father for help yet?"

"Yes, but he never got back to us."

"Marrock!" seethed Zayla. "He certainly won't be interested in helping Nick. Or in my father keeping in touch with friends and relatives. Marrock wants to isolate him, just like he tried to isolate me."

"I've been able to talk Nick into doing a regression with one of you two to see if his situation might be related to a past life," Tahnee blurted out.

"I thought you didn't believe in that?"

She heard Tahnee sigh. "I have no idea what to believe, honestly. Ever since Logan returned to the U.S., Nick has been having the same cruel nightmares over and over again. A hypnosis session with you is our last hope. Can we meet you in London, Zayla?"

"We could also hold a session via video call if you don't want to make the long trip."

"That works?"

"Sure. It's up to you guys to decide. But we should do it soon. I scheduled my due date for three weeks from now."

"You made a C-section appointment?"

"Yes. I don't want to go through all the birth trauma with her."

"It's a girl?"

"It's a girl."

"What are you going to do with her, Zayla?"

"Give her away. I don't want her, even though I am deeply sorry that I feel that way about her. I have found a woman here who has contacts with a good adoption agency. Unfortunately,

I can't give my final approval for her adoption until six weeks after they cut the little one out of me."

"Are you happy with your choice of parents?" asked Tahnee. Zayla sensed her cousin was disturbed by the coldness of her decision.

"Yes, they are nice people, and I have a good feeling about them."

"What if you regret it later?"

"I won't regret it."

"I want a child so much ..." Tahnee broke off, and Zayla understood her cousin's marriage was not at its best at the moment.

"We could be in London the night after tomorrow," Tahnee blurted out. "Does that suit you?"

"Where will you stay?"

"Maybe at the Mandarin Oriental near Hyde Park. I'll let you know tomorrow. Can I reach you at this number?"

"No, but I'll call you again and we'll make an exact appointment."

Two days later, Zayla was sitting with Tahnee and Nick in a five-star hotel suite in central London. They had closed the curtains, dimmed the lights, and put on soothing music. Zayla was startled by how haggard and emaciated Nick looked. For an hour, he had bombarded her with all the questions he could think of about past life regression.

How long would such a session last? How exactly did it proceed? What chances of success did Zayla expect from it? Could anything go wrong? What if he did not believe in concepts like reincarnation? What if he only used his imagination during such a session?

"Your powers of imagination are the language of your soul

and the gateway to it," Zayla answered him. "Just think of it this way: put your rational mind on the couch next to you for a few hours. It can observe, and when the session is over, it may comment and pick apart everything as it likes. If your mind then tells you that what you experienced during hypnosis was mere fantasy or woolgathering, and you feel better with the thought that reincarnation is just a figment of your imagination, then that's perfectly fine with me. I don't preach and I don't cajole anyone. The decision to participate in this session or not is yours alone, Nick. But if you conclude that our session could possibly support you in gaining insights about yourself and initiate healing, does it make any difference if it was 'just' your imagination that helped you along? What do you have to lose?"

"Not much anymore," Nick replied, appearing to relent.

"Do you trust me?" asked Zayla.

He looked at her intently. "My father trusts you. That is beyond remarkable and reason enough for me to engage in such a session with you."

Zayla blushed. "How is Deimos?"

"Good."

"I'm glad."

"He was the only one who kept his cool when everyone was worried about where you might be. You'd be in touch when the time was right for you to resurface, he said."

"And yet Tahnee told me on the phone that Deimos had hired a private investigator to look for me."

"That was just a week ago because I wouldn't have wanted anyone else to accompany me on this regression journey but you. Especially after your father didn't get back to us."

Zayla smiled. "Shall we begin then?"

To Zayla's amazement, the first half hour of the session went like something out of a manual. Nick quickly and easily sunk into a deep trance state. When, after the scenes of his childhood and the memories of the time in his mother's womb, she asked him to dive into a past life that was of special significance to him, he abruptly slipped into the images of his nightmares that broke Zayla's heart.

"I see soldiers and civilians attacking a camp," he stammered. "Tents that are on fire. Villagers being slaughtered. I see children pleading for their lives. Babies torn from their mothers' arms and their heads smashed on rocks ..." Tears ran down Nick's cheeks in torrents. "A woman, in complete panic, is clinging to one of the children. She is one of the white captives we came to rescue from the clutches of the reds. I can see unborn babies and how they are cut out of the bodies of the pregnant women. Anything young and wearing a dress is raped. Some have their breasts cut off." Nick sobbed. "I'm standing next to the body of my horse, and I can't comprehend this unbelievable brutality. Some of my comrades are riding toward me. They are holding the severed genitals of the reds in their hands. I have to throw up. One of them hands me the reins of a new horse. I jump on and see this woman. We separate her and her child from the others."

"When you look into her eyes, do you recognize her?" asked Zayla, who shook with excitement at Nick's description of the massacre, which resembled in every detail the scenes she had seen during the regression with her father in Brighton. Goosebumps covered her throughout the entire session.

"It's you!" exclaimed Nick in horror. "Oh God, it can't be! Zayla, is it really you?"

Zayla squeezed his hand. "Yes, I'm the sandy-haired woman," she murmured to herself, casting a cautious glance at Tahnee, who sat open-mouthed at the head of the couch on which they had bedded her husband.

"My comrades are riding away with her," Nick continued to sputter out. "I see a fallen warrior on the ground. He took a bullet to the head and his body was mutilated. His eyes are wide open. *Logan!*" Nick screamed out his adopted brother's name and shifted back and forth on the sofa. Zayla made every effort to calm him down. He was crying and sobbing and thrashing about.

Zayla guided him back to the safe place he had named at the beginning of the hypnosis and told Nick to rest there. After a while, when she gave him the choice of coming out of hypnosis or entering a new scene of the life they had just watched together, Nick, with a heavy sigh, chose to continue.

"Where are you now?" asked Zayla after leading him deeper into hypnosis again.

"On an army base ... at a fort on the Great Plains," he replied. "I am ... the son of the commanding officer there."

"Do you know your name?"

Nick was silent for a very long time. "I'm a ... lieutenant. Lieutenant Charles ... Montgomery," he then said.

Zayla was struck by each new realization like a blow. Spellbound and overlapped by her own memories of this life together with him, she guided Nick through the session. Her consciousness had split. She found herself simultaneously in the roles of hypnotherapist and sandy-haired woman. In the moments it took Nick to respond to her questions, she was immersed in her own memories and became a witness to the same scenes Nick was describing, while Tahnee rubbed her eyes and let out one incredulous sound after another.

Zayla recognizes the lieutenant, who threw up at the massacre on the Lakȟóta people, next to her. His father, the Colonel and commander of the fort, stands at his side and looks down on her and her young son.

Deimos! thought Zayla, and she groaned.

At the same moment, Nick confirmed that he, too, recognized his father. "The Colonel is my father! Deimos! He loves that sandy-haired woman … But he also knows he has to let you go."

Zayla glances at one of the chiefs who has been negotiating with the officers since morning. At the colonel's request, she has translated the talks for both sides. The leader is an impressive man, tall like all the warriors of his people, lean but sinewy and with piercing eyes that can uncover the soul of a man.

She grew up with him and has not seen him since the massacre. He is the brother-friend of her dead husband, who was shot and maimed in the attack. When the men were boys, she loved them both. But a decision was taken from her when the Black Wolf Chief followed his father into exile. When he returned to the Lakȟóta years later, her husband, the Standing Elk — in whom Zayla and Nick recognized Logan — fought with the young warriors, and against the will of the older ones, to have his brother-friend reinstated.

The Black Wolf Chief revels in the respect of his men and the fear his enemies have for him. With other Lakȟóta leaders, he has come to the fort and buried any hope of a good negotiation before he arrived.

Zayla can see it in his eyes and read it in his energy body. Her abilities are more pronounced than today, and unlike the soldiers, the Lakȟóta are not afraid of them.

The gaze of the Black Wolf Chief touches his old childhood sweetheart and her child. She makes a gesture that means she wants to speak. The Black Wolf Chief breaks away from the group of headmen and does something outrageous. He walks toward the sandy-haired woman and the Colonel, raising his hands in front of his chest to make it clear that he is not a threat.

"Speak, Rock-With-Horns-Woman," he encourages her in the

language of his people.

Zayla lowers her eyes and her child pushes close behind her. "Let us both go with you," she pleads.

"The Standing Elk's son," the Black Wolf Chief nods to the boy, "is also my son."

He is a smart child and Zayla smiles when she sees him approach the warrior. She hears some soldiers start whispering around them, and then everything happens very quickly.

"Colonel Montgomery!" the Black Wolf Chief now addresses the commander in English. Not a trace of an accent can be heard. The many years he has lived as an exile among the whites show clearly. He speaks only loud enough for the Colonel, his son, and a few bystanders to still understand him. "Bluecoats and civilians attacked one of our camps and cruelly murdered my people. My brother-friend was also among the dead. The Rock-With-Horns-Woman is his widow, this child his son. She is now my wife and her child my son. This is the custom of my people. Will you let the Rock-With-Horns-Woman go, Colonel?"

Zayla's heart is pounding in her throat. She knows that the Colonel loves her. She knows how much the soldiers despise her because she gave birth to a savage's child and did not have the decency to take her own life. Without the Colonel's protection, some of the soldiers would surely have abused her, forgetting that she was a white woman whom they had pretended to free from the clutches of the Lakȟóta. She turns to the Colonel. "Robert," she says softly. "Please. I want to go back. I have to go back. I can't live here. My home is with them."

Zayla sees a corner of the Colonel's mouth twitch. He can't allow himself to be exposed in front of his men, but she senses how much he is struggling. "Go on, Miss Brooke," he says, emphatically patronizing. "It's certainly better that way for your little one there. My son and I will find a new maid."

The Rock-With-Horns-Woman knows how to put on a mask and

put on as much theater as the Colonel. She swallows the public disparagement — another in the long line of things she's had to endure over the past year. She sees the Black Wolf Chief's eyes blaze. Wordlessly, he signals her and the child to follow him.

"They're going with him now," Nick told them. "It has been inconclusive negotiations so far. The Lakȟóta gathered want to retire for a consultation. The Colonel, my father, loves this woman. Elizabeth ... Brooke is her name, and I'm not sure she hasn't also given her body to him to live in safety at the fort. Life out here is hard. With that Indian bastard on her hands, she's considered spoiled goods. Unimaginable that a white woman would give herself to a red man! But since my father took her under his wing and has her working for us as a housekeeper and as an interpreter, the snide remarks have diminished. My father had a soldier who behaved insolently toward her thrown in the hole."

"Was the Colonel responsible for the massacre of the Lakȟóta?"

"No. He wasn't even there."

"Were *you* responsible?"

Nick groaned. "Damn it, I don't know!"

Zayla prompted him with more relaxation suggestions to dive deeper into his memory worlds. After a while, she repeated her question.

"Were you responsible for this massacre, Charles Montgomery?"

Nick began to cry. "I was there. But the whole attack got completely out of hand! There were more civilians than soldiers among the attackers. They were full of hate and undermined my authority. They trampled the reds as if they were vermin."

After a marathon five-hour session that had drained Zayla's energies, she sat in the hotel restaurant over coffee and a mighty chocolate cream pie with Tahnee. Nick had stayed behind in the room, exhausted, and fallen asleep. Tahnee ran her fingers through her hair and shook her head again and again.

"I just can't believe all this. Please explain the connections to me again," she said softly, "so my brain understands it is not dreaming."

Zayla exhaled slowly. "Well, the paths of Nick, Deimos, Logan, Travis, and me crossed almost 200 years ago during the so-called Indian Wars in North America. Deimos was Colonel Robert Montgomery, commander of a fort on the Great Plains. Nick was also his son once in that life: Lieutenant Charles Montgomery. The latter was partly responsible for the massacre that took the life of Logan, who was a Lakȟóta warrior named Standing Elk. I was his wife and the daughter of European parents who had grown up among his people from childhood. Logan's and my young daughter was also killed in that raid. The Black Wolf Chief, Logan's great-great grandfather, was the brother-friend of the Standing Elk and later took care of his brother's widow and her son. The sandy-haired woman, the Rock-With-Horns-Woman, or Elizabeth Brooke, became the first of his three wives after meeting the Black Wolf Chief again at the fort."

"The sandy-haired woman, this Elizabeth Brooke ... she ... *you* were the wife of Logan *and* the Black Wolf Chief?"

Zayla nodded, surprised by the softness that had been in her cousin's voice when she spoke Logan's name. "He, Travis, and I have also lived a life together in Australia, as an Aboriginal family. Travis was one of our children. In that life in North America, however, Travis was my brother, as well as in a very ancient life among Celts, Christians, and Templars, along with Deimos," Zayla replied, striving to find another clue to her suspicion that her cousin must have loved Logan.

"In the life in North America, Travis was named Nathaniel Brooke. He and I lived among the Lakȟóta. Years later Travis — or Nathaniel — along with the Black Wolf Chief, found one of their camps completely burned out. The Black Wolf Chief almost killed him out of desperation and anger at the whites. This was a scene Travis had already shared with me two years ago in Brighton. The army and white civilians were raiding a Lakȟóta village under the pretext of freeing white prisoners. By this they meant Nathaniel and Elizabeth Brooke."

"But they both grew up there!" Tahnee was indignant.

"Fatally, their presence was the perfect cover for the whites to raid the camp."

"And Nick was responsible for that?"

"Nick, as Charles Montgomery, did not want the raid. He was a young officer, and the civilians traveling with him and his small band of soldiers undermined his authority. Nick's nightmares, his entire mental and physical state, all of it certainly stemmed from those images of horror — and the knowledge that he had incurred a tremendous debt. But now that he knows what he did and can face the responsibility for his actions, his symptoms will probably improve. I have seen this happen many times. Once the cause of a phobia or trauma becomes clear, people begin to heal."

"And Deimos?" whispered Tahnee.

"Deimos, as Colonel Montgomery, hunted the Black Wolf Chief across the Northern Great Plains years later and confronted him and his men just short of the Canadian border. He too loved Elizabeth Brooke, but he could never have her. During the escape and especially after the Black Wolf Chief's killing, she wished only for his death."

"Did *Deimos* kill the Black Wolf Chief?"

"No. That was one of his own warriors who had turned on him."

Tahnee swallowed. "With all this terrible knowledge, can Logan, Deimos and Nick still remain a close-knit family?"

Zayla shrugged her shoulders. "I certainly hope so. Haven't they proven how much they appreciate each other? It would be madness to give up such a bond just because the three of them faced each other as enemies in another life."

"Marrock," Zayla added thoughtfully, "was the murderer of the Black Wolf Chief, by the way."

"Goodness gracious! And you ...?"

"Yes, I'm carrying that killer's child. But not for long."

The expression on her cousin's face distorted. She closed her eyes, and a bad premonition stirred in Zayla.

"Zayla, I ..." Tahnee looked at her pleadingly. "I'm so sorry, but I didn't know."

"Oh, how *could* you!" cried Zayla angrily, shoving her chair backwards and jumping up. "You told them I was here with you guys today? I trusted you, you bitch!" Zayla bit her tongue and tears welled up in Tahnee's eyes.

"I'm so sorry, but your father was crazy with worry! And he said Marrock was, too. Even Deimos was at his wits' end."

"Is he here, too?" asked Zayla incredulously.

"No, but he wants you to call him." Tahnee held out a small envelope the size of a business card to her cousin. The latter shook her head vigorously.

"Who does he think he is? Let him get his own butt in gear and track me down if I'm important enough to him. He could have helped me back in Mystery Bay, but he didn't. Now I don't need his help anymore."

Zayla knew how unfairly she judged, but anger boiled up inside her. Anger at Tahnee and her betrayal; anger at her father, at his symbiosis with Marrock and the fact that her beloved papa, of all people, had withdrawn his trust from her;

anger at Deimos, who supposedly could have set everything right for her in Mystery Bay; anger at herself, her immaturity, her vulnerability, and how much she had let herself be played by Marrock. She snatched the envelope from Tahnee's hand and opened it.

Call me, love of my many lives, she read on the back of Deimos's business card. Zayla scoffed and flipped the card and envelope back onto the table. Wordlessly, she reached for her bag and left the hotel.

Hope had suggested she take Zayla to Glastonbury in Somerset, England, after the birth of her child to a still-secret retreat of the mystical Avalon, where Zayla could hide from the world for as long as she wished. There, Hope had promised her, she could return to the birthplace of her soul and learn from the other descendants of the great Celtic priestesses.

"Provided you muster the strength to face your own inner darkness and make the journey back into the womb of the Great Mother," Hope had said.

For only then, Zayla had understood, would she be able to advance her own healing process in this place shrouded in legend.

There are two powers in the world:
One is the sword and the other is the pen.
There is a third power stronger than both: that of women.

Malala Yousafsai

Afterword

Dear Reader,

A debut like *Night Dance: Shadow Worlds,* whose plot accompanied me for forty years and whose storylines kept branching out, deepening, and changing, did not come without outside influences. My inspirations flowed abundantly and from very different quarters. At this point I would like to pay tribute to the most significant catalyst for the creation of my book.

As a teenager, I first encountered the works of ancient historian Dr. Liselotte Welskopf-Henrich (who was acquainted with *American Indian Movement* activists Dennis Banks and Vernon Bellecourt) in the public library of my birthplace. The story of her brilliant series of novels *Die Söhne der Großen Bärin* (The Sons of the Great [Female] Bear) and *Das Blut des Adlers* (The Blood of the Eagle) — both of which have never been translated into English — gripped me at the deepest level of my soul and has never let me go. In retrospect, the encounter with the texts of this great writer and historian was probably a twist of fate for me.

To this day, the events of *Die Söhne der Großen Bärin* captivated me in a way no other story has: It spoke of the life and suffering of a Lakota boy who follows his father into exile as a twelve-year-old and becomes a fratricide as a youth and an (unwilling) traitor to all sides as a man. Professor Welskopf-Henrich masterfully created the psychologically deep and multi-layered lead character of Harka Stone-With-Horns, who temporarily finds a home among his enemies and is then forced to leave it again as well; she skilfully brought to life the drama of the outsider who, as a twenty-four-year-old, finds his way back to his people, is later detained by the U.S. Army, flees, and with a handful of Lakota men, women and children is finally able to build a self-determined life as a farmer and rancher in Canada.

I devoured Professor Liselotte Welskopf-Henrich's novel cycle for days and nights and immediately started rereading it after the last page.

In Chapter 3 of *Night Dance: Shadow Worlds*, those familiar with her works will recognize the themes of exile, the life of father and son among the hostile Siksika, and Harka's return to the Lakota in a highly alienated form in the figure of the Black Wolf Chief and his biography as outlined by Uŋčí.

At the same time, the story of the Black Wolf Chief is completely different from that of Harka, but more about that in the upcoming prequel to *Night Dance* (Book 3: *Prelude*). It will tell what was only touched upon in *Night Dance: Shadow Worlds* (Book 1) and the subsequent *Night Dance: Glimmer of Light* (Book 2): the story of the sandy-haired Rock-With-Horns-Woman (aka Elizabeth Brooke) and her brother Nathaniel; her husband, the Standing Elk, and his brother-friend, the Black Wolf Chief; as well as the intertwining of the lives of Colonel Robert Montgomery and his son Charles with theirs.

I thank Ms. Welskopf-Henrich from the bottom of my heart for her masterpiece and for the dream of my childhood self, triggered by her, to one day as an adult be able to write a thoroughly powerful and multifaceted story with heart, passion, and depth.

Incidentally, the name of the Rock-With-Horns-Woman in *Night Dance* is not a deliberate homage to the figure of Harka Stone-With-Horns of Welskopf-Henrich, but owed to research that made it clear that Welskopf-Henrich's translation *Tokei-itho* (for Stone-With-Horns) was an error, but that there must have actually been a *Tȟuŋkáŋ Hetȟúŋ-wiŋ*, Rock-with-Horns-Woman, among the Lakȟóta. *Tȟuŋkáŋ* here is not the same kind of stone as *íŋyaŋ* (Welskopf-Henrich's later corrected translation for the name Stone-With-Horns: *Inyan-he-yukan*), but "rock" or "stone" as a spiritual entity.

If you, dear reader, enjoyed this novel, I would like to invite you to the following:

1. A positive review on Amazon and other platforms helps a debut and underdog book like *Night Dance* gain visibility and reach more people interested in reading it. I would therefore be heartily grateful for your benevolent feedback!
2. Feel free to visit my website at nightdance.net, and sign up for my *Night Dance Mail* newsletter to stay up to date regarding the releases of *Night Dance Part 2* and *Part 3* (its prequel).
3. If you have any questions or comments about my novel, please email me at Kory@nachttanz.net. I really look forward to your messages. 😊

Kory Wynykom
January 21, 2023

Sources and References

Prologue, chapters 2, 9, 11, 15:
The descriptions of regressions into "past lives" as well as into the so-called "in-between lives" were either inspired by my own training and regression experiences with hypnotherapists and hypnosis coaches of various stripes or they are purely fictitious.

The example of the multiple sclerosis patient in Chapter 2 from Professor Kirkpatrick's practice, isolated and expanded upon for *Night Dance*, was inspired by reading **Dr. Michael Newton**'s book *The Journey of Souls*.

The phenomenon of *xenoglossy* (speaking a language you never learned) is surprisingly also described on Wikipedia. However, Wikipedia seems to have generally made it its business to put all "paranormal" phenomena, and even those scientists who deal with the supposedly supernatural in a very serious way, in an unflattering light.

Chapter 1:
The abhorrence that the Lakota (and many other indigenous peoples of North America) felt toward sexual violence in their traditional cultures, and the absolute exception with which they themselves raped prisoners of war, is confirmed in *Toward an Indigenous Jurisprudence of Rape* by **Sarah Deer** (2004) here, among other places:
https://open.mitchellhamline.edu/cgi/viewcontent.cgi?article=1082&context=facsch (last accessed December 2021).

For a penetrating study of historically, politically, and colonially motivated violence against indigenous women, see also:
The Beginning and End of Rape. Confronting Sexual Violence in

Native America by **Sarah Deer** (2015).

For a brief review of the issue of domestic violence on the Lakota Reservations, see this article and others posted on the independent, nonprofit news source *Indian Country Today*:
https://indiancountrytoday.com/archive/yes-i-am-a-batterer-the-first-step-to-stopping-domestic-violence (2015 with a 2018 update; last accessed December 2021).

Chapter 3:

Uŋčí's remarks on the Lakȟóta ideal of masculine beauty and continence are taken from **Charles Alexander Eastman**'s reflections on his people, the Santee Sioux (Dakȟóta), in *Soul of the Indian* (1911).

Chapter 4:

There are several videos on YouTube about the suffering of orangutan females.

Chapter 6:

For references regarding **Max Planck,** see: www.weloennig.de/MaxPlanck.html (in particular also Dr. Wolf-Ekkehard Lönnig's comment on the authenticity of the Max Planck quotation reproduced by Zayla, mutatis mutandis, at the end of the above internet page).

Zayla and Travis mention two YouTube videos in their conversation. One, non-fictional, can be found here: www.youtube.com/watch?v=85hbMtegrLc (What Comes After Tragedy? Forgiveness. By Azim Khamisa and Ples Felix)

Chapter 7:

For the words of late Dr. Haunani-Kay Trask, Hawaiian activist, educator, author, which echo in Logan's mind, see:

www.youtube.com/watch?v=SDsx1mUpiI4

For the role of Lakȟóta-Code Talkers during World War II and the surprise of the Japanese General that indigenous languages were used to decode communication, see here: www.southdakotamagazine.com/clarence-wolf-guts

As Tiya mentions in her conversation with Logan, the statement that the Sioux (i.e., Lakȟóta / Lakota and Dakȟóta / Dakota) have occupied all the platforms of indigenous coolness comes from Ojibwe academic **Dr. David Treuer**. (Treuer's original wording in his book *Rez Life*: "The Sioux have corned the market on Indian cool"). The small conversation segment between Tiya and Logan on the relationship of the formerly hostile Sioux and Ojibwe to each other was also somewhat inspired by reading Dr. David Treuer's (funny, partly ironically witty) remarks in the introduction to his book *Rez Life* (2012).

The conversation among Tiya, Logan, and Nick in Uŋčí's log cabin about the Bureau of Indian Affairs (BIA), the Department of the Interior, and the fictional character of Anne Sixkiller came about after several internet searches about the BIA, the so-called "Five Civilized Nations," and newspaper articles from 2020 and 2021 about the appointment of Deb Haaland as the first female Indigenous minister in the United States. In addition, there was a *Red Nation* podcast from 2021.

(In fact, however, Deb Haaland was not the first indigenous figure at the cabinet level: Charles Curtis, a member of the Kaw Nation from Kansas, had already served as vice president of the United States from 1929 to 1933.)

Chapter 8:
Tina Michelle Fontaine's tragic story can be read on Wikipedia and elsewhere.

Logan's comments in Chapter 8 as well as in Chapter 1 are

(incomplete) summaries of various internet research on the topic of *Missing and Murdered Indigenous Women,* as well as various (Native) Twitter and Facebook posts.

Chapter 9:

The facts about the Australian platypus and Ignaz Semmelweis are a summary of various journal articles and internet research.

The idea for Dorothea Nicols and her school in London-Leytonstone came about after a *We Don't Die Radio*® interview by podcaster Sandra Champlain with **Nicola Farmer** and my subsequent research on Nicola Farmer's website: www.icuacademy.co.uk/.

Leytonstone Academy and Dorothea Nicols, however, are fictional. So are the events described in Chapter 9, except for the amazing abilities Emma, James, and Charlotte possess. They are based on my research into Nicola Farmer and her fascinating *Inspiring Children Universally Academy*. The children in Chapter 9 themselves, however, are fictional characters.

Chapter 12:

The information about the heroines of the six women on Avalon Beach is real and can be found on countless websites.

In **Turia Pitt**'s case, in addition to her website www.turiapitt.com, highly informative and impressive videos can also be found on YouTube (including a TED Talk).

For **Dr. Kim TallBear,** her own website https://kimtallbear.com/ as well as her interviews as a guest on the podcasts *All My Relations* and *Breakdancing With Wolves* have been a treasure trove of information.

The information about **Dr. Judy Atkinson** comes from here:

- *The Value of Deep Listening - The Aboriginal Gift to the Nation* | Judy Atkinson | TEDxSydney (www.youtube.com/watch?

v=L6wiBKClHqY)

  - *Trauma Trails - Recreating Song Lines: The Transgenerational Effects of Trauma in Indigenous Australia* by Judy Atkinson (2002)

  On **Elizabeth Blake,** see *The Direct Voice* by N. Riley Heagerty (2017)

Chapter 13:

The items needed to counter a black magic attack (including the holy water and black candles) are based on information from a now deceased medium from northern Germany who reported having experienced such an attack herself and successfully warding it off.

Note to the novel: Since Zayla and Deimos (partly together with Travis) knew how to handle the forces of light *and* darkness in an ancient common incarnation (see chapter 6: the story of the former Templar and the daughter of the High Priestess), it makes sense at this point that the three of them remember the ritual mentioned here.

The Black Wolf Chief's statement "Know yourself. Know your friends. Know the enemy. Lead the way!" is the second subtitle of a book by **Joseph M. Marshall III,** *The Power of Four: Leadership Lessons of Crazy Horse* (2009).

  The images of Native American children in Logan's vision echo the narratives of indigenous survivors of Canadian *residential schools* (referred to in the U.S. as *boarding schools*). A deeply uncomfortable documentary on this subject titled **Unrepentant: Kevin Annett and Canada's Genocide - il genocidio del Canada** can be found here: www.youtube.com/watch?v=swGEK8duSiU.

  Also recommended and eye-opening are these two publications: ***Unrelenting: Between Sodom and Zion*** by **Reverend**

Kevin D. Annett (2016) and **Murder by Decree: The Crime of Genocide in Canada - A Counter Report to the Truth and Reconciliation Commission** (2016), published by the *International Tribunal for the Disappeared of Canada.*

Travis's remarks on the subject of nothing being lost on a spiritual level come, as he already mentions to Logan, from the Aboriginal Soundhealer **Eshua Bolton**. One of his interviews, the content of which Travis reproduces in conversation with Logan, can be found here in the video titled *Ancient wisdom & Light codes - Eshua didgeridoo healer:* www.youtube.com/watch?v=YkJocnrJbW0

Chapter 14:

The story that gave Mystery Bay its name is real, a summary of which can be found on several websites and YouTube videos.

Chapter 15:

I first encountered the term *"unfuckwithable"* in the context of appearances (podcasts, YouTube videos, books) by Mindvalley founder **Vishen Lakhiani.** Whether this is *his* neologism or whether the term already existed before (as internet research suggests), I cannot say for sure. In any case, the word *"unfuckwithable"* is unfortunately not my own creation.

Hope's explanations of narcissistic abuse are essentially based on conversations with those affected and a longstanding preoccupation with this subject. In addition, the following publications have been integrated in some places:

Melanie Tonia Evens: *You Can Thrive After Narcissistic Abuse* (2018)

andreas-gauger.de/narzissmus-manipulation/ (last accessed January 2022)

Nachttanz - Night Dance -
Haŋwáčhipi

Looking at the prequel to the present novel, which I originally intended to write first, the title of my trilogy was inspired years ago by reading Clark Wissler's description of the *Lakota Night Dance* (*Haŋwáčhipi*) below.

Since **Night Dance** is not only about making collective and individual shadows visible, but also about ancient soul connections and the power of hearts, this title seemed more than appropriate to me on many levels ("shadow dance," shadow work, „courtship", historical reference).

From Lakota Classics (facsimiles of the earliest publications on Lakota history, language, and culture): Societies of the Oglala, a reprint of the Anthropological Papers of the American Museum of Natural History Vo. XI, Part I: Societies and Ceremonial Associations in the Oglala Division of the Teton-Dakota by Clark Wissler (1912):

"**Night-Dance**. The members were unmarried, but two men acting as leaders were usually married. They opened the ceremony by recounting their deeds. The young men sat on one side of the tipi, the young women on the other. As the songs for this dance were sung, a man would rise and dance with a present which he then presented to one of the young women. In the same way the young women danced with presents for young men. [...] At the close a feast was made".

A more recent source confirms some of the information: see Lakota Dictionary, Lakota Language Consortium (2nd ed.,

2011):

"**Haŋwáčhipi** - **Night Dance**. One of the societies was common to both young men and young women and it was called **Night Dance**, they would get together and dance almost all night long. [...] they usually dance[d] holding each other in the arms (men with women)."

Acknowledgements

My special thanks go to Nadja Bobik, Nadine Balazs, my dearest friend Ursel (who already accompanied the reading of the first bumpy drafts of *Night Dance* with encouraging comments three decades ago), as well as these amazing women: Heidi R., Nadine, Nicole, and Dr. Monika.

Your belief in me and my heart project, your valuable feedback and your manifold support made it possible for me to dare step out of my comfort zone and bring *Night Dance* into the world.

A super special thank you goes to Elise Ryan! Your help with proofreading the (American) English version of *Nachttanz* was invaluable! I am so incredibly grateful for your support, and all your empathic input and commentary.

Another huge and heartfelt thank you goes to Majona of MajonaDawn.com (host of Life After Life Radio podcast) for your final review of *Night Dance* despite tragic personal circumstances and your supporting comments pertaining to indigenous and mediumistic matters.

@Nadja: For birthing heart projects, you are the best midwife ever!

About the author

Kory Wynykom finds herself in the Human Design System as a "lighthouse" (a projector), a storyteller, and a "heretical investigator." She is also a mother and a bookworm and holds a university degree in Social Sciences and Anglistics (English).

Born in Germany in 1968 she spent longer periods in Australia and Great Britain. Night Dance is her heart's unrivaled project, which has accompanied her for four decades. Only toward the end of 2012 did her vision gradually become wide enough to put her research, her numerous thoughts and inspirations down on paper, cast in a dense and multi-layered plot.

For more information about the author and her books visit **www.nightdance.net**.

List of characters

21st century:

Zayla Victoria Kirkpatrick:
Highly gifted outsider with metaphysical abilities that most people fear; only child of renowned British psychologist and hypnotherapist Professor Matthew Kirkpatrick.

Logan Black Wolf Chief Diamandis:
Descendant of the legendary Black Wolf Chief; Oglála-Lakȟóta with U.S. and Australian citizenship; adopted son of Deimos Aleksander Diamandis.

Deimos Aleksander Diamandis:
Australian media mogul with Greek-Iranian roots; power player on the international stage; father of Nick and adoptive father of Logan.

Travis Mason:
Australian with British and First Nations roots; like Zayla, endowed with metaphysical abilities; partner of professional surfer Carl Freeman (Zayla's cousin).

Marrock Lovell:
Former investment banker in London's Canary Wharf financial district and the City of London.

Nicholas "Nick" Castor Diamandis:
Logan's adopted brother and son of Deimos.

Tahnee Carlynda Diamandis, née Freeman:
Cousin of Zayla with British and Wiradjuri-Australian ancestry.

Tiya-Alea Redbird:
Member of the Canadian Ojibwe-Anishinabe; journalist, radio host, podcaster, political activist. Later wife of Logan.

Carl Freeman:
Professional surfer with British and Wiradjuri-Australian ancestry; brother of Tahnee; partner of Travis and cousin of Zayla.

Yarran Freeman:
Australian and Wiradjuri Aboriginal; renowned journalist; father of Tahnee and Carl; uncle of Zayla.

Florence Freeman, née Kirkpatrick:
Mother of Tahnee and Carl; only sister of Professor Kirkpatrick.

Prof. Dr. Matthew Kirkpatrick and Nazneen Kirkpatrick:
Zayla's parents. Her father is a renowned British university professor, psychologist, and hypnotherapist; her mother an Englishwoman with Persian roots who had second sight.

Uŋčí [Oongtschi] Black Wolf Chief:
Logan's grandmother; Oglála-Lakȟóta; spiritual leader of her people; descendant of the Black Wolf Chief.

Phoebe Black Wolf Chief:
Logan's (half) sister, Oglála-Lakȟóta, descendant of the Black Wolf Chief.

Mary Black Wolf Chief:
Logan's mother, Oglála-Lakȟóta, descendant of the Black Wolf Chief.

Dorothea Nicols:
Headmistress of an extraordinary school in Leytonstone, London, and friend of the Kirkpatricks.

19th century:

Šuŋgmánitu Tȟáŋka Sápe - Black Wolf Chief:
Ancestor of Logan; Oglála-Lakȟóta, brother-friend of the Standing Elk; became one of the most legendary resistance fighters, controversial headmen and warrior leaders of his people.

Heȟáka Nážiŋ - Standing Elk:
Oglála-Lakȟóta, brother-friend of the Black Wolf Chief and first husband of the Rock-With-Horns-Woman.

Tȟuŋkáŋ Hetȟúŋ-wiŋ - Rock-with-Horns-Woman / the sandy-haired woman / Elizabeth Brooke / Kimímela (Butterfly):
Twelfth child of French and Irish settlers; raised from birth among the Oglála-Lakȟóta; wife of the Standing Elk.

Nathaniel Brooke:
Brother of Elizabeth Brooke, raised from an early age among the Oglála-Lakȟóta; childhood friend of the Standing Elk and the Black Wolf Chief.

Colonel Robert John Montgomery:
Commanding officer of a U.S. Army fort on the Great Plains; hunter of the Black Wolf Chief; admirer of Elizabeth Brooke.

Lieutenant Charles William Montgomery:
Son of the Colonel.

Printed in Great Britain
by Amazon

20029180R00157